I stopped dead in my tracks.

I realized it was not my mother, as I had expected. It was the vibrant and sexy Anita Bell, the only woman I'd ever loved, or at least thought I loved.

"Anita." I gasped as my eyes quickly roamed over her body. Anita was dressed in a very conservative white church dress with white heels, but her voluptuous body made anything she wore look provocative.

"Dante." She smiled.

She locked the door then stepped closer to me. She kissed me with her full lips. "I missed you, Dante," she whispered.

She kissed me again before I could respond. This time she wrapped her arms around me and I did the same, closing my eyes. Our kiss was so passionate it took my breath away. When it was finally over, we stayed wrapped in each other's arms and stared lustfully into each other's eyes.

"God, I missed you, Dante," she whispered.

"I missed you, too," I said as I gently pushed her away. "Just not enough to commit adultery. Where's your husband?"

Also by Carl Weber

The Church Series
The Preacher's Son
So You Call Yourself a Man
The First Lady
Up to No Good
The Choir Director

A Man's World Series
Lookin' for Luv
Married Men
Baby Momma Drama
Player Haters
So You Call Yourself a Man
She Ain't the One (with Mary B. Morrison)

Big Girls Book Club Series
Something on the Side
Big Girls Do Cry
Torn Between Two Lovers

Published by Kensington Publishing Corp.

The PREACHER'S SON

Carl Weber

Kensington Publishing Corp.
http://www.kensingtonbooks.com

DAFINA BOOKS are published by

Kensington Publishing Corp.
119 West 40th Street
New York, NY 10018

All Kensington titles, imprints and distributed lines are available at special quantity discounts for bulk purchases for sales promotion, premiums, fund-raising, educational or institutional use.

Special book excerpts or customized printings can also be created to fit specific needs. For details, write or phone the office of the Kensington Special Sales Manager: Kensington Publishing Corp., 119 West 40th Street, New York, NY, 10018. Attn. Special Sales Department. Phone: 1-800-221-2647.

Dafina and the Dafina logo Reg. U.S. Pat. & TM Off.

ISBN-13: 978-1-4967-2232-4
ISBN-10: 1-4967-2232-9
First Kensington Hardcover Printing: January 2005
First Kensington Trade Paperback Printing: December 2005
First Kensington Mass Market Printing: December 2006

eISBN-13: 978-0-7582-5988-2
eISBN-10: 0-7582-5988-3
Kensington Electronic Edition: December 2006

10 9 8 7

Printed in the United States of America

This book is dedicated to the late minister
Tyrone Thompson,
the man who taught me more about God, the church,
and living on this earth than anyone else.
Rest in peace, my friend.
I'll see you when I get there.

Acknowledgments

First off, I have to thank God. Without Him none of this would be possible.

Thanks to all the book clubs and fans who have read my books. It's you who make this whole thing worthwhile and get me up at three in the morning to write. I know this story is a little different from the kind I usually write, but I think you'll enjoy it.

To Karen Thomas, my editor and my friend. You've taught me so much about the industry, more than you probably realize. Thanks. I'll always be grateful.

To Walter Zacharius, Steven Zacharius, Laurie Parkin. Thanks for believing in me and my dream for Urban Books.

To Robilyn Heath, my right hand, and Roy Glenn, my left hand, thanks for all your hard work and help with Urban Books. To my Urban Books family, you are some of the most talented people in this business. With a little hard work I'm sure you will all achieve your dreams.

Thanks to Paul Chin, my attorney. Thanks for watching my back as I crawl through the maze of the publishing world.

Thanks to Linda Williams, Linda Gurrant, Valerie Skinner, Marlene Hernandez, and Ann Murphy—my readers. You have been a help that I can't even explain.

Thanks to Maxine Thompson. I could not have done this book without your help. Good luck in all you do.

Thanks to Marie Brown, my agent and second mother. You've done a great job, and I may not say it enough, but thanks. Your hard work and support are highly appreciated. Last but not least, I'd like to thank all the black bookstores that helped to make my career a success. I'd especially like to thank Gwen Richardson at Cush City in Houston, Texas. Gwen, I know it seems like every time I'm supposed to be headed your way something comes up. But these things are really happening. I hope you'll let me make it up to you and your customers. ☺

Well folks, until *So You Call Yourself a Man* hits the stores next year, thanks for the ride. It's been great.

Oh, and if you get a chance, holler at your boy. *UrbanBooks@ hotmail.com.*

Prologue

"Family values . . ." Bishop T.K. Wilson paused for effect and looked down upon the crowd of people. He took a breath and repeated his words in his strong, baritone voice. "Family values . . . Family values!" Each repetition was more animated than the last. He was holding a microphone in one hand, waving a Bible in the other, as he moved back and forth across the stage in what he liked to call his preacher's strut. "What has happened to family values in this community? In this country?" he shouted, then paused again, as if expecting a response from his audience.

T.K. Wilson was the pastor of First Jamaica Ministries, arguably the largest African-American church in Queens, New York. A tall, handsome man with chiseled features and a well-maintained salt-and-pepper beard, he was not only a very good minister and administrator, but a dynamic speaker as well. You could almost see him reeling in each and every one of the five hundred or so people who'd flooded into Roy Wilkins Park for the free hot dogs, sodas, and balloons for the kids that his church was giving away. It was all part of First Jamaica Ministries' voter registration campaign. This year the registration campaign was even more crucial, because it was also the year that their pastor hoped to become the next borough president of Queens.

"I'll tell you what has happened to this country and this community," T.K. continued. "They've gone to hell in a handbasket! That's what's happened to them. And why have they gone to hell in a handbasket?" He used his signature dramatic pause again, then emphasized his words with a wave of his hands. "Because *this community* has no role models! No one to look up to. No one they can go to when there's a problem. No one they can rely on to make sure your children and homes are safe. And to be quite frank, no one who cares." He lowered his voice. "Well, brothers and sisters, that ends today, right here and now." He pointed to the stage before him. " 'Cause if no one else will step up and be the role model that this community needs, then I will. And that's why I'm running for Queens borough president!"

There was an immediate explosion of applause, and everyone in the audience rose to their feet. When the crowd finally calmed down, the bishop smiled. "Thank you, thank you so very much." He took a handkerchief out of his breast pocket and wiped the sweat from his forehead before continuing. "For almost seventeen years I've been the pastor of First Jamaica Ministries, and I've tried to lead by example. During that time, I've accomplished quite a bit. We've built senior homes, a school, Section Eight housing for the needy, a free health clinic for the children, and we even have a homeless shelter for those who need to come in out of the cold. And if I'm elected borough president, I think I can do more."

There was some applause, and an older woman yelled from the crowd, "We love you, Bishop!"

"Well, thank you, Sister Adeline. I love you, too. However, I need more than your love. I need your help. I need all of your help. I need you to go over to that table and register to vote. Register so that when Election Day comes, I won't be just a role model for First Jamaica Ministries, but a role model for the entire community. The entire borough of Queens."

The crowd exploded into another round of cheers. First a few voices started, then it seemed like every voice in the crowd was chanting, "Bishop . . . Bishop . . . Bishop!"

Bishop Wilson stood there smiling proudly. For a moment he felt like the most powerful man in the world. It was a strange feeling for him, because he'd never aspired to be involved in politics. That had been his now-deceased father-in-law, Reverend Dr. Charles Jackson's dream, not his. Reverend Jackson had been T.K.'s mentor and predecessor as pastor of First Jamaica Ministries, and had always dreamed of seeing his son-in-law hold office. T.K.'s only ambition had been to serve the Lord and be the best husband and father that he could be.

T.K. glanced to the right side of the stage and smiled at his wife, Charlene, the only child of Reverend Jackson. She gave him a subtle thumbs-up, making T.K.'s smile widen. T.K. and Charlene had been married for over twenty years and had a good, blessed life as the pastor and first lady. She took her position as first lady very seriously, and in truth, she was just as responsible for T.K.'s rise to power in the church as he was. It was Charlene who went to her father's deathbed and secured a letter to the deacons board asking them to forgo interviews with other ministers and name her husband the next pastor of the church. It was a decision that the deacons board reluctantly agreed to, only out of respect for their deceased pastor. Years later, though, they had not once regretted the decision.

Charlene was also responsible for raising a sizable donation for the near-bankrupt Northeast Black Church Council, First Jamaica Ministries' governing body. She then talked the council's trustee board into bestowing T.K. with the title of bishop and naming him to their board. There was no doubt that Charlene was dedicated to her husband's career and she held high hopes for his future.

Charlene, like her father, wanted to see T.K. embark on a political career. She had pushed him for years to run for office. He finally gave in when his good friend Helen Marshall, who stepped down as borough president due to term limits, asked T.K. to run. Charlene, of course, was thrilled with Helen's request, and some people even believed she had somehow orchestrated the whole turn of events.

From his beautiful wife, the bishop glanced into the crowd at his lovely twenty-year-old daughter, Donna, who was surrounded by young men, many of whom were eager to court the bishop's daughter. She was T.K.'s pride and joy, his little princess, as he still called her. He was proud of the job he and his wife had done with her, and it saddened him to think that she was now a woman attending college and he would soon be losing her to the young men of the world.

He searched out his son, Dante, who was sitting behind a table helping people register to vote. Dante had just recently graduated from St. John's University with a degree in business administration. He was working for the First Jamaica Ministries as director of church activities, although his mother had much higher aspirations for him. It was her belief that someday Dante would step into his father's shoes as pastor of the church. This was also the bishop's hope, although he was a little more realistic about the situation than his wife was. He knew that being a minister was a calling, and he wasn't quite sure if his son had or would ever receive that calling. His wife, on the other hand, imagined that her son becoming pastor was a matter of birthright, and she would not hear of anything else.

1

Dante

It was late afternoon when my best friend, Shorty Jefferson, and I rolled east down Jamaica Avenue in his metallic blue Jeep Cherokee. Shorty and I were rocking our heads to the music as we flirted with one pretty woman after another. We'd just finished handing out my father's campaign flyers in front of Gertz Plaza Mall, and the radio was blasting G-Unit's "Poppin' Those Thangs." The bass was so loud that not only could nearby pedestrians hear the music, they could feel it too. When Shorty stopped at a traffic light, I winked at a beautiful twenty-something-year-old woman who'd pulled up next to us in a red Honda Civic. She winked back with a smile. I gestured for her to roll down her window, then turned toward Shorty, my face now flush with color. One thing was for sure—she was as fine as they came.

"Yo, check out baby over here in the Civic," I yelled, reaching for the button to roll down the window. I turned back in her direction, smiling as if I were on a toothpaste commercial. I wasn't a real believer in picking up women off the street with corny-ass lines, but this sister was worth taking a shot at. "What's up, baby girl? Can a brotha get them digi—" I stopped myself abruptly and Shorty fell out laughing. I hadn't seen quite what I was expecting. Oh, there was a woman there all right, but it wasn't the fine sister I'd been flirting with just seconds before. She and her red Civic had made an illegal right on red and were halfway around the corner. In place of her car was a black Lincoln Continental. The driver was a mocha-colored, heavyset woman in her late fifties, wearing a very expensive but ugly bronze-colored wig. Both Shorty and I knew her quite well, and by the scowl on her face, it was clear she didn't appreciate my comment, our music, or Shorty's laughter in the background. Her name was Deaconess Lillian Wright, better known in whispers around my father's church as The Bitch. She was one of my mother's closest friends along with being one of my father's biggest political supporters.

"How you doing, Deaconess?" I raised my hand as I smiled meekly. She remained stone-faced, offering no reply. I rolled the window up and turned back toward Shorty, who'd stopped laughing and was back to rocking his head to the music.

"Shorty, turn the radio down," I told him through gritted teeth.

"What?" Shorty shouted, obviously wondering why I was whispering.

"I said turn the motherfuckin' radio down!" I yelled this time. Then I reached for the volume knob, turning the radio down myself. I turned back toward Deaconess Wright, who was already punching the buttons on her cell phone. I knew that could only mean one thing—*trouble*—especially when I saw her flailing her other arm as she yelled into the phone. I wasn't a lip reader, but her mouth looked like it was forming the word *drunk* several times. I sank into the seat, wishing I could take back the last few minutes of my life.

The light turned green, but before Shorty could hit the accelerator, Deaconess Wright swerved out of the right turn lane and into his, speeding down Jamaica Avenue and turning on Merrick Boulevard.

"Aw, shit." I slammed my hand on the dashboard. "Man, I bet that bitch is headed straight to the church to see my momma."

"So what?" Shorty shrugged.

"So what? Do you realize how much trouble I'm gonna get into?" I screwed up my face with disgust as I imagined the choice words my mother would have for me when I got to the church.

"Trouble for what?" Shorty sighed, rolling his eyes at me. "How old are you, Dante?"

"Man, you know how old I am," I snapped with attitude. "Same age as you."

"Okay, so you're old enough to drink in this state and buy cigarettes, right?" Shorty asked sarcastically.

"Yeah, what's the point, Shorty?"

"The point is . . ." Shorty took his eyes off the road and glared at me. "Why the fuck are you so worried about some old church biddy with droopy titties calling your momma? You a grown man. What your moms gonna do, give you a beatin'?"

I hesitated before I responded as if that was exactly what I was afraid of. "Look, Shorty, I been trying to explain this to you for years. Everything that my sister Donna and I do is a reflection of my parents, and a reflection of the church. My pops is Bishop T.K. Wilson, for crying out loud. He's one of the most influential ministers in the city, possibly even the state. Jesus, he's running for borough president."

"And? What's that supposed to mean? You know I like the bishop, Dante, but he ain't God. He's just a man. He likes pussy just like the rest of us heathens; otherwise you and your sister wouldn't be here."

I couldn't help it. I let out a frustrated laugh. Shorty had a way with words that was always colorful, if not true. Hell, I still heard my parents doing their thing every once in a while late at night.

"You don't understand how hard it is being the bishop's son, Shorty. They all think I'm the heir apparent to the bishop."

"Yeah, and they're right. Except maybe for Reverend Reynolds, you the only candidate."

"But I don't wanna be—"

Shorty cut me off. "Don't even start that shit, Dante. Not unless you're willing to tell your folks the truth."

"I can't tell them the truth. Not yet, anyway. My momma wants me to be the pastor one day, and so does the bishop. I can't let them down."

"Let them down! What about letting yourself down, Dante? You got a damn near perfect score on the LSATs and you don't even have the guts to apply to law school because of your parents." Shorty's face looked pained at the thought of me passing up that opportunity. "Man, you need to stand up to your parents. Shit, man, you don't even wanna be a minister. How you gonna be a pastor?"

I shrugged but remained silent. We'd had this conversation a hundred times before, and the result was always the same. I ended up agreeing with Shorty, but I never actually had the nerve to admit to my parents my true aspirations.

Shorty turned his attention back to the road, but not before he turned up the volume again. After a brief drive, he pulled his truck in front of the church and smiled as he stuck out his fist for me to tap. I smiled back as I tapped it then stepped out of the truck and stretched. At an even six feet three inches tall, I'm a well-built man with a basketball player's body and smooth, handsome, almond-colored features. I'm not trying to brag or anything, but everyone says I look like my dad minus the beard, and women have been calling him good-looking for as long as I can remember. My friend Shorty, not a bad-looking guy himself, isn't an inch over five six. He, too, is well built, but with a darker, mahogany complexion. His real name is John, but I can't remember anyone other than a few teachers calling him anything but Shorty since we met. He and I have been friends since the sixth grade, and much to my mother's chagrin, we've remained friends throughout the years.

"Yo, I'll check you later. Why don't we shoot by Scandalous, that new place in Long Island City, tonight?"

"Please. You know I can't be seen in a place like that," I replied. Even if I didn't have to worry about my public image as the preacher's son, I wasn't in the mood to go to a strip club anyway. I didn't mind hanging out with Shorty, but lately I'd been looking for a woman to settle down with, and a strip club isn't exactly the kind of place you're gonna find a woman to take home to your momma. "Yo, Shorty, why don't you come on in?"

Shorty never replied because a tall, voluptuous, olive-skinned woman exited the side door of the church, distracting him. She was wearing a short, black miniskirt and a tight-fitting red blouse. She was a big-boned woman with shapely thighs and a huge butt. She was what we brothers like to refer to as thick. Her name was Donna, my younger sister. Shorty had been infatuated with her for as long as I could remember. When we were younger, the two of them were actually pretty close. When Shorty couldn't find a date to the prom, he asked Donna and she went. You should have seen their prom picture. The two of them looked like Laurel and Hardy, my sister being a good four inches taller than him, even without her heels. Still, Shorty never seemed happier than he was that night at the prom with Donna.

"Hey, Donna." Shorty waved his hand eagerly. Donna waved back politely then walked up to me and kissed my cheek.

"Hey, sis, what's up?"

"My car's in the shop. Can I borrow yours, pleeeease?" She gave me this sad, pleading look then turned toward the church, watching the side door nervously. She must have been afraid my mother was gonna pop out those doors and make her change her clothes. What she was wearing was pretty provocative, and I was surprised she got out the house, let alone the church, without our mother's scrutiny. That's when the thought hit me that she had probably just changed in my office, which she had done before, and had been waiting by the window for my return so she could borrow my car and get out of Dodge.

"Where you going dressed like that?" I asked with brotherly concern.

"I'm going to see my friend. We're going to dinner at the Soul Café on Forty-second Street." She smiled. "Why? Is there a problem?" She gave me that don't-even-go-there-after-everything-I've-done-for-you look. Donna had done everything from helping me sneak girls into our house to pretending my girlfriends were her friends so they could sneak into my room after our parents were asleep. The last thing I wanted to do now was be a hypocrite.

"Nah, no problem." I sighed, trying to hold back my true feelings. "I just don't want you to get hurt, Donna. I hope you're taking the proper precautions."

"Don't worry about that, because I took them right out your dresser drawer." Donna blushed while I didn't even crack a smile. I hated the thought that my sister might be having sex, but she was twenty years old and there really wasn't anything I could do about it. "So can I borrow your truck, Dante? Please! I gotta get out of here before Mommy comes out."

I stared at my sister, then handed her the keys to the new Lincoln Aviator truck my parents had given me as a graduation present. "Don't you get in no accident with my car." I loved my sister, but she was a horrible driver; that was why her car was in the shop now.

"I won't. I promise." Donna smiled, wrapping her arms around me and kissing me on the cheek. "Oh, Dante, can you tell Mommy that I'm studying at Susan's?"

I hesitated, then thought about how many times she'd lied for me. "Yeah, sure. No problem."

"Thanks." She kissed me again then waved. "Bye, Shorty."

"Bye, Donna." Shorty and I watched her walk toward my car, then he turned to me with an unhappy look on his face. "She's got a boyfriend, doesn't she?"

"Yep."

"When did this all happen?" Shorty, like myself, had never known Donna to date. Matter of fact, after the prom, he pursued Donna for over a year. For a while I thought they might even hook up for real, but for the past few years Donna had been treating him like he barely existed. Even though it hurt Shorty, as far as I was concerned, it was a good thing. Best friends and sisters shouldn't be mixed.

I shrugged my shoulders. "I guess she's been seeing him for a couple of months."

"What? Why didn't you tell me?" There was obvious jealousy in his voice. That was exactly why I hadn't told him.

I stared at my lovesick friend. " 'Cause it's none of your business. You don't go around telling me who your sister is dating."

Shorty rolled his eyes. "So who is this guy, anyway?"

"I don't know, but whoever he is, he's got her nose wide open. She's used up about half the condoms in my drawer."

I could see the disappointment in Shorty's face and I felt sorry for him. He really liked my sister. I guess I just never knew how much until now, so I decided to try to take his mind off it.

"Hey, man, forget about my sister. Why don't you come on inside? The women's choir rehearsal's about to get out and you know they gonna have some food and some good-looking honeys down there."

Shorty glanced over at Deaconess Wright's Lincoln Continental and my mother's champagne-colored Mercedes-Benz parked in the church's parking lot. I could tell my offer was tempting. We hadn't eaten all day, and a lot of those church girls were hot in the ass. Still, the look in his eyes said he really wasn't up for any drama. With my mom and Deaconess Wright around, there was sure to be some. If things went the way they usually did, Shorty would be the one who ended up getting blamed for it, too.

"I think I'll pass, bro." He pointed at the two cars in the

church's reserved parking spaces. I guess he figured if he was going to deal with that, there was going to have to be a good reason, and that reason had just pulled away in my truck to see another guy. "It looks like you about to have some drama with your momma. Ain't no need for me to stick around. I'll just make things worse for you."

"Chicken. What, are you scared of my mother?" I teased.

"Pretty much." He nodded.

"I thought you said I should stand up to her."

"I said *you* should stand up to her. You're her son. Me, I'm just the guy from around the block. Only time your moms wants to see me is on Sunday morning and that's *only* if I'm putting something in the collection plate."

I chuckled. "You know she loves you, Shorty."

"Yeah, like a snake loves a rat. Did you forget what she did last Saturday?" I figured that was best left unsaid, so I remained quiet. I hoped Shorty would do the same, but he continued. "Your moms got on the mike at the church bazaar and told everyone who'd listen to hold on to their daughters 'cause Satan just walked in. Them people started staring at me like I had horns and shit. Now, I've been called a lot of things, Dante, but to have the first lady of the church you belong to call you the Devil has got to be the worst."

I lowered my head, laughing at my mother's antics. Despite her actions, I really don't think my mother disliked Shorty. She just loved the hell outta me and didn't want to admit that I'm human and can make mistakes. It was easier for her to make Shorty the scapegoat for my missteps. "She didn't mean anything by it, Shorty."

Shorty rolled his eyes. "Dante, face it, man. Your mom doesn't like me. She never has, and she probably never will. She thinks I'm a bad influence on you."

"Yeah, little does she know I'm probably a worse one on you." We both laughed as I said goodbye and headed for the side entrance to the church.

2

Donna

I entered the Soul Café on Forty-second Street and headed straight for the bar, relieved that no one had stopped me to check my ID. I searched for an empty table. I was early for my date with Terrance and I wanted to have a drink to calm my nerves before he arrived. Just the thought of being alone with him had me so excited that my hands were shaking. I'd been dating Terrance for a little over four months now and he continued to have the same overwhelming effect on me as he had the first day we met. He was unlike any other man that I'd ever dated, and there was no doubt in my mind that I was in love with him.

I spotted an empty booth on the other side of the bar where I was sure Terrance would see me. I immediately headed toward it. I could feel the eyes of almost every man in the place on me as I walked across the room. A few of them tried to stop me for idle chitchat, but I ignored them and kept right on going. There wasn't anything in that room that interested me other than a drink, but those fools were persistent as hell. Maybe it wasn't a good idea for me to wear such a micro-miniskirt, but Terrance had mentioned on more than one occasion that he liked seeing me in skirts because of my shapely legs. Truth is, I think he liked the easy access to what was under my skirt a little more, but either way, I was hoping that when he came in, *he'd* be pleased. I never imagined I'd end up being eye candy for every horny guy in Manhattan, though. Oh well, I guess that's just the price you pay when you're trying to please the man you love.

I'd known I wanted Terrance the second he showed up at the church two years before. He was everything I'd ever hoped for in a man. He was handsome, caring, intelligent, funny, and as I would find out later, a phenomenal lover. Everything a girl would want to take home to her momma—that is, if her momma weren't a bitch like mine. From the moment I had showed an interest in boys, my mother made it clear that no one was good enough for her daughter. That was ironic, though, because it also seemed like no matter how hard I tried to please her, nothing I did was ever good enough for her. Any time I was less than perfect, she would remind me what a disappointment I was. My mother was a hard woman to please, which was why I didn't make my interest in Terrance public knowledge.

However, I wasn't the only one interested in him, and the others weren't shy about hiding their feelings. It seemed like every woman in the church was after him—including my best friend, RaShanda Wright. With all that competition, I had my work cut out for me just to get his attention, but I knew one day he was going to be mine. One day he was gonna take my gift of virginity and make me his woman. I would just have to be patient. Besides, my real dilemma wasn't RaShanda or the other girls in the church. It was my mother, the biggest cock blocker in New York. The way she acted you could have made a case that she wanted Terrance for herself. So, unlike the other girls in the church, it took a little longer for him to notice me than I would have liked. I didn't mind, though, because after all those lonely Friday and Saturday nights I spent dreaming about him, Terrance finally asked me out to dinner and we'd been a couple ever since.

When I finally arrived at the booth, it didn't take long for the waitress to appear. I ordered an apple martini and drank about half of it before I nearly choked on what was left of it. I couldn't believe my eyes when I spotted Shorty headed my way. I was tempted to duck under the table, but by then it was obvious he'd seen me. Three seconds later he slid into the seat across from me and smiled.

"Shorty? What are you doing here?" I whispered. My voice was filled with paranoia and agitation as I glanced around the bar, expecting Dante to pop up at any moment.

"I heard you tell Dante where you were going," he replied.

"You followed me?" My jaw dropped and my eyes were as wide as silver dollars. I glanced at my watch nervously. I only had about ten minutes to get rid of him before Terrance showed up.

"Yeah, I wanted to see if we had the same taste in women," he said sarcastically. "I mean, you are gay, aren't you? That's the excuse you used when you rejected me." There was anger in his eyes and his voice was testy.

"What are you getting an attitude about? You're not my man. And I do not appreciate you following me. My social life is my business, Shorty. I don't be chasin' around after you and Dante when y'all be messin' with them hootchies. Now, if you don't mind, I'm waiting for someone and you're sitting in their seat." I picked up my drink and turned my head toward the door.

"You want me to leave? Okay, I'll leave, but I'm just going over to the bar to have a drink." He started to slide out of the booth and I grabbed his arm with my free hand.

"Go home, Shorty."

"For what, Donna? Is there something you don't want me to see?"

"No. I just don't want you to get hurt."

"Why? Are you seeing someone I know?"

"That's none of your business. Where's Dante? I know he's lurking around here somewhere." I changed the subject.

"He's at the church."

Well, thank God for small favors, I thought.

"Good. Now go home, Shorty." I tried to convey my point with my most serious expression.

"You want me to leave, Donna? Okay, I'll go, but just answer one question for me." I was desperate so I agreed with a nod. "Why'd you lie to me?"

"Lie to you about what? I didn't lie to you, Shorty."

"Yes, you did. You lied to me about being gay."

I looked around to see if anyone had heard him. "Who said I lied?"

"You did when you told Dante you took condoms out his drawer. Why'd you take the condoms out of his drawer if you're with a woman?"

I lowered my head because his face had *go 'head, tell me another lie* written all over it.

"Donna, you're not a lesbian. You know it and I know. You're seeing a man."

Suddenly I felt bad. Shorty and I had fooled around a little during my late teens. Nothing serious like Terrance and me, or even as serious as Dante and his ex, Anita. Hell, I'd never even let Shorty get to third base, but as far as he was concerned, we were a couple. I didn't mind letting him have his little fantasy, though, as long as he didn't tell my brother or my parents about us. Truth is, I kinda liked the idea of pulling the wool over my mother's eyes, so everything was cool for a while. Our problem came when Terrance showed up at the church and captured my heart. From that point on, I had no interest in Shorty. That's when I told him that story about being gay. After that, he never pushed up on me again, and to my surprise, he was mature about it and kept it to himself. But I could tell from the way he looked at me now that he still cared. Don't get me wrong, I thought Shorty was a sweet boy, but that was just it. He was a boy, and Terrance was a man.

"So what's up, Donna? You're messing with some dude, aren't you?"

"Shorty, I'm sorry. I was just trying not to hurt your feelings. I care about you—"

He raised his hand to stop me so that he could finish my sentence. "But just not the way I care about you, right?" I nodded and he frowned.

"So who is he? Do I know him?"

I didn't say a word; my facial expression said it all.

"We could have been good together, Donna. I would have done anything for you."

"I know that, Shorty, but sometimes what's good to you is not good for you. Besides, it would have never worked."

"Why not?"

"Because of my mother and because of Dante. He doesn't want us to be together, Shorty. He never did. He's afraid he's gonna lose his best friend to his sister." I was trying to soften the blow, but Shorty wasn't making it easy.

"Fuck Dante! Fuck your mother, too. I'm in love with you, Donna. You never even gave me a chance. Just give me a chance."

"I'm sorry, Shorty, but I can't do that. I'm not in love with you. I'm in love with someone else." I felt so bad and he looked so sad.

"No one is ever gonna love you like I do, Donna. No one." He got up from the seat and looked down at me with these sad, dark eyes. "Just remember this: One day you're going to end up on my doorstep looking for that love. You just better pray that I open the door."

I can't explain how bad I felt as I watched Shorty walk away. My sadness was not long lived, though, because a few seconds after Shorty walked out the door, Terrance walked in. I waved at him in an attempt to get his attention. He glanced my way, but I don't think he saw me, because this high-yellow bitch was grinning in his face like she was a contestant for Miss Black America and he was one of the judges. I was tempted to get up out of my seat and snatch her fake-ass ponytail right out of her head, but Terrance had made it very clear that he didn't like drama. So I sat there and waited for my boo to notice me. Besides, I didn't have anything to worry about. He'd never disrespected me. Well, at least not until now. I couldn't believe my eyes when he leaned over and whispered something in that heifer's ear, and you better believe I was livid when her grinning ass handed him a piece of paper and he took out a pen and started writing. He might not have liked drama, but he was about to get some. I'd given that man my heart, not to mention my virginity. He was not going to make a fool out of me.

"Excuse me, miss. Can I buy you a drink?" I looked up as a handsome, thirty-something-year-old man stepped directly in front of me, blocking my line of sight to Terrance and that bitch. He was dressed in a very expensive suit and looked like he was probably making big bucks. Not that it mattered to me. He could've been Denzel Washington holding a suitcase full of money. The only thing that brother could do for me was move out of the way so I could see what that bitch was doing with my man. "Miss, can I buy you a drink?" he inquired again politely.

"No, I already have a drink," I told him with hostility as I leaned to my right in an attempt to see around him. "Now, could you move out my way?"

"Well, do you mind if I sit down?" This guy just didn't get the hint. I was about two seconds from cursing his ass out.

"I don't care what you do." I sighed. "I just want you to get out my way. Can't you see I'm trying to look at something? Now move!"

I guess he got the message, because he finally walked away. When he did, I almost passed out, because neither Terrance nor that high-yellow bitch was anywhere to be found and that scared the hell out of me. The only thing that came to mind was that Terrance had taken her somewhere to fuck. I knew I shouldn't have been thinking that way, but sometimes you've just got to face facts. Terrance was always horny and loved spontaneous sex. We'd done it everywhere and anywhere in the few months we'd been together. The freakier the situation, the more he seemed to like it. Now it looked like he'd taken that bitch into an alley, or perhaps the restaurant bathroom, and was doing to her what I'd expected to have done to me. I could feel the tears threatening to run down my face. Before then you couldn't have paid me a million dollars to believe Terrance would do this to me. I lowered my head on the table and let the tears flow. Part of me wanted to get up and check the bathroom or the alley behind the restaurant, but I was scared of what I might find. How the hell could this be happening to me?

"Miss, you okay?"

Don't ask me how long I had my head down, but when I looked up, the waitress was standing there.

"No, I'm not all right. Do I look all right to you?" I snapped.

"Look, I was just trying to help." She started to walk away.

"Hey," I called to her and she turned around. "I'm sorry. I just saw my boyfriend leave with another woman. I'm a little pissed, if you know what I mean."

"Yeah, if you're going to be pissed, that's a good reason. These men are getting bolder and bolder these days." I didn't reply. I just sat up and wiped my eyes. "Hey, how about a drink on the house? You want another apple martini?"

"Can you bring me something strong? Real strong." I lowered my eyes to the table again.

"Sure. How about a Long Island Iced Tea?"

"Yeah, that'll work. Thanks."

She walked away. When I finally looked up again, every muscle in my body tightened as I spotted the high-yellow bitch come from around the corner that separated the restaurant from the bar. That bitch had the nerve to be adjusting her ponytail as she headed in my direction. A vision of Terrance holding on to her ponytail as he screwed her from behind in a bathroom stall popped into my head and I became furious. The closer she got, the angrier I got. Oh, it was about to be on.

"Is your name Donna?" she asked rudely when she reached my table. She had the nerve to look like she was trying to hide a smirk behind a smile, and her body language was saying *Yeah, bitch, I just fucked your man and it was good*. I wondered if she was actually gonna have the nerve to speak those words to me. I held on tight to my purse, because if she said something smart, I was gonna beat her ass with it.

I stood quickly and was in her face. "Yeah, I'm Donna, bitch. Why?"

She took a step back as if she was surprised by my aggression.

"Your boyfriend asked me to give this to you." She raised her hand and I lifted my purse in the air. If she made one wrong move, they were going to be picking her ass up off the floor.

"That's right, bitch, he's my boyfriend. *My man*," I growled. I'm sorry but I couldn't keep that shit in.

She took another step back, raising both her hands defensively. "Look, I don't know what the problem is, but I'm just the hostess here. I'm not looking for trouble. Your boyfriend asked me to give you this note. I'm sorry. I would have given it to you earlier, but I had customers who had to be seated in the restaurant." She waved her hand, and that's when I noticed the folded paper in her hand.

"What's this?" I snarled.

"I don't know. He just asked me to give it to you." She handed me the note. I felt stupid for jumping to conclusions once I saw my name written with hearts around it.

"Look, I'm sorry about the way I acted. I'm PMSing," I lied.

"Whatever," she replied, then walked away in a huff. That's when I realized half the bar was staring at me and I'd just made a real ass out of myself. I sat down and unfolded the note.

Hey Baby,

I see you over there in that sexy skirt. It's a real turn-on. Look, I've decided that maybe we should skip dinner and get right to dessert. I've kind of fixed up something special for you across the street at the Howard Johnson motel. I'm in room 345. Why don't you come over and join me?

Tee

As stupid as I felt about wanting to fight the hostess, I had to smile. Terrance was always coming up with some creative way to make my life interesting. A million things ran through my mind as I thought about what type of surprise he might have waiting for me in that hotel room. With him you just couldn't be sure. One thing I was sure of, though. It was going to involve some mind-blowing sex. Like earlier, just the thought of having Terrance inside me had my panties moist. I glanced around for my waitress, then ended up just leaving a twenty-dollar bill on my table and rushing to the door.

3

Dante

When I entered the church, I was greeted by the loud cackling of women gossiping, then a sudden silence. I smiled as I approached the thirty or so women of the First Jamaica Ministries award-winning women's choir standing in the church recreation area. "Hi, Dante." One woman smiled.

"What's up, Latrice?" I replied with a nod. That started a chain reaction of greetings, shy waves, and blushing if I happened to make eye contact. The women seemed to part like the Red Sea to allow me to pass through and enter the hallway to my office. I could feel their eyes still on me. I thought I even heard a few sighs.

I'd been given this type of attention from the young women of the church for years and it seemed like most of their mothers encouraged it. As the son of the bishop, I was treated like royalty, the crown prince of the church. As with all princes, every young woman in the village wanted to be my princess. For years I'd taken advantage of that, fooling around with half of the young women in the congregation. Strip clubs and bars didn't have anything on a good church function if you were looking to get some.

I walked into my office and closed the door. I sat behind my desk and listened to the women of the choir leaving, then I checked over the schedule for the youth basketball league, which I ran as director of church activities. Not long after I sat down, there was a knock on the door, a knock I'd been expecting ever since Shorty and I pulled in front of the building. I got up and approached the door, but there was no need. The door opened before I could get there.

I stopped dead in my tracks when I realized it was not my mother, as I had expected. It was the vibrant and sexy Anita Bell, the only woman I'd ever loved, or at least thought I loved.

"Anita." I gasped as my eyes quickly roamed over her body. Anita was dressed in a very conservative white church dress with white heels, but her voluptuous body made anything she wore look provocative.

"Dante." She smiled. "I guess some things never change."

"What's that supposed to mean?" I tried to play it cool, but I was truly confused until Anita pointed at my crotch. I looked down and cringed. When it came to Anita, it was obvious which one of my heads was in control. I lowered the folder I was holding to cover my swollen manhood.

"Don't hide it now. I've already seen it." She smirked, locking the door then stepping closer to me. She kissed me with her full lips. "I missed you, Dante," she whispered.

She kissed me again before I could respond. This time she wrapped her arms around me and I did the same, closing my eyes. Our kiss was so passionate it took my breath away. When it was finally over, we stayed wrapped in each other's arms and stared lustfully into each other's eyes.

"God, I missed you, Dante," she whispered as her right hand moved from my backside to my crotch.

"I missed you, too," I said as I gently pushed her away. "Just not enough to commit adultery. Where's your husband?"

Anita took a step forward and looked up at me with a frown. "Why'd you have to go and mention him?"

"I don't know," I said sarcastically. "It seemed kind of important when I realized you were unzipping my fly." Anita sighed. "So where is he, Anita? Where's your husband?"

"He's at our new house, unpacking our things. But you don't have to worry about that. Only thing you need to be worried about is what's in front of you. I want you, Dante. And I missed you. I've been thinking about you every day since I left."

I looked at her and my mind traveled down memory lane. Anita and I had been lovers for almost two years, although very few people other than Shorty and my sister knew about it. We'd kept things on the low because Anita was my father's secretary and ten years my senior. The age difference didn't bother me, though. I wanted to tell the world. As far as I was concerned, I was going to marry Anita. But Anita was scared and wanted to keep everything a secret. She swore that my mother and father would never go for us being together. That's why she started dating Deacon Robert Emerson behind my back. Deacon Emerson was an arm amputee in his early forties. He was well known around the church and had considerable assets. He'd been trying to get Anita to date him since she'd started working at the church. For almost four years she'd told him no, but one day she agreed to go out with him. Three months later, much to my chagrin, they were married and moved to Florida at Anita's request. She knew she needed to get as far away from me as possible. She may have denied it then, but she was in love with me. Now a little under a year later, she and the deacon were back, and since she had mentioned a new house, it appeared they were back to stay.

"I love you, Dante, and now that your father has given me my old job back, we can get right back to doing everything the way we did before. And I mean everything." She posed flirtatiously and gave me this sexy look that made my hard dick even harder.

"What about your husband?"

"What about him? We kept your parents in the dark for almost two years. What makes you think we can't keep his stupid ass in the dark, too?" She stepped closer, rubbing her hands on my chest the way I liked it. "I need you, Dante. I need your love and I need your body. He can't satisfy me the way you can. I haven't had an orgasm since I was with you." She pouted like a child who had been punished.

I thought about how easy it was for me to satisfy her. I knew Anita's body better than I knew my own. I ran my finger down her spine and she shuddered with excitement, then I lowered my head and blew in her ear. Anita moaned. *How could the deacon not be able to do that?* I wondered, then smiled at my own ego. Anita was my pussy. She had always been my pussy. I looked at her. I looked at her in the manner a man reserves only for his woman. Oh, those feelings were starting to come back. But instead of making me want her, they made me angry. I pushed her away.

"Well, I don't want you. Not if you're married. Not if you're his wife instead of mine. What are you doing back here anyway, Anita?"

"I hated Florida. I hate him. I needed to get back to you. I love you, Dante, and I'm never gonna let you go. Please, baby, let me show you how much I love you," she begged.

I didn't say a word. I just silently watched Anita unbutton her dress until she was no longer wearing a conservative church dress. She was still wearing all white, though—a white push-up bra, white panties, white garter belt with white stockings, and of course, those sexy white stiletto heels. The contrast against her mahogany skin was stunning.

"Please, baby. Let me show you how much I love you." Anita rubbed her hands on my chest again then kissed me gently before she started to slowly kneel. I knew what she was about to do and was virtually powerless to stop her. Oral sex was my weakness and Anita was an expert.

"I can't do this, Anita," I whispered repeatedly, but that didn't stop her from struggling with me to get my pants down. Finally I just decided to give in. When it came to Anita, my big head went on autopilot and my little head took over. I placed my hand gently on her hair and stared blankly at the wall as I waited eagerly for the pleasure she would soon give me. Anita licked her lips as she stared at my pulsating manhood and I could tell she was preparing to swallow it whole. Unfortunately, before she could move, there was a knock on the door and a jiggling of the doorknob.

"Dante, are you in here, son?" my mother called through the door.

Without thinking, I instinctively answered, "Yes," as both Anita and I stared at each other with panicked expressions. We knew that if I didn't open that door quickly, my mother, a suspicious woman by nature, would put two and two together the second she saw Anita in my office. And Lord help us both if she had Deaconess Wright with her as I suspected. Anita reached down and picked up her dress then turned back to me, looking to get some direction.

"Hide!" I was as panic-stricken as Anita. I fumbled with my belt buckle as she glared at me.

"Where?" she asked.

My eyes searched the room for a hiding place. I jumped when my mother knocked on the door again. I pointed toward my desk.

"Dante, open this door," my mother said sternly.

"Under my desk," I whispered to Anita. She scrambled over there as I approached the door. I waited until she was out of sight then opened the door. My mother and my father greeted me.

"Have you been drinking?"

"No, Ma," I replied, opening my arms to give my mother a hug. In my mind, I was cursing the woman in the black Continental. *Damn, that bitch Deaconess Wright lied on me again.*

My mother sniffed me like a dog as she kissed my cheek, then smiled with satisfaction. If I knew her, she'd been defending me tooth and nail and now felt vindicated. "Why was this door locked?"

"Huh? Oh, uh," I searched my mind for an excuse as my mother stared into my eyes, "because I was changing my clothes and I didn't want any of the women's choir walking in and seeing my private parts. I just came from the gym and wanted to get out of those sweaty clothes." I casually turned my back and zipped up my pants as my mother walked by. She was surveying my office as if she knew I was lying.

"Hey, Bishop." I offered my father my hand, still keeping my eyes on my mother and my desk. "So what brings you two down here?" My mother's suspicious look instantly became a jubilated smile and she spoke before my father had a chance to get out a word.

"Oh, Dante. We have the best news. Come sit down so we can tell you." I moved over to my desk quickly and sat down. My father had a habit of sitting at my desk and that wasn't something I could risk right now. As my parents settled in the chairs on the other side, I glanced under my desk. Anita, still half-naked, smiled at me. I pushed my chair back about a foot when she stroked the inside of my leg. I knew Anita too well. She was a freak and I wouldn't put it past her to try something crazy like pulling out my manhood to finish what she'd tried to start earlier.

"So, what's this great news?" I asked, subtly removing Anita's hand as she tried to unzip my pants.

"Well, Dante . . ." My mother turned to my father with a huge smile. She looked like she was gonna bust a gasket she was so excited. "I'm going to let your father tell you."

I turned my attention to my father, who leaned forward with a paternal smile. "Well, son. Your mother and I just found out you've been accepted into Howard University's School of Divinity."

"I have?" All expression left my face as I looked from one parent to the other then back again.

"You sure have, son." My father smiled.

"Dante, I'm so proud of you." My mother had tears in her eyes.

"But, but I never applied to Howard's School of Divinity," I stuttered.

"I know. I applied for you," my smiling mother replied. "I know how busy you can get with all these church activities." She was so clearly pleased with herself and expected the same from me.

"Congratulations, son." My father nodded as he stood and offered his hand. "Howard's Divinity School is a fine institution. I'm sure you'll do well."

"Thanks, Bishop," I replied meekly, taking my father's hand without thinking.

"Come on, Charlene. We're supposed to be over at the mayor's office in thirty minutes."

My mother smiled. "I think the mayor is going to endorse your father for borough president."

"That's great news, Bishop."

"Thanks, son, but not as good as yours."

My mother stood and leaned over my desk to kiss me. "Dante, I'm so proud of you. I can't wait to tell everyone in the church the good news."

"Neither can I, Mom," I answered weakly, glad that she stepped away from my desk without noticing Anita under there.

I watched my parents walk toward the door and suddenly I had a surge of courage. I had to tell them. I had to tell them I didn't want to go to Howard's Divinity School. I didn't want to go to anyone's seminary, and I had to tell them before they started to blab their news to everyone in the church because then I'd be painted into a corner.

"Ma," I called, standing up quickly. Just as the words left my mouth, I realized I had to sit down because my fly was unzipped and Anita's hand was reaching for my dick.

"Yes," my mother replied as she turned around. I sat down just in the nick of time.

"Ah, nothin'. Just wanted to say thanks." I gave her a fake smile.

"Oh, you're welcome, baby." My mother took my father's arm and smiled contentedly as she shut the door with her free hand. When they were both out of sight, I exhaled loudly and stared down at Anita.

"Jesus Christ," Anita said from under my desk. "I didn't think they were ever gonna leave." She tugged at my pants.

"Stop it, Anita!" I slapped her hand then pushed my chair back about three feet to get away.

"No, Dante. You stop it," she said adamantly as she crawled out from under my desk. "Stop fighting me. Stop fighting us."

"That's just it, Anita. There is no us. Not since you got married." There was hurt in my voice. Anita stepped forward until her hands were close enough to touch me. She smiled as she rubbed her hands along my chest, probably surprised that I didn't stop her. Not that it mattered. I could never resist her for long and she knew it. All she had to do was be patient.

I took a deep breath, trying to keep my hormones under control. "Put your clothes on, Anita."

"Why, are you finding it hard to control yourself?" She grabbed my arms and pulled me closer until her breasts were rubbing against my chest and our lips were close enough to kiss. I knew I was in trouble because I wanted to touch her, to kiss her, to be with her. So she was right. I was finding it hard to control myself, and by the time she pressed her lips against mine, I had lost control. Thank God I heard some shuffling outside my door.

"Did you hear that?" I broke the kiss.

"Hear what?" she replied in frustration.

"I just heard someone outside the door." She gave me a skeptical look, trying to kiss me again, but then stopped abruptly when she heard the noise.

"You think it's your parents again?" she whispered.

I glanced at my watch. "No, it's probably one of the deacons. Their choir rehearsal starts in about five minutes."

"The deacons' choir? Oh, Lord," Anita muttered, almost instantly picking up her dress. She was more panicked now than when she was under my desk with my parents in the room. "All my husband's friends are members of that choir. I can't let them see me like this."

I frowned as I watched her get dressed. A large part of me wished she'd just say fuck it and stay, but I knew she wouldn't do that. Anita wanted the best of both worlds. She wanted the deacon's money and my body. What she didn't know was that, by picking up her clothes, she had just lost the latter.

"Don't look so sad, baby. I'm gonna make it up to you," she promised. "We just have to get out of here. Why don't we meet at the Jet Motel? You know, just like old times." She gave me a smile before glancing at the door nervously.

"I don't think so, Anita. As long as you're with the deacon, we're over." I picked up my briefcase and walked past Anita toward the door.

Anita's eyes got small and her face got this real evil look. "You don't get it, do you, Dante? We're not over until I say we're over. And I haven't said we're over, so I'll see you at work tomorrow. You might wanna bring some condoms."

Her voice gave me goose bumps but I didn't back down.

"Go home, Anita, 'cause you're starting to scare me," I told her as I left the office.

4

Tanisha

I'd been dreaming one of those good dreams. You know, the kind that you can control. The kind where everything you want just seems to happen exactly the way you want it to happen. Well, in my dream, I was on a deserted beach lying on a blanket while Morris Chestnut rubbed suntan lotion on my back and Nelly fed me grapes. It was one of those dreams where neither of them seemed to care about sex. All they cared about was making *me* happy, and believe it or not, that turned me on. There is nothing sexier than a guy who wants to be with you just because you're you and not because his hormones or his boys are telling him he needs to get between your legs, because we all know guys don't care 'bout nothing and no one but themselves.

"Nelly," I whispered. "Why don't you take off your clothes?"

"You sure?" he asked, smiling at me with those bedroom eyes of his.

I nodded and he placed the bowl of grapes on the blanket. He stood in front of me then snapped his fingers and this slow, erotic music started playing. A few seconds later, he was swaying his hips to the beat, teasing me with his movements. Not long after that, Morris was standing next to him and the two of them were both taking off their shirts like they were Chippendale's dancers.

"Tanisha. Tanisha." A voice called, but it wasn't Nelly and it wasn't Morris either. It was a familiar voice but I just couldn't make it out, and to be honest, I didn't want to. I had other things on my mind. Nelly and Morris were just about to take their pants off, but the voice just kept calling me. The more it called, the more my dream guys seemed to fade away until finally they were both gone.

"Tanisha! Tanisha!"

"What?" I growled angrily in frustration. I was awake now, and when I opened my eyes, there was my twelve-year-old brother Aubrey standing in front of the living room sofa I used for a bed. All he was wearing was a dingy pair of drawers. "What you want, Aubrey?"

"I'm hungry," he whined.

"So? Go make you a bowl of Cap'n Crunch," I snapped, closing my eyes as I tried to snuggle under the covers and get back to my dream. "I just got home from work a couple of hours ago."

"There ain't no Cap'n Crunch and there ain't no milk," he answered.

"Stop lying, Aubrey." I lifted my head, shooting him a dirty look.

"I'm not lying, Tanisha. Mommy's friends came over last night and ate all the cereal and drank up all the milk." His words angered me. I'd bought that cereal and a quart of milk before I left for work last night just so he'd have something to eat before he went to school.

"Goddammit!" Now I was pissed off. Not at my brother, but my mother. This shit didn't make any sense. What kind of mother lets people come in her house and eat the only food she has for her children? I turned back over and stared at my little brother. He was a pain in the ass at times, but he was a good kid. Unlike me, he liked school and was good at it. He was gonna make something of himself one day. Go to college and possibly be a doctor, or maybe a lawyer. I was gonna make sure of that.

"Where's Mommy?" I asked angrily.

"I don't know." He shrugged. "She wasn't in her room when I got up."

"It figures," I mumbled.

I glanced at the clock on the living room wall. It was 7:15 A.M. I'd only been home from work a couple of hours, but when I came into the house, my mother had been in her bedroom with the door shut, talking to somebody. Probably some trick or one of her smoking buddies—and I don't mean cigarettes. I hate to admit it, but my mom's a crackhead. Been one for years.

"What you want for breakfast, Aubrey?" I sighed.

"Pancakes." He smiled.

"Okay." I sat up on the sofa. Morris and Nelly were gonna have to wait until I got my little brother off to school. "Hand me my sweatpants." He handed them to me and I slipped into them. Then I reached over on the sofa and searched for my scarf before heading into the bathroom.

Five minutes later I was walking down 109th Street toward Guy Brewer Boulevard and the little C-Town supermarket three blocks away. I could have gone to the bodega a block away, but I was hoping to spot my mother on the boulevard and give her a piece of my mind. Unfortunately, she was nowhere to be found. The only people I saw on the boulevard were those who were waiting for the bus, and the losers who hung around the corner near the supermarket.

When I walked up, the losers started whistling and catcalling at me like a bunch of dogs in heat. I didn't pay them no mind, though. I was used to it. Even with a scarf, a beat-up T-shirt, and a baggy old pair of sweatpants, there was no hiding my body. God had blessed me with a pair of perfect D-cup titties that stood straight up and an ass that could make Jennifer Lopez jealous. I was used to the attention from both men and women, but I knew the bitch in me was about to come out when one of those fools ran to the supermarket entrance and blocked my way.

"What's up, *baby?* You sure lookin' good today." His name was Joe-Joe and he had so much alcohol on his breath it almost knocked me down. The one major drawback to living in my neighborhood was you never meet any real men, just thugs and creeps like Joe-Joe.

"Thank you," I said politely, hoping that I could just sidestep him and go into the market. But as always when it came to these fools on the boulevard, he took my kindness for weakness and wouldn't let me pass.

"Hey, baby. Where you going in such a rush? I wanna talk to you. You remember me, don't you? I'm Joe-Joe. We talked at the club a couple weeks ago. I'm the guy that knows your momma, 'member?" I glanced at my watch. I didn't have time for this shit. I had to get Aubrey off to school so he wouldn't be late.

"Yeah, Joe-Joe, I remember you. Now could you please let me pass? I got some shopping to do." I tried to push my way past but he grabbed my arm.

"What, you too good to talk to me or something? You wasn't too good to take my money two weeks ago, was you?" He started grinning like there was more to it than there really was, and his friends all started laughing. I pulled my arm free and got up in his face.

"Please, nigga, don't be acting like you some big spender, 'cause your ass only gave me a dollar. Matter of fact, you can have that shit back right now with interest if you want it. What I owe you, a dollar twenty-five?" His friends laughed even harder this time and I was hoping this little scene was over, but unfortunately it wasn't.

"Yeah, that's about right, since everyone knows you ain't but a quarter of the woman your momma is, and she ain't nothin' but a five-dollar ho." Of course his little peanut gallery was damn near on the ground cracking up now. It was a good thing I didn't have my blade, because I'd probably be on my way to central booking for attempted murder.

"Well, if we hoes, at least we get paid, Joe-Joe. From what I hear, everyone on the block done had your wife for free. Everyone but you, that is. But now's your chance. I just passed your house and the line outside your door was down to about ten. Matter of fact, if you ask my twelve-year-old brother, he might let you cut the line."

His friends were laughing so loud it sounded like they were crying. Joe-Joe didn't have a comeback for this one. He just stood there stunned. That's when I took the opportunity to push my way past him and into the safety of the store.

"That'll be six seventy-six," the cashier said nonchalantly, staring at her fingernails as if behind her register was the last place she wanted to be at seven-thirty in the morning. I nodded then reached in my bag for my wallet, only to pull my hand out empty.

"Where the fuck is my wallet?" I thought out loud, looking up at the cashier in a panic. She shrugged her shoulders as if to say, "Don't look at me."

The first thing that came to my mind was that my mother had stolen it. She had a habit of going through my things while I was asleep and stealing whatever money she could find. But then I remembered I'd purposely taken my wallet out of my bag and placed it under the sofa cushion just for that reason. I let out a thankful sigh then gave the cashier a weak, embarrassed smile.

"I left my wallet at my house. Can you hold this to the side while I run home and get it? I'll be back in five minutes. I promise. I only live down the block."

She rolled her eyes and shook her head. "Damn, now I

gotta void this shit outta my register. Do you know how much of a pain in the ass that is?" she mumbled as she picked up the intercom from next to her register.

I wanted to say, "No, and I really don't care. Just do your fucking job," but instead I smiled weakly and said, "Sorry."

The girl sucked her teeth then spoke into the intercom. Her voice echoed throughout the store. "I need a manager at register one for a void. A manager at register one, please, for a void."

There was an immediate grumbling from the five or six customers who were standing behind me. Not that I could blame them. The store only had one register open, and now, thanks to me, it was closed.

"How much is her stuff?" a male voice asked from behind.

"Six seventy-six," the girl replied.

"I got her. Just add this to it." I turned around and had to check myself because the brother who stepped out of the line was drop-dead gorgeous. I flashed him my patented you-know-you-want-me smile, but he barely looked at me as he handed the cashier a bottle of water, a sandwich, and a twenty-dollar bill. Damn, of all the times to come out the house lookin' busted. I musta looked like a female version of Flava Flav with that multicolored scarf wrapped around my head and no makeup. Not to mention the fact that my sweat-suit didn't match and had a big bleach stain on it. But busted or not, I wanted that brother to notice me.

"Thanks," I said in my sexiest voice. "I can pay you back. We just have to run by my house. I live right up the block." If I could get him to the house, then at least I could run upstairs and take off the scarf and put on some makeup before he left.

"Don't worry about it, sister. I'm in a little bit of a rush." He took his change then picked up my bag and handed it to me before heading toward the door.

"But, but . . ." I had to catch my breath as I watched him

walk away. Not only was he tall and fine, he was bowlegged, too. *Mmm, mmm, mmm,* I thought, *that was so damn fine!* I also appreciated the fact that he wasn't thugged out like the rest of the brothers around my way. He was wearing a New York Jets throwback jersey and a pair of baggy jeans, but he carried himself like a gentleman, not a wannabe killer. Still, it was obvious from his muscular arms and V-shaped chest that he was far from being a punk. *Shit, why the fuck didn't I get dressed before I left the house?*

I glanced at the cashier and she said, "Fuck it. If he don't want the money, let his ass go."

"I don't care about the money," I said. "Did you see how fine he was? I want him."

"Yeah, he was cute, but he wasn't all that."

"Yes he was," I stated before heading toward him and the front door. I wasn't quite sure what I was going to say when I caught up to him, but I'm the type of woman who knows what she wants, and I wanted him.

"Excuse me, excuse me!" I yelled, hoping to catch his attention. I caught up to him right in front of the automatic doors and he looked my way. He just wasn't looking at me the way I was looking at him.

"Did I forget something?" he asked.

I contemplated saying, "Yeah—me," but instead I said, "Sorta," as I leaned against the storefront glass.

"Look, I can't let you pay for this stuff without paying you back. Is there any way for me to get in touch with you so I can give you back your money?"

He patted his shirt pocket impatiently then checked his pants pocket, pulling out some kind of postcard or party flyer. "I don't have any business cards on me and I'm headed over to Brooklyn right now. Just forget the money, sister, aw'ight? It's no big deal."

He turned to the door and I grabbed his arm.

"It's a big deal to me," I said firmly. "I don't need charity. I work for a living."

"You sure are persistent, aren't you?"

"I usually get what I want," I told him with a smile. I was hoping that he might at least look at my titties or my ass or something to show he had some interest, but the way he was acting I was starting to think he might be gay.

"I'm starting to believe you. You think I can have my arm back?"

"Oh, sorry." I gave him an embarrassed look as I let him go. I'd completely forgotten that I was holding on to his arm.

"Okay, look, if you really wanna pay me back, I'm gonna be at the African Poetry Theater tomorrow night. You can bring it to me there." He handed me the postcard he was carrying and I read the bold type that announced an open mike poetry reading.

"Okay, I'll see you then. I like poetry." I smiled.

He nodded then motioned toward the door with his hand as if to say, *After you.* I took his cue and exited. It was nice to be treated like a lady for once, even if he didn't seem interested in me. That feeling didn't last long, though, because when I got outside, Joe-Joe and his cronies were still hanging around.

"So, what was that shit you was talking a little while ago?" Joe-Joe asked as he approached me.

I was about to tell Joe-Joe not to start no shit, but before I could speak, Mr. Tall, Dark, and Handsome stepped up and got in Joe-Joe's face.

"Yo, my man! Is there a problem?" Once Joe-Joe realized I was with him, it was a wrap.

"Nah, man, no problem. No problem at all," Joe-Joe explained. He turned around and started talking to his boys like nothing had ever happened.

"Thanks. I guess that's twice you saved me this morning, and I don't even know your name," I told him as we walked toward the corner.

"Oh, my bad. I'm sorry. My mom taught me better than that. My name's Dante." He stuck out his hand.

"Well, your mother sounds like someone I'd like to meet, Dante." I took his hand. "Everyone calls me Tanisha."

"Tanisha, huh? All right, Ms. Tanisha, it's a pleasure to meet you." He smiled and I saw his pearly white teeth for the first time.

"The pleasure's all mine." I blushed and shook his hand. We walked up the block a little ways toward my house and he stopped in front of a pretty silver SUV. "So, Dante, how come I've never seen you before?"

"Probably because I don't hang out around here too tough. I was just dropping off a friend up the block. Figured I'd get a sandwich."

Lucky me, I thought.

"So this friend, are you and her close?" I know it was bold, but I wanted to know if he had a woman.

He stared at me and laughed as he shook his head. I knew that look. It was the same look I gave guys when they came up with corny-ass lines. "Yeah, actually we are pretty close. But she is a he, and he's my best friend, not my girlfriend."

"Oh," I gave him a lighthearted laugh. "So you don't have a girlfriend or a boyfriend?"

"I don't have a girlfriend," he said calmly then raised his voice. "And I damn sure don't have a boyfriend."

"What about kids?"

"No kids. Why you asking me all these questions anyway? You with the police? If you are, I want a lawyer."

Oops. Time to chill. I knew he was joking, but maybe I had pushed a little too far. Some brothers don't like such personal questions right off the bat, and his expression and comment let me know he was probably one of them. Not that it mattered. I'd found out all I needed to know. He didn't have a girlfriend, he didn't have any kids, and he definitely wasn't gay. Three points for the home team.

"Oh, I'm sorry. I didn't mean to offend you. I was just making conversation. You know how we women can just run off at the mouth sometimes."

"I guess," he replied suspiciously. "Look, I'll see you tomorrow if you stop by the poetry theater."

"Oh, you better believe I'll be there." I gave him a wink. "Matter of fact, why don't you pick me up? Like I said, I really like poetry."

"You do?" He looked surprised.

"Yeah, I do. I've been to Def Poetry Jam like four times, and I got all of Nikki Giovanni's books. That sister is bad."

He nodded as if he was impressed, but he still hadn't said yes, so it was time to be a little more persistent.

"So what's up? You gonna pick me up or what?"

He hesitated like he had no idea what to say. Either that or he was about to hurt my feelings by saying no; but I wasn't about to take no as an answer.

"Hey, what are you afraid of? I won't bite. You did say you like girls, didn't you?"

"Yeah, I like girls." He gave me an ice-cold stare. I guess he was touchy about that subject or something.

"Well, then what's wrong with me? I know I don't have no makeup on and my hair ain't done, but I just woke up, and at seven-thirty in the morning even Halle Berry don't look this good." I placed my hand on my hip and posed, trying my best to show off my slammin' figure. "Besides, you can't ask me out on a second date if we don't have a first." It was time for the direct approach.

"So now we're going on a date?"

"Yep."

"Do I have any say in this?" He chuckled.

"Yeah, you get to pick out what restaurant we're going to when we leave the poetry theater."

I held my breath as I waited for his reaction. I was relieved to see a smile on his face and even more relieved when he finally gave me the once-over with his eyes, stopping briefly at my titties then my hips. He made me work for it, but I'd finally worn him down. "Okay, how about I pick you up about seven?"

"Six sounds good. What restaurant we going to?"

"I hope you're not allergic to seafood, because I was thinking Red Lobster."

"Nah, that's cool. I love Red Lobster," I told him as I tried to contain my smile. "I stay over in Forty Projects, Building two, Apartment L." I pointed in the direction of my building. "Think you can remember that?"

"Uh-huh, I can remember. Apartment L, like in lake."

"I like to think of it as L, like in lucky. As in be on time and you might get *lucky.*"

He turned his head, probably because he didn't want me to see him blushing. Now that I'd reeled him in, I was laying it on thick.

"I'll see you tomorrow, Tanisha."

"I'll be waiting," I told him flirtatiously.

I watched him get in his car, then I rushed home to get my brother off to school. I also needed to get down to Jamaica Avenue to buy me some hair and a new outfit to wear the next night. The next time I saw Mr. Dante, I wasn't the one who was gonna be sweating him. He was going to be sweating me.

5

Donna

It was Saturday afternoon, the one day of the week that Terrance and I always found time to slip away to his apartment, a hotel, or some inconspicuous place to spend some quality time. When we were together on Saturdays, it was as if we were man and wife. Yeah, I'll admit we spent most of our time in bed getting our groove on—or as I liked to think of it, making love—but making love on the weekend was always more satisfying than the quickies we snuck in during the week. On Saturdays, Terrance always took his time and we tried new things. He would take me to places physically and mentally that I had never been to before and honestly never wanted to come back from.

As I approached his house, I could hear the sounds of Reuben Studdard playing on the other side of the door, and I had to smile. I'd made the comment to Terrance that I could make love while listening to that man's singing all night long, and it looked like he was about to take me up on it. I could feel myself getting moist as I thought about the fun we were going to have, but I also had another plan for our afternoon together—a plan that involved our future.

I'd decided it was time for us to take our relationship to the next level. I wanted—no, I needed Terrance to profess his love for me. Oh, deep down inside I knew he loved me, but if I could get him to say the words, I would be one step closer to my goal of being his wife. I could already see myself walking down the aisle while all the other young women from the church who wanted Terrance sat there watching.

I knocked on the door and I heard Terrance shout, "Come in." I opened the door and was greeted by what seemed like a thousand shimmering candles. God knows that man was always doing something to put a smile on my face. I glanced down at my feet and saw a path of white rose petals leading through the small living room and into the kitchen. I followed them to where they stopped at the back door, which I opened, only to find Terrance sitting in a Jacuzzi I'd never seen before.

"When'd you get this?" I asked curiously as I stared at the Jacuzzi. I couldn't help it; I was grinning from ear to ear. I'd always wanted to make love in a Jacuzzi.

"They brought it this morning."

"Who brought it?"

He smiled. "Rent-A-Center. You'd be surprised what those people have to rent. Now stop wasting time. You did tell me one of your fantasies was to make love in a hot tub, wasn't it?"

I nodded, trying my best to keep from blushing.

"All right, then." He pointed at the patio table. "There's a bottle of champagne in the ice bucket. Why don't you pour yourself a drink and join me?"

He didn't have to ask me twice. I kicked off my shoes right away. Even so, to prolong the moment, I did a slow striptease, which Terrance let me know he thoroughly enjoyed. I walked over to the table and grabbed the bottle of champagne and a glass. From there I eased my foot into the tub, trying to adjust to the heat of the foaming water.

"Oooh, Terrance, this feels so good."

"If you think that feels good, you ain't seen nothing yet." Terrance licked his lips suggestively.

"Oh yeah? What you got for me?" I asked eagerly.

"Come on in here and find out." Terrance lifted his eyebrows in that sexy way I loved.

I did as he suggested, first pouring myself a glass of champagne then easing into the Jacuzzi completely. "Okay, I'm here. The next move is yours. What you gonna do?" I teased.

"I'm about to take deep-sea diving to a whole 'nother level." He smiled then dove under the water. The next thing I knew, his head was between my legs and I was holding on to the sides of the Jacuzzi moaning loudly.

Three hours later Terrance and I were making love in his bed. We'd made love twice in the Jacuzzi and he'd just carried me into his bedroom so we could do it again. He used almond oil to rub my back and massage my feet before we got busy again. The bottle of champagne had been polished off sometime between our first and second rounds in the hot tub. I'm not ashamed to say I was still feeling its effects.

"Oh, Terrance," I whispered repeatedly, clinging to his back as I climaxed.

"Yeah, baby, that's it." He was kissing my neck and it was about to make me climax again.

"I . . . I love you, Terrance. I love you more than anything in this world," I cried out as one orgasm took over for another.

Even in my moment of ecstasy I noticed that he did not reciprocate my confession of love. Although I wanted him to say he loved me first, the champagne had loosened up my tongue. Oh, well. I waited . . . The air turned still. I could tell by his rigid posture that he was caught off guard by my confession, but I couldn't hold it in any longer. I was in love with Terrance and I *knew* he was in love with me. We'd just never said the words to one another. But now that I'd said them to him, I desperately wanted to hear him tell me the same.

"I love you, Terrance," I repeated. For three months I'd been trying to entice that man to say he loved me, and at this point I probably would have settled for a "me too," but that was not going to be the case.

"Donna, I'm not gonna lie to you—" I could tell by the look in his eyes that I didn't want to hear whatever he was about to say, so I placed my index finger on his lips.

"Shhhh. I know we've only been dating a few months. You don't have to say it back," I lied. "I just wanted you to know how I feel, and that I'd do anything in the world for you." I rested my head on his shoulder, hoping he wouldn't sense my disappointment.

"Donna," he whispered a few seconds later.

"Yes," I whispered back, trying to contain my excitement. I had a feeling he was about to say those magical words.

"Do you mean it?"

"Mean what?" I was confused.

"That you love me and you'd do anything for me?" I lifted my head off his shoulder and stared into his eyes. I wanted him to know exactly how serious I was.

"I've never meant anything so much in my life. I'll do anything for you, Terrance."

He blinked, then I noticed a sparkle in his eyes.

"Would you give me some of this?" Terrance playfully slapped my buttocks, reminding me how he'd slap my butt when I was coming. I know it sounds kinky but I love to have my butt slapped when I make love.

"What did you say, baby?" I wasn't quite sure I understood what he meant.

"I said how about some of this?" He grabbed my ass.

"You just got some of that, but you know you can have some more any time you want."

"No, not that." Terrance moved his finger between my butt cheeks until it was at the entrance to my anus. He poked me with his finger and every muscle in my body tensed. "Some of this. I wanna have anal sex with you."

He said the words quickly and avoided looking directly into my eyes, so I couldn't tell if he was actually serious. I stared at him like he'd lost his mind. Goose bumps rose along my arms. I shivered with the thought of the pain. Now, I loved Terrance and all, and he was the only man I'd ever been with, but that—that was just out of the question.

"Forget about it," he finally said, then rolled away from me and stared at the ceiling. "It was just a thought, a fantasy. You know, like the Jacuzzi was for you."

"That was different, Terrance."

"How?" he asked, rolling over on his side. "Your fantasy was to make love in a Jacuzzi, mine is to have anal sex. I made yours happen, and you have the ability to make mine happen." He stared at me then continued in the sad, pathetic voice. "I think I've proven I'd do anything for you, Donna."

"I know that, Terrance," I replied, though I hardly thought renting a Jacuzzi was anywhere equal to allowing a man into that part of my body.

"Well, how come you aren't willing to do the same for me?" He actually sounded upset.

"I am, b—"

He cut me off before I could finish.

"Good, 'cause I wanna try it. I don't think I'm asking a lot."

"You're kidding, aren't you?" My voice went soprano and cracked with hope on the last two words. *Please Lord, let him be playing.*

"No, I'm serious as a heart attack." This time he looked me in the eyes as he spoke, which let me know he really was.

"Terrance, I can't," I whimpered. "It's gonna hurt."

"You don't have to worry. It won't hurt. I'll be just as gentle as I was when you gave me your virginity."

I sat upright in the bed, pulling the sheet up around me in a protective gesture. I was flabbergasted. I couldn't believe it. He really wanted to go in the back door! I couldn't think of anything to say. My mind went blank. Speechless, I

glanced over at Terrance. He remained absolutely quiet, res-
olute.

Finally, he broke the silence. "Donna."

"What?" I'm sure I sounded annoyed.

He lowered his head. "Just forget about it, all right? If
you don't wanna do it, I'm not gonna force you. Matter of
fact, I'll never bring it up again."

He leaned over and kissed me, then got out of bed and
headed for the bathroom. Thank you, Lord, 'cause if he had
pressed the issue, I don't know what I would have done.
Then a thought hit me and an icicle lodged in my throat. If
that was what he really wanted, how long would it be before
he found someone else who would do it?

6

Dante

I was headed down Liberty Avenue toward Forty Projects to pick up Tanisha. Believe it or not, I was kinda excited about taking her to the poetry theater and dinner. She wasn't like the girls I usually dated from the church. She kind of reminded me of a female version of my best friend Shorty. She had a directness about her that I liked. Oh, don't get me wrong. Those church girls aren't exactly angels, either. Most of them are pretty bold, too, in their own way. Just look at my ex, Anita. But what I liked about Tanisha was that she didn't try to hide her wildness behind closed doors by acting prudish and virginal. After all the fraud perpetrated by some of these church girls, Tanisha's directness was appealing. And with that body of hers, I could see us having some good times a few weeks down the road once we got to know each other.

I must admit, though, I couldn't imagine us being together long-term. Oh, she seemed like a nice girl and all, but I couldn't see myself bringing her home to the bishop and the first lady. The minute my mother found out Tanisha was from the projects, she'd lose her mind and make both Tanisha's and my life miserable. Sooner or later I'd have to settle down with one of those church girls, but for the time being, I was looking forward to getting to know Tanisha. She was definitely going to be a welcome distraction from my feelings for Anita.

When I was about three blocks from Tanisha's building, my phone started ringing. I looked at the caller ID and saw the number to my house. I answered on the third ring and was greeted by the troubled sound of my mother's voice.

"Dante. Have you seen your sister?"

"Nah, I haven't seen her since this morning. Why, is something wrong? She didn't have another accident, did she?" I crossed my fingers.

"No, not that I know of, but Anita Emerson just called. Your sister was supposed to open up the church recreation hall and help the Emersons run tonight's Bingo game, but she never showed up. I tried calling her cell phone, but she's not answering. She's probably out with them ghetto hooligans she calls friends."

Or getting laid by her mystery boyfriend, I thought.

"She probably just forgot today was Bingo night, Ma." I was starting to get a bad feeling about this call.

"Nonetheless, I need you to go over to the church and take care of things."

"But Ma, I'm on my way to pick someone up. I've got a date tonight. I can't cancel this late. She'll never go out with me again."

"Well, I'm sure whoever she is won't mind spending a few hours at the church helping you run the Bingo game." No doubt my mother assumed my date was with some member of the church. She was so determined to marry me off to one of those church girls that I don't think it ever crossed her mind that I might be attracted to someone who didn't worship at First Jamaica Ministries.

"Ma, can't you get someone else to do this? Why don't you and the bishop go over there? You know how he likes to call the numbers."

"Your father and I have some other business we have to take care of tonight. We need you to take care of this, Dante. There is no one else we can call."

"What about Reverend Reynolds?" I was still trying to talk my way out of it. The last thing I wanted to do was cancel my date with Tanisha in order to spend three hours with Anita and her husband.

"I couldn't get in touch with him."

"Well, I'm sorry, Ma, but I can't do it."

"Dante, you are the director of church activities. When these things happen, you're supposed to be there to pick up the slack. You have a responsibility. How do you expect to become pastor one day if you can't handle being director? I'm sorry, but this is your job. If this young lady doesn't understand that, then she's not worth it. Now you get your behind over to the church and open up the recreation hall. Bingo starts at seven-thirty sharp and I'm counting on you." She hung up without waiting for my reply.

I folded my cell phone just as I pulled up in front of Tanisha's building. I turned off my truck and stared at the entrance. Now what was I going to do? There was no way I was going to ask a girl like Tanisha to go to the church with me. She'd probably laugh me out her house. I thought about just leaving. I mean, she was a nice girl with a terrific body, but it wasn't like she was Tyra Banks or anything. Besides, she didn't have my number or my last name. She also didn't go to our church, so the chances of me running into her again weren't that great. I started the truck and slid the shift into drive, but my conscience wouldn't let me put my foot on the gas. I owed her an explanation; whether she was cool with it or not was up to her. At least I'd know I'd done my part. So I sat there another two minutes then willed myself to get out of the truck.

Once I got in the building, it took no time to find Apartment L. I knocked on the door. A few seconds later a scarecrow-thin woman who looked like she hadn't combed her hair in about two weeks answered. She was scratching her arms like she had fleas or something. I was sure I was at the wrong apartment. In fact, I must have gone into the wrong building, because this was obviously a crack spot.

"What you want?" the woman asked. She was still scratching her arms.

"I'm sorry. I think I have the wrong apartment. I was looking for Tanisha."

I took a step back, preparing to leave until she said, "She's here. Come on in. I'll get her." In between her scratching, the woman gestured for me to come in, then turned toward the back of the apartment and screamed, "Tanisha! Somebody here to see you!"

I followed her into the apartment and felt like I was in another world. It was what my mother would call a well-kept mess. There was stuff everywhere, but you could also see where someone had tried to straighten up and keep the place neat. From the looks of the woman in front of me, I figured that must have been Tanisha.

"You can sit down," the woman told me. She was back to her scratching and it was starting to make me feel like I had an itch too. She ran over to the couch and scooped up a handful of clothes to clear a spot, then she gestured for me to sit down. She called for Tanisha again at the top of her lungs, as if the apartment were the size of a mansion.

"I'm coming," I heard Tanisha shout from behind a closed door.

By the time I walked over and sat down, the woman had scooped up another pile of clothes and was sitting next to me, still scratching. I figured if she wasn't going to introduce herself, I might as well.

"How you doing? I'm Dante." I offered her my hand and she stopped scratching long enough to shake it.

"My name's Marlene. I'm Tanisha's mother." She was so bony I felt like I was shaking the hand of a skeleton.

"Nice to meet you, Marlene." As soon as I let go of her hand, she was back to scratching her arm again, and now I was scratching right along with her. It was like that shit was contagious.

"Hey, Dante, you got a cigarette?"

"Sorry, I don't smoke."

"Think you could loan me five dollars so I can get a pack?"

"I'm sorry, Marlene, but I don't have any cash on me. I was planning on going to the ATM when I left here," I lied. I didn't mind loaning her money for cigarettes, but I was afraid she might use it to buy something stronger.

"So bring me a pack of Newports when you come back, and I'll let y'all use my room." She smiled and I had to look away so I wouldn't gasp. That woman didn't have but one tooth in her entire mouth.

"I'll see what I can do."

"Okay, and bring me back a doggie bag. Y'all are going out to eat, ain't you?"

"We were supposed to, but—"

"But what? You taking me somewhere else instead?"

I recognized Tanisha's voice right away, but when I looked up, I damn sure didn't recognize the woman standing in front of me. She bore a resemblance to the woman in the baggy sweats I had met the day before, but if this was Tanisha, she must have gone on that show *Extreme Make-overs*. The woman standing in front of me was so fine she looked like she should have been on a rap video. She had these tight, baby blue low-rise jeans on with a matching jean jacket. Under the jacket she was wearing a thin white halter that didn't leave anything to the imagination. And that was just her outfit.

Her hair was hooked up in a curly brown style that fell down to her shoulders, accented by a baby blue Kangol that was cocked to the side. All this was accessorized with a pair of blue-tinted sunglasses, freshly manicured nails, and a pair of blue boots that made her a full three inches taller. She was looking so good I was glad I was wearing baggy pants, because my little head immediately took over for my big one, and he was telling me, *The hell with Bingo! We need to take her to dinner and a hotel*.

"Tanisha?"

I must have sounded unsure, because she looked at me like I was stupid and said, "Yeah, were you expecting someone else?"

"No, I just didn't expect for you to look this goo—I mean, you look damn good."

She rolled her eyes at my foolishness. "Thanks, I think."

I was relieved that my phone rang so I could get my foot out of my mouth, but then I realized it was probably my mother calling back to nag some more about my Bingo obligations.

"Aren't you gonna answer it?"

I sighed then nodded. "Hello?"

"Dante, where are you?" It wasn't my mother. It was Anita. "Your mother said you were going to be here ten minutes ago. There are over a hundred people out here waiting to get into the rec hall." I was brought back to reality and my little head relinquished control to my big head.

"I'm coming, Anita. I had to make a stop first. I'll be there in five minutes." I hung up the phone and looked at Tanisha with a frown.

"I hope Anita works at the poetry theater." Tanisha was glaring at me over the top of her blue-tinted glasses.

"Well, not exactly."

She jumped in before I could explain. "What do you mean not exactly?" I could hear the disappointment in her voice, but I was sure that was going to turn into B.W.A.—Black Woman's Attitude—at any moment.

"Tanisha, I'm sorry, but I have to cancel our date."

All the expression left her face as she leaned back in an Oh-no-you-didn't-just-cancel-our-date pose. "What? I don't wanna hear that shit. You mean to tell me I spent all day getting ready for nothing? Do you know how long it took me to put this weave in my head?"

"Look, Tanisha, I'm sorry. You see—"

She cut me off again. "You know what, Dante? You're full of shit." She took her sunglasses off. She was no longer disappointed. Now I could see anger in her eyes.

"I'm sorry. But it's not my fault."

"Whose fault is it?" She was starting to raise her voice.

"Tanisha, calm down for a minute and let him explain," her mother chimed in. I'd completely forgotten she was there until just then, although I was grateful, because Tanisha looked like she wanted to pluck my eyeballs out.

Tanisha folded her arms. "Okay, I'm listening. Why can't you go?"

"Something came up and I gotta work."

She uncrossed her arms and pointed a finger in my face.

"Do I look stupid to you? Do I look like I have *Tanisha's a stupid bitch* written all over my face?" she spat.

"No, but—"

"Then why the fuck you tryin' to play me?" she yelled.

"I'm not trying to play you. I really gotta go to work." I turned to her mother for some help, but she looked just as skeptical as her daughter.

"So I guess you work with this Anita, right?" Tanisha asked, giving me a look that told me she wasn't going to believe whatever answer I gave her.

"Uh-huh. Yeah, I work with her."

She sucked her teeth, then rolled her eyes as she walked over to the door. "You are such a fucking liar."

I stood up. "I'm not lying, Tanisha. I swear to God. If you want, you can come to the church with me."

Both Tanisha and her mother started laughing. "Church?

Now I've heard everything. You niggas be coming up with some of the corniest shit. What are you, the preacher?"

I was about to tell her I was the preacher's son, but instead I just gave her the basics. "No, I'm supposed to be running the Bingo game tonight."

She and her mother laughed even harder than the first time. "Yeah, you running game, all right. 'Cept it's not even good game."

Tanisha opened the door, glanced at me, then looked outside to the hall. I took her hint and walked toward the open door, stopping at the threshold. I decided to give it one last-ditch effort.

"I'm not lying, Tanisha. If you don't believe me, you can come by First Jamaica Ministries on Merrick. I'll be there all night."

"I ain't going nowhere looking for you. Now get out my house."

As I stepped past her to exit the apartment, she put a hand on my shoulder. I turned to face her and she said, "You know what, Dante? I wish you had never paid for my groceries." She reached in her pocket and pulled out some money, forcing it in my hand. "I hope you have fun with Anita, but believe me, it won't be as much fun as you could have had with me."

"Tanisha . . ." I looked in her face and she raised her hand as if she was about to smack me. I ducked out of the way just in case she swung. That's when I knew it was time to get out of there. She was about to take things to the next level and the last thing I needed was to wind up in jail for fighting a woman. I walked out the door without another word.

7

Tanisha

It was a little after ten when I walked out of the house and stepped into a waiting cab. I decided to go in to work to take my mind off the fact that Dante had canceled our date to be with another woman. Maybe making some money would take my mind off the fact that I was hurt. I hated to admit it, but I was really feeling that brother, and it wasn't just his looks. I would have bet money that he was one of the good ones, but I guess I was wrong, because he sure made a fool outta me. I just wish I hadn't spent all my money on a new outfit and begged my boss to give me the night off. Trust me, he had not been a happy camper when I told him I wasn't coming in. Saturday was our busiest night at the club, and the last couple of weeks we'd been short-handed. I thought he was gonna give me a hard time when I called in and told him I was coming in after all, but he was so happy I thought he would jump through the phone and kiss me. Well, at least somebody cared, even if he was a fifty-year-old, overweight, balding white man.

"Where to, miss?" the driver asked.

"Take me to the F train at the corner of Hillside Avenue and 168th," I replied as he headed toward Merrick Boulevard. We hadn't gone two blocks before my cell phone started ringing. I fumbled through my bag to find it.

"Hello?"

"How's it going?" a female voice whispered.

It was my friend Natasha, the head bartender at work. She was probably the closest girlfriend I had, despite our ten-year age difference and considering I didn't get along with women too tough. I'm sorry, but they're just too petty and catty for me. My grandmother used to have a saying before she died: Where there's a woman, there's bound to be trouble—especially if there's a man around—so stay as far away as you can. And she was right. Ever since I was a teenager, whenever I got close to a woman, there was trouble. I've had four best friends in my life, and I'd lost all of them because of something to do with a man. I lost one because she thought I liked her man, another because her man liked me, the third because she liked my man, and the last one . . . well, I'm not proud of it, but I liked her man and he liked me too, so we ended up sleeping together. I know I shouldn't have done it, but I got mine in the end. Not only did I lose my best friend but I lost the man, too. They got back together, and I think they're happily married now. From that day on I learned a lesson about other women and myself. We just don't mix. Nevertheless, Natasha and I were cool, even if I still tried to keep my distance. I just didn't wanna meet her man, and when I got one, I wouldn't want her to meet mine.

"How's what goin'?"

"Your date. How's your date going?" she asked.

I wanted to lie and say it was fine, but if she saw me at work later on, she'd know I was lying. She'd come over and helped me fix my hair that afternoon and I'd made the mistake of telling her how excited I was to be going out with Dante.

"What date? Girl, that nigga had the nerve to come over to my house and cancel five minutes before we were supposed to go out."

"Get the fuck outta here."

"For real. Oh, and get this. While he was there, he got a phone call and told some other bitch that he'd be there in five minutes."

"No he didn't!" I could imagine Natasha's expression.

"Yes he did. And then after he was busted, he had the nerve to try and change shit up by telling me she was his coworker, and that he had to meet her at the church."

"At the church? What kinda job he got at the church?"

"He said he runs the Bingo game. Imagine that." I laughed.

"A Bingo game?"

"Uh-huh, a goddamn Bingo game! Can you believe that shit?"

She laughed. "You know, Tanisha, that story sounds so crazy, it could be true."

Natasha was all right. She knew Dante was a dog just like all the rest, but she was still trying to make me feel better. I just wasn't in the mood. Sometimes you just wanna be miserable.

"At a church? Running a Bingo game? Come on, Natasha. Now I know why you got three baby daddies, 'cause you'll believe anything these niggas tell you."

"Now why you gotta go there?" Natasha barked half-jokingly. She was very sensitive about and protective of her children's fathers. I was about to apologize until my cab pulled up to a light at the corner of 109 and Merrick and a huge sign across the street grabbed my attention. It read: BINGO, THURSDAYS AND SATURDAYS, 7:30–10:30 PM. The sign was in front of a huge church I'd passed a thousand times before, but this was the first time I paid any attention to it.

"You know, that was wrong, Tani—"

"Hold on a minute, Natasha," I told her as I read the sign for the second time.

I leaned forward and asked the driver, "What church is that?"

"That's Bishop T.K. Wilson's church. Everybody knows him. He's the man running for borough president." He pointed at a campaign billboard.

"I didn't ask you who the preacher was, I asked you the name of the church."

"Oh, sorry. I think it's called First Jamaica Ministries." I glanced at the sign again and my stomach did a flip. Was it possible that Dante had been telling the truth? Had I kicked him out of my house for no reason? Did he really have to go to work? There was only one way to find out.

The light turned green. When the cab started to move I said, "Pull in there. I wanna see something." Then I placed the phone against my ear and told Natasha I'd call her back. "I gotta check something out."

A few minutes later I was following a series of Bingo signs that led me to a short flight of stairs and the side entrance of the church. I took a long, deep breath. As much as I wanted to walk down those stairs to find out if Dante was inside, part of me was afraid that he might not be there and I'd have to relive his lie again. Another part of me was concerned about what he might say if indeed he was inside. After all, I did call him a liar and kick him out of my house.

Finally, after standing there like a fool for five minutes, I walked down the stairs and opened the door. The Bingo hall was much larger and more crowded than I had expected. I'd never seen so many old people in my entire life. There had to be over five hundred people in that room, and all their eyes seemed to be glued to the colorful Bingo pads in front of them as they waited for the next number to be called. I felt like I was at a grandparents convention. I scanned the room twice, but there was no sign of Dante. Finding him, if he was there, was going to be much harder than I thought.

"Can I help you? You look a little lost. Are you here to pick someone up?" a woman asked.

I turned toward the voice and saw an attractive woman in her thirties sitting behind a desk to the right of the entrance. I'd been so fascinated by the number of people playing Bingo and my search for Dante that I hadn't even noticed her or the older, one-armed gentleman sitting next to her.

"No. I'm not picking anyone up. I was wondering if there's a man named Dante who works here."

The woman gave me the once-over with her eyes then asked, "And you are?" She had a little too much attitude in her voice for me and the way she was looking at me was just as rude. I tried to keep my cool. I was in a church, after all.

"Oh, I'm sorry. I'm his friend Tanisha," I replied with a smile. "Are you his mother? I can see where he gets his good looks."

"I am not his mother," the woman snapped angrily. She was halfway out of her seat.

"Calm down, sweetheart. She didn't mean any harm." The man reached up and gently pulled her back down to her chair.

"Oh, I'm sorry. I didn't mean to offend you."

I was lying through my teeth. I knew the woman was too young to be Dante's mother, but I wanted to put her nosy ass in place. From her reaction, I'd succeeded. She just sat there and glared at me evilly with her mouth open. I know this sounds crazy, but she was giving off this hostile vibe like she considered me her enemy, but we'd never even met. From the way she was looking at me, I was sure that if we were in any other place, she'd have had plenty more to say.

"Dante's over there, young lady." The man pointed with his one arm and my eyes followed his hand until they were focused on Dante's handsome face.

Well, I'll be damned. He really is one of the good ones. A big smile crept onto my face as I observed him sitting at a table on a small platform, calling the Bingo numbers into a microphone. I didn't recognize his voice at first because the cheap church speakers were distorting it.

"He should be done in about ten minutes. We only have two cards to go," the old man told me. The woman was still glaring at me.

"Thank you," I said as I walked toward an empty seat. I sat down and watched Dante as he called the last two cards. When he was finished, I let the majority of the people exit the building, then walked up to the platform where he was cleaning up. When he saw me, his eyes got wide and he rubbed them with both hands as if he wasn't quite sure if what he was seeing was real.

"Tanisha." His tone was neutral. I couldn't tell if he was happy to see me or upset about the way I'd acted before. Either way, it was probably good that we were in a church so he had to stay calm.

I walked up two steps to the platform and leaned against the table where he had been sitting.

"What are you doing here?" I still didn't know if he was happy to see me, but he was definitely confused.

I didn't reply at first. I just shrugged my shoulders, trying my best to avoid eye contact. It was awkward for a moment, until I finally built up the courage to look at him and say, "I'm sorry I didn't believe you."

A timid smile crept upon his face as he responded. "It's aw'ight. I thought about it, and I probably wouldn't have believed me either."

I let out a sigh of relief. "So we're cool?"

"Yeah, we're cool."

He nodded, then surprised me by wrapping his arm around my shoulder, pulling me in for a hug that I didn't resist. I wrapped my arms around his waist and closed my eyes briefly, taking in the sweet, masculine scent of his cologne. He lowered his head and I was hoping that he would kiss me, but things never got quite that far, because we were rudely interrupted by a woman's voice.

"Dante! What are you doing?" I opened my eyes and there was the woman from the desk. She had her hand on her hip and was staring at me like I was holding on to her man. "Get your hands off of him, you, you little . . . don't you have any shame? This is the house of the Lord."

We both dropped our hands to our sides. I was upset at the fact that she had the nerve to blame it on me so loudly. After all, Dante was the one who wrapped his arms around me first. Thank goodness we were the only ones left in the church.

"Anita, leave them young people alone. They weren't doing anything wrong. Don't you remember what it was like to be like that?" The one-armed man walked over and placed his arm around her. "I seem to remember us doing a lot more than that upstairs in the church pews," he teased.

"Hush, Deacon. That's not the same. And they're not in love." She removed his arm from her shoulder.

"So you and Anita were doing your thing up in the church, huh, Deacon Emerson?" Dante asked. Damn, people were nosy around here.

"We had our share of fun before we were married, young fella, but some things we saved till after we were married." He winked at Dante then smiled at his wife. "You ready to go, dear?"

She nodded, but something about her expression told me she really didn't want to let Dante and me out of her sight. "What about them?" she asked. "We can't just leave them here alone."

He looked at us, then at her. "Why can't we? He's the one with the keys."

She was no longer staring at me. She was looking directly at Dante. "You gonna be all right? We can stay until everything's locked up." She was trying to sound sweet, but the way she was staring at Dante, I was sure something else was going on in her head.

"We're gonna be fine, Anita." Dante placed his arm around my shoulder and I thought I saw a smirk pass across his face for a second. "Go on home with your husband. I'll take care of everything here."

"See there, now come on," the woman's husband said. "Let's go home. I wanna see what's on HBO." We watched the two of them walk out. Every few steps the woman looked back at us until they were finally out the door.

"I take it that's the Anita you work with?"

"Yep, that's Anita," he said flatly. He stepped down from the platform and gestured for me to follow.

"So how long you two been fooling around?" I asked.

Dante stopped abruptly. His shoulders tensed and his face became flushed. It was clear from his body language that I'd hit a nerve. He turned, trying his best to sound innocent. "What do you mean? We're not fooling around. She's a married woman."

"Yeah, right. Don't play stupid with me, Dante. That woman looked like she wanted to scratch my eyes out. It's pretty obvious something's going on between you two. The only one who can't see it is her husband."

"We're not fooling around." I gave him a skeptical look and he fessed up. "Well, not anymore. I ended it about a year and a half ago. Right before she got married to him."

"*You* may have ended it, but it sure don't look like she has."

"That's not my problem." He placed his hands around my waist and looked at me as if Anita was the last thing on his mind. "She made her choice. She married him. Now she has to live with it."

"You sound like you're over her."

He lowered his head until his lips were inches from mine. "Let's just say I'm ready to move on."

"Well, why don't I just help you with that?" I gently pulled his head toward mine then I closed my eyes and kissed him like I'd never kissed anyone before. I was determined to make him forget that Anita ever existed, and if the way he kissed me back was any indication, I was well on my way to my objective.

A few moments later he broke our kiss and smiled. "The poetry reading is over, but we can still hit Red Lobster if you want."

I looked up at him with a disappointed half-smile. "That sounds good, Dante, but I can't go tonight."

He loosened his hold on me. He must have thought this was my way of getting back at him for breaking our date earlier, but that couldn't have been further from the truth.

"Don't be mad." I gave him a pleading look. "After you left my house, I called my boss and asked if I could come in. I can't cancel on him twice. How 'bout tomorrow?"

His expression relaxed. "Aw'ight. But can we make it Monday? I have something to do tomorrow."

I nodded and he smiled.

"You need a ride to work?"

"You can give me a ride to the train."

"You don't want a ride to work? I'm not a stalker, you know," he said half jokingly.

"It's just that I don't mix business with pleasure. I try to keep my relationships as far away from work as I can."

"So what are you doing here? I'm at work," he teased.

"The sign outside says they only have Bingo two nights a week, and I know you don't pay a note on that pretty truck I saw you driving off calling out Bingo numbers. Besides, you invited me to come here."

"I did, didn't I?" He smiled and squeezed me a little harder as he kissed me again. "You know, I like you, Tanisha. A lot more than I wanted to admit at first."

"Good, 'cause I like you, too, Dante."

"I know you don't have time for dinner but how about I buy you a cup of coffee before you go to work?"

I smiled. I definitely liked the idea of spending more time with him. "Sure. There's a coffee shop right by the subway."

He reached out and took my hand. "Then it's a date. Let's get outta here."

8

Dante

I pulled into my driveway feeling like I was floating on air. I'd had kisses before, but I'd never had a kiss like the one Tanisha laid on me at the church and again at the subway station. Her lips were so soft and she smelled so good she made every other woman I'd ever been with easy to forget, and that included Anita. We sat in my car outside the subway talking and I was enjoying it so much I considered begging her not to leave. I hate to admit it, but she had me open. I couldn't wait for Monday so I could see her again.

As I exited my truck, my thoughts of Tanisha were interrupted and I was nearly frightened to death. A dark figure appeared from the bushes surrounding my house. I was so scared that I jumped back, tripping over my own feet, and landed right on my ass. Whoever it was could have killed me in a snap if they wanted to.

"Where have you been?" the figure growled.

At first I thought it was my mother because the voice, although distorted, was obviously female. My mother had a tendency to trip every once in a while when I came in later than she expected, but when this person took a step out of the shadows, I couldn't believe who I saw.

"Anita?" I whispered in confusion.

"I asked you a question, Dante. Where have you been? The deacon and I left you and that little hussy over two hours ago." She was acting as if she'd just caught me cheating.

I ignored her question and asked one of my own as I got up from the ground. "Anita, what are you doing here?" I brushed myself off as I waited for her answer, glancing nervously toward my house.

At first I thought maybe she and her husband had stopped by to see my parents after Bingo and she'd just stepped out back to smoke a cigarette. Deacon Emerson and my father were close, and that would have answered my question about the lights being on so late. But then I realized I wasn't going to be that lucky. Anita was wearing a raincoat on a humid, eighty-degree night. I could only imagine what she was wearing underneath it, if anything. Despite the objections from my big head, my little head once again took over.

"I've been waiting to talk to you. I've been waiting out here for almost two hours," she growled with attitude. She made it sound like I'd stood her up and she was the one who should be upset.

"You've been waiting here? For what? I never told you to meet me here." This was starting to get a little scary.

"I came here because you've been avoiding me, Dante. You won't answer my phone calls, you avoid me at work, but bringing that tramp to Bingo tonight was the last straw. I will not be humiliated. Why are you doing this to me?" I couldn't believe it. She was jealous.

"How the hell am I humiliating you? I'm not the one who got married, Anita. You are. You had your chance, but you chose Deacon Emerson over me, so don't get mad at me or Tanisha. Be mad at yourself because this is all your doing."

"I know that, Dante, and that's why I'm here. I wanna make it up to you."

She walked toward me, and with each step she unbuttoned her raincoat until she was two feet away from me and I could see her completely naked body underneath the coat. Just like that day in my office, I knew I was in trouble, so I took a step back only to find that I was pinned between her and my car. I raised my hands to try and keep her at arm's distance, but she grabbed my wrists, pulling my hands toward her breasts. I tried to resist touching them, but by now my little head had completely taken over. Her breasts were soft yet firm in my hands. I probably could have caressed them all night as she nibbled on my neck, but two things stopped me.

One was the thought of my date with Tanisha. Obviously it was too soon for us to make any commitment to each other, but I saw potential with this woman. Sure, it had surprised me to feel it, but during the short time we spent together earlier that night, she proved to be much deeper than I had given her credit for. In spite of where she lived and the way her mother acted, Tanisha had something special about her. Something I hadn't felt since me and Anita first got together. I wasn't thinking marriage or anything, but I was definitely looking forward to getting to know her, and I wasn't about to let Anita get in the way.

The other thing that stopped me was the kitchen light that had just come on in my house. I grabbed Anita and dove onto the grass in the shadow of the bushes just as my mother pulled back the curtains and peered out the window.

I think Anita took my action the wrong way because she started to plaster my face with kisses as she moaned, "Ohhh, Dante, I love it when you get rough. Take me. Take me, baby. Take me right here on the grass under the moonlight." She opened her legs and wrapped them around me.

"Shhhhh," I whispered.

"What? What's the matter?" she asked.

I pointed at my mother in the window and she froze. We watched my mother stare out that window for a good thirty seconds before she opened the door just enough to shout, "Dante? Is that you, son?"

I don't know if it was stupidity or what but I yelled, "Yeah, Mom. I'll be in in a minute."

"Is there someone with you? I thought I heard you talking to someone."

"Ah, no, I'm just putting some Armor All on my tires, Ma." It was a stupid lie, but she bought it.

"Okay, come on in. I have something important I wanna talk to you about."

"Sure, Ma. I'll be right in." She closed the door and I pushed myself away from Anita.

"Why the heck did you do that? She couldn't see us," Anita snapped.

"I did it because she knows I'm home, Anita. She might not be able to see us, but she could see my truck. If I didn't answer her, she would have come out here to investigate, and I know you didn't want her to see you dressed like this."

Anita didn't reply to that. She just got up from the ground and tried to hug me. I pushed her away.

"Now what's the matter?" she asked.

"You need to go home to your husband."

"He's 'sleep, Dante. He won't be up for hours. Why don't you go pacify your mother then come back out? We've got all night." She tried to kiss me again.

"No," I said sternly as I sidestepped her grasp. I stepped out of the shadows and into the safety of the light where I knew Anita dared not come because of my mother's prying eyes. "Anita, we're over. We are through."

"This isn't over, Dante. You know you want me, and I want you. It's just a matter of time. That little hussy I saw you with tonight can't do for you what I can."

I couldn't help it. I had to laugh.

"What's so funny?"

"You know, earlier tonight she said the same thing about you." She glared at me. "But you're right about one thing,

Anita. I do love you. I'll always love you. You're the woman who made me a man. But my father always told me that the best way to get over someone you love is to find someone else to love. And that's exactly what I'm trying to do."

"I'm not gonna let you go, Dante. You're mine and you are always gonna be mine, so don't think you're just gonna walk away from me and be with some other bitch."

"You know, Anita, that's exactly what I'm afraid of, that this whole thing could get real ugly and real personal."

"It's already gotten personal, Dante. You tell that bitch to watch her back, because one of these days I might be standing behind her, and that's the day she's gonna get her ass whipped."

I turned and looked at Anita. Her expression was dead serious, almost scary.

"If I were you, Anita, I wouldn't sleep on Tanisha. She ain't one of these scared church girls. You mess with her and you might be the one who gets her ass whipped. Now go home to your husband." On that note, I walked away from her and headed into my house.

9

Donna

I took the candied yams I had cooked and placed them on the counter with a smile. I loved Sundays and I loved cooking Sunday dinner even more. I guess it was because I was such a good cook and everyone complimented me, including my mother. If there was ever a day I needed a compliment from my mother, it was today. She was already angry enough with me for coming home late and not opening the church for Bingo the night before. Usually, after she got on me, I'd be moping around the rest of the day, but after making love to Terrance four times last night, I was in such a good mood I was humming. I guess that's what good loving will do for a sister. Maybe I would talk to the bishop and see if I could get him to give my mom some. That might get her panties out of that permanent bunch. Yeah, some good hard loving was exactly what she needed. A sudden chill ran through my body at the image of my parents having sex. Now that was nasty.

Anyhow, this Sunday after church, I had cooked pork roast garnished with parsley sprigs, a large pot of turnip and mustard greens, candied yams, golden brown corn bread, macaroni and cheese, and a peach cobbler. I could already imagine everyone seated around the table "throwing down," reminding me of a scene from the movie *Soul Food*.

"It sure smells good in here. Anything we can do to help?" The bishop smiled as he walked into the kitchen, inspecting the food. He was followed by his right-hand man and protégé, Reverend Reynolds.

Reverend Reynolds, a much younger man than my father, was the youth and prison outreach minister. The last couple of years he'd been like family, coming over for Sunday dinner whenever he wasn't out of town or at a conference. If it weren't for my parents' desire for Dante to be the next pastor, Reverend Reynolds would be the most logical choice. And I still wouldn't count him out, especially since Dante was secretly yearning to be a lawyer. Reverend Reynolds was probably one of the most well-liked men in the church, and with the right woman by his side, he could end up being the pastor someday.

"Dinner's just abo—" I didn't finish my sentence because I had to smack both their hands with the serving spoon when they tried to steal a piece of the roast pork I had just sliced.

"Ouch!" Reverend Reynolds laughed. "You sure swing a mean spoon, Donna."

"I'ma swing more than that if you two don't get out my kitchen. Dinner will be ready in a few minutes. Go and get washed up."

I pointed at the door with a smile and they both turned to leave, but not before the bishop reached out and snatched two pieces of pork, handing one to Reverend Reynolds.

"Lord, you two should be ashamed of yourselves. You got what you came for, now get out my kitchen and tell Dante to come help me bring this food out."

I went back to the stove and stirred the pot of greens. I glanced up as Dante swept into the kitchen and bowed graciously like Jeffery, the butler on *The Fresh Prince of Bel Aire*.

"Hey, sis, what's up? Reverend Reynolds said you wanted me."

"Yeah, help me bring this food out for dinner."

"No problem." He approached the counter and looked me dead in the eye. "So, where were *you* last night?"

"Don't start, aw'ight, Dante?" I groaned. "Mom is already giving me enough grief about that."

"She should. Guess who had to work Bingo with Anita and Deacon Emerson last night because of you? Do you know how unpleasant that was?"

"Oops, my bad." Now I felt sorry. "I had no idea she would call you when I didn't show up. I'll make it up to you, I promise." I gave him a sincere smile.

"You better."

"I will. So what'd you end up getting into after Bingo?"

He didn't give me an answer at first. He just broke into this goofy smile that raised a thousand flags in my mind.

"Nothin' much."

"Nothin' much, like what? And why you grinning so much?" I studied his face. "What're you up to?"

He gave me this innocent look. "What? I'm not up to nothin'. I was just thinking about something that happened last night."

"Like what?" I was in interrogation mode now.

"None of your business. You have your secrets, I've got mine." He reached for a platter and walked out of the room. He returned a few seconds later with the same goofy smile. Oh, there was no doubt in my mind something was going on and it was killing me not to know. I took a long look at my brother. There was a look about him that I hadn't seen in a long time. A look that was familiar, but I just couldn't quite put my finger on. Then it hit me.

"Oooh, Dante . . . you think you're slick, don't you?" I whispered.

"What?" He tried to look innocent.

"I haven't seen you smile like that since you was knocking boots with Anita." I put the spoon down and placed my hands on my hips, shaking my head. "You slept with her again, didn't you? You slept with Anita!"

Dante raised his finger to his lips, shaking his head to quiet me. "No! Hell no. I ain't messin' with her," he scolded through gritted teeth. "Look, sis, she's married, so as far as I'm concerned, that woman is off-limits."

"You sure? I know how you feel about her. They say love can make you do strange things."

"Yeah, but I'm not the one you got to worry about. She's the one chasing me. Last night when I got home, she was staked out in the bushes waiting for me."

"For real? Why would she do that?" I asked, wide-eyed.

"Don't ask me, but if she could, I think she would have raped me. That bitch is crazy, Donna. She's obsessed." From the look on his face I could tell he was concerned, but I wasn't sure if it was because of Anita or himself.

"Is she? I know you have feelings for her. Are you sure your actions haven't led to any of this?"

He hesitated. "I'm not gonna lie. I love Anita, Donna. I always will, but God hasn't come up with the pu-pu that could make me play second fiddle to Deacon Emerson." He picked up another platter and smiled. "Besides, I'm seeing someone else."

"You are? Who is she? Don't tell me it's that Sherrie McDonald I saw you with last week. Oooo, Dante, didn't you mess with her sister a while back?" Now I wanted all the details. Dante and I used to share all our secrets, but things had changed lately, ever since I had a secret too deep to share even with my brother.

"Oh, so you wanna know who I'm see but you're not willing to tell me who you've been creeping with?"

I froze for a moment. I wanted to tell Dante, but I promised Terrance I wouldn't say anything until he said the time was right. "Touché. You're right. It's none of my business." To get Dante out of my Kool-Aid, I turned the tables back around on him. "Anyhow, I'm worried about you. You stay away from Anita. If she finds out about you dating someone else, she could be trouble."

"She already has and already is."

"Oh, Lord, what happened?"

"Nothin' yet, but she made a lot of threats."

"Dante, please be careful. Anita doesn't sound too stable."

"She isn't." He started to walk out the door with a platter and I grabbed his arm.

"Seriously, Deacon Emerson has a lot of guns in that house. If Anita's as crazy as we think she is . . ."

Dante pulled his arm free as if he didn't want to hear it. "I know, Donna. I've already thought about that, okay?"

"Sure, but when you come back, I need to ask you something."

"Does it have to do with Anita?"

"No."

"Good. I'll be right back." He walked out the door.

When he returned, I went straight to the point of what had been on my mind all night. "Can I ask you that question now?"

"Look, don't take all day. We've got some hungry folks in there. The bishop and Reverend Reynolds look like they're about to eat their napkins."

"Don't worry. This won't take long."

"Aw'ight, what's the question?"

"How can a woman tell if a man loves her?"

"What?" A frown took over Dante's face. "What you wanna know that for? You think you're in love or something?"

"Maybe . . . or maybe I'm trying to find out if someone else is in love. Now can you just answer the question so we can go eat?"

He exhaled. "Hmmm. You can probably tell by how he treats you, not by what he says. Most men are willing to say anything to get some. It's the ones who don't push you that usually care."

"So if a man asks for something, he usually doesn't care?"

"Nah, I wouldn't say that. I mean, wanting some pu-pu is a natural thing. I don't care who he is, he could be the nicest guy in the world. He's still gonna wanna get some ass. I guess it's the way he goes about trying to get some that's important."

That made me feel a lot better. Terrance never pushed me when we first started to date. It was me who ended up giving him the condom.

"Well, let's say the man has proven he loves the woman. Do you think a woman should do everything a man asks her to do?"

"Baby sister, it depends on what it is. You can't just do anything a man asks. You have to use some common sense. Ain't no man worth going to jail for."

"What if it's something in the bedroom? Should a woman do everything a man asks her to do in the bedroom?"

"Donna, this is not a conversation I wanna have with you." He picked up the last platter.

"But . . . but I need some advice, Dante. Look, we been through a lot together. I've been there for you."

"I can't. This is something you need to talk to one of your girls or Mom about."

"Mom? You know I can't talk to her. She lost her virginity the night of her wedding."

"Well, what about RaShanda? Why don't you talk to her?"

"No. I want a man's perspective."

He exhaled again, this time louder. "Okay. Let me put it like this, and don't ever forget this. If a woman gives a man everything he wants, he loses interest. Men are hunters. It's just the nature of the beast."

"What do you mean?"

"Well, a lot of men like to go after women. They like the chase, the hunt. And women have to know how to give just enough, but not so much that the man gets bored. But a good man, he'll be loyal and true to the one woman."

"Like the bishop?"

"Yeah, like the bishop. Although, I think they mighta broke the mold when they made him. If you could find his clone, then that's the man I'd want you to marry."

I left the kitchen with a big smile on my face 'cause that's the man I felt I had.

"Amen," we all repeated as the bishop finally finished up his rather lengthy blessing of the food. Unlike most Sundays when our dinner table consisted of only Reverend Reynolds and my immediate family, today's table had some extra last-minute guests. Right before we were about to sit down to eat, we received a visit from Deacon Emerson and my brother's ex, Anita. Of course they apologized when they heard we were about to eat dinner, but they just happened to be in the neighborhood, the deacon explained, and decided to stop by. Now, I'll give the deacon the benefit of the doubt, but Anita knew we always ate Sunday dinner between five-thirty and six o'clock so the bishop could watch his favorite show, *60 Minutes*. The bishop, of course, said there was no reason for them to apologize and invited them to dinner. Anita, much to Dante's chagrin, quickly accepted the invitation without even a glance at her husband. I wasn't sure what she was up to, but I was glad my mother didn't place her next to Dante, because that woman had hands like an octopus.

Despite the obvious awkward situation for Dante, things were pretty decent for a while. I could tell that the food was good from the way all conversation stopped as everyone filled their plates and dug in. This was a relief to me because I was hoping to score a few brownie points with my mother since I was still not forgiven for missing Bingo the night before. As it turned out, Bingo was the last thing on anyone's mind once my father noticed that my brother didn't seem too happy.

"Dante," the bishop called, "are you all right? You barely touched your candied yams. And we all know you love candied yams."

Dante glanced in Anita's direction then plastered a fake smile on his face as he answered. "I'm fine, Bishop."

But I could tell he wasn't fine. He did not want to be there.

"You sure? You look a little distant."

"He must be thinking about that half-dressed woman who came looking for him at the church last night, Bishop Wilson," Anita announced. I swear I thought that witch was about to cackle after she said it.

The room fell silent—no more silverware clinking against plates, not a word from anyone—as every person at the table turned toward Anita. Everyone but me, that is. I was looking at my brother, who was glaring at Anita, his eyes telling her everything he couldn't say.

"What half-naked woman?" my mother asked.

"Dante's new little girlfriend. Hasn't he told you about her? Everyone at Bingo was talking about them. They really put on a show. Isn't that right, Emerson?"

"I don't know if I'd call it a show. They were just showing each other some affection."

"Affection! In the church? Is this true, Dante?" my mother asked, continuing her interrogation. All eyes were now on my brother. I guess he wasn't lying when he said he was seeing someone new. Now I wanted all the scoop.

"It's not what you think, Ma," Dante protested. "I just gave her a little kiss."

"Just a little kiss? Hmph, it was more than a little kiss," Anita corrected him. For anyone paying attention, her jealousy was transparent. "What'd you call it, Emerson? Young love. It was more like lust. Kissing on each other like they was married. I tried to tell them they were in the house of the Lord, but they wouldn't listen to me."

Now, ain't that a bitch? She had the nerve to complain about Dante kissing in the Bingo hall when she and Dante probably screwed in every room of the church. And only the Lord knows what she and Deacon Emerson did.

"Who is this woman?" my mother asked. She was staring at Dante so hard she looked like she could see through him. "Do I know her? Is she a member of our congregation?"

"No. We just met a few days ago."

"And you're carrying on with her like that in the church? What is wrong with you? Don't you have any shame?" I wasn't used to hearing our mother get on Dante like this. Usually I was the one she felt she had to put in place.

"Ma, we were just kissing. Anita's exaggerating. It wasn't like we were doing anything X-rated."

My mother gasped. "Don't get fresh with me, young man. We may have guests but I'm still your mother, and you still live under my roof." Now that was embarrassing. I could see Reverend Reynolds trying to hide a smirk.

Dante sighed but kept his mouth shut.

"Now, you need to thank Anita for bringing this to our attention. If you're going to be a minister, you've got to watch these fast women. They don't care about you, they—"

Dante cut her off. "Ma, she's not fast."

"Oh no? Well, it doesn't sound that way to me."

My father finally spoke up. "Son, how a woman presents herself is very important and is a direct reflection on you. Isn't that right, Deacon Emerson?"

"Your father's right, Dante. A woman can make a man or break a man." He wrapped his good arm around Anita and beamed with pride. She had a smile on her face, but I knew that inside she was smirking. If only her husband knew what kind of woman she really was.

"What are y'all sweating me about?" Dante's brow

furled. "She wouldn't have even been at the church if Donna had shown up for Bingo like she was supposed to."

I kicked Dante under the table. Of course, now Mom turned her attention to me and pointed. "And you, I don't even wanna talk about. What were you thinking last night?"

I heaved an exasperated sigh. "I said I was sorry. It won't happen again."

"It better not." My mother turned back to my brother, never missing a beat. "Dante, we're not trying to sweat you, as you put it. We're just concerned. You've got so much potential. I don't want to see it all go down the drain for a fifteen-minute thrill."

"I know, Ma, but you and the bishop gotta trust me because I really like this girl." I was the only one who noticed Anita rolling her eyes after Dante's statement.

"Well, if you really like her, maybe we should meet this girl. When are you going to bring her by?" the bishop asked.

"Soon, I hope."

10

Tanisha

"Why you so quiet?" Dante whispered in my ear.

I looked back at him and smiled. We'd just had dinner at Umberto's, a seafood restaurant on the water in Bayville, Long Island. After we finished eating, we left the restaurant, walked over to the beach, and climbed up onto one of the lifeguard chairs. I was sitting between Dante's legs and he had his arms wrapped around my waist as we gazed at the moonlight reflecting off the water and listened to the crashing waves. It was the most romantic moment I'd ever had, and I was utterly speechless.

Not that I'd said more than a few words since we arrived at the restaurant anyway. For the first time in my life I let someone else do most of the talking. In all honesty, I was afraid I might open my big mouth and say the wrong thing. I'd already done that once, right before we arrived at the restaurant, and I had no plans of making the same mistake twice. Especially since Dante had worked so hard to make sure everything about this evening was perfect. Now it seemed so stupid that I had gotten an attitude earlier when he told me we were going to Umberto's instead of Red

Lobster. I didn't even give him a chance to explain before I started rolling my eyes and mumbling under my breath about how I hated cheap-ass niggas. I know I was acting ghetto, but at the time I was really looking forward to going to Red Lobster. Besides, I'd never even heard of Umberto's. Not to mention the fact that I promised my mother I'd bring her home one of those fancy glasses Red Lobster gives you when you order one of their tropical drinks.

For a minute I was so angry I contemplated getting out of the car and telling Dante to shove Umberto's up his ass, but in retrospect I'm glad I didn't. Once we pulled in front of the restaurant, it didn't take me long to figure out that Umberto's was a big step up from Red Lobster and that the first thing I should order off the menu was some humble pie. Not only did they have valets who opened our doors like we were VIPs, but Dante had reserved a table outside overlooking the ocean. And the food—oh, my God, the food was *da bomb*. Dante even ordered a bottle of Moët and you know how much that must have cost him. If that wasn't enough, the restaurant had a man playing the violin who went from table to table to serenade the customers. I'm not into that classical music stuff, but holding Dante's hand, sipping on that expensive champagne, and hearing that music made me feel real special, like I was Julia Roberts in *Pretty Woman* and not just a girl from the projects. If this was what it was like to be Dante's girl, then I knew why that chick Anita was fighting so hard to get him back. Not only was he cute, he had a lot more class than any man I'd ever dealt with.

"Hey, you okay? You're not still upset about not going to Red Lobster, are you?"

I wasn't sure if he was joking or not so I took hold of his arms, pulling them gently until he got the hint that I wanted him to hold me tighter.

"No, I'm not upset. I'm not upset at all. I'm just savoring the moment." I hesitated, trying to find the words to express my feelings. "This place, this night . . . it's perfect. I know

I'm not supposed to say things like this but I like you, Dante. I like you a lot and I don't think I ever want this date to end."

"Good, 'cause I like you too, Tanisha, and believe me, this is just the beginning."

"I'm gonna hold you to that." I smiled, leaning back in hopes that he might kiss me.

"I hope you do."

He pressed his soft lips on mine. I damn near melted in his arms when his tongue entered my mouth. If this was just the beginning, I was afraid to think of what he had planned next.

"Come on, let's go." He playfully nudged me from behind.

"Where we going?"

He kissed me again quickly then stood and jumped off the six-foot-high lifeguard chair, looking up at me when he landed on the sand.

"Come on. You'll see." He encouraged me to jump down. "I told you before, this is just the beginning."

Just the beginning. Just the beginning of what? A thousand things ran through my mind but one stuck out. Did his words mean what I think they meant? Was he insinuating that we were going to make love that night? That he was gonna give me some of what my dreams had been filled with the past few nights? Well, if he was, then I was down for that, except for one problem. I was on my period.

Then again, maybe that was an omen. I had promised myself that I wasn't gonna give him any for at least two weeks. I had a rule that if a guy stuck around two weeks, he was probably gonna stick around at least two more. There were exceptions to the rule, of course, but it had worked pretty well for me in the past. The way Dante was making me feel, though, I was gonna be hard-pressed to hold out the two weeks. And after all the money he had spent on our date, I doubted he planned on going home to take a cold shower. I can't say that I blamed him, though. Anyone who'd gone to this much trouble to set up a date deserved to get a little somethin'.

"You coming?" he shouted up at me again.

"Yeah, but you have to catch me." He opened his arms and I leaped. He caught me, and our lips met as he lowered me to the ground. Within seconds his hands were easing their way down my back to massage my ass, and his passionate kisses were making my knees weak. At that point, my monthly visitor was the only thing keeping me from climbing back up on that lifeguard chair and getting busy right there under the stars.

"Let's get out of here," he whispered between kisses.

"Aw'ight, but there's something I need to tell you before we go," I whispered back.

"What's that?" he asked, kissing my neck. I could feel his hard penis rub up against me and that just made matters worse. I wanted him more than I ever wanted any man before in my life.

"I hope this doesn't mess up your plans, but, but I'm . . . I'm on my period. I can't do anything tonight. I mean I want to, but—"

"What?" His neck snapped back and he immediately stopped caressing my ass and dropped his hands to his sides. It was obvious that he was disappointed and that I had done exactly what I said I wouldn't do. I had opened my big mouth and ruined our date. I wanted to smack myself. Why the hell did I have to tell him that? I could have come up with some excuse about my period just starting when we got to his place. But now I was in trouble, 'cause if what I knew about men was true, he was about to make an excuse to take me home, and that was the last thing I wanted him to do.

"Please don't be mad, Dante. I can still take care of you if you want."

He had this bewildered look on his face and a twinge of confusion in his voice. "Take care of me? Take care of me how?"

"You know. Take *care* of you?" I raised my eyebrows a couple of times then smiled bashfully as I twisted nervously in front of him. Can you believe he still didn't get the hint? I stepped closer to him and placed my hand on his waist as I stared into his eyes. "What I'm trying to say is that even though I'm on my period, this date doesn't have to end. I like you, Dante, and I'm willing to do whatever it takes to make you happy." I gave him a wicked smile. "And believe me. I know how to make a man happy."

He took another step back, tilting his head as he studied my face. "Are you saying what I think you're saying?"

Thank God he was finally starting to get the hint, but both his expression and his words told me he wanted it confirmed. Why, I don't know. What did he want me to do, spell it out for him? Did he actually want me to just come out and say that I would suck his dick? What the hell was this, some type of test? I glanced at him and he still had this look of uncertainty on his face. I knew it was a front, but I finally said to myself, *What the fuck. If he wants me to say it, then I'll say it. I ain't got no shame to my game.*

"Look, Dante, I'm not stupid and neither are you. I know you spent a lot of money tonight trying to impress me so you could get some ass. Well, I'm impressed, and although I'm on my period, I'm going to give you the best blow job you've ever had. I know it's not the same as getting some, but I'm pretty good at it. Shit, I'm better than good," I bragged with a smile. "I'm da bomb."

There. I'd said it, but instead of him smiling or looking happy or even grateful, he just shook his head and tried to hide a smirk. I'm not gonna front; that shit pissed me off. I mean damn, I did just offer to suck his dick, and now he was looking at me like I was a ho. I was no longer feeling like a pretty woman.

"What the fuck is so funny?" I snapped.

He stopped smirking and stepped closer. He even tried to grasp my hand, but I pulled it away. "Tanisha, I wasn't planning on having sex with you tonight. Look, this is only our first date. I respect you too much for that."

"You respect me too much?" I just stared at him, thinking, *This motherfucker is gay. Don't no straight man say no to me.* "You expect me to believe that you spent all this money and you wasn't planning on getting some 'cause you respect me too much?"

"Yeah, it's the truth. I was planning on taking you to Coney Island to see the fireworks, not to a hotel." I was starting to feel sick.

"So you had no intentions of getting any tonight?" I wanted to call him a liar, but the last time I did that, he proved me wrong.

"None," he said in this sincere voice that made my stomach turn. "I didn't think sex was something we'd get into until at least a couple of weeks down the road."

"And you don't want me to go down on you?" I was starting to feel like I was shrinking in front of him.

He hesitated for a second to think, which told me he wasn't gay, but I still didn't like his answer. "Nah, it's too soon."

Can you say *fool?* That's how I felt: like the biggest fool in the world. His facial expression was so serious I had no choice but to believe him. I swear if I had a gun, I would have shot myself for being so damn stupid. I'd never been so embarrassed in my entire life. How in the world could I be with him after this? God, why the fuck did I just tell him I would suck his dick? He must have thought I was a straight-up ho, and the way I was feeling, I couldn't blame him.

I was so embarrassed I couldn't look at him. I didn't think I could ever look at him again, so I just said, "Dante, can you please take me home?"

"Take you home for what?"

"Because I wanna go home," I snapped with attitude. At that moment all I wanted to do was get home and as far away from him as possible.

"Come on, Tanisha. Don't be like this." He tried to kiss me and I pushed him away.

"Look, I said I wanna go home, aw'ight?" I turned and started walking toward the car.

"What about the fireworks?"

"Like I give a shit about some damn fireworks now."

11

Dante

I pulled my truck in front of Tanisha's building and turned to her, hoping I'd find the words to make things right. She'd barely said a word during the ride home and in truth I was afraid things between us were over before they had begun. All this because I didn't have the common sense to smile and say yes when she offered to go down on me. Things were going so perfectly. If I had just stopped trying to impress her by being Mr. Respectful, I'd probably be on the beach at Coney Island watching the fireworks, having who knows what done to me. Damn, of all the times in my life to let my big head take control from my little one.

"Bye," Tanisha said, emotionless as she leaned over and kissed my cheek, a telltale sign that things between us were truly over.

"Call you tomorrow?" I tried to make it sound like a casual question, but it was actually a plea to give us one more try; a plea that I knew was painfully rejected when she glanced at me coldly and stepped out of the car. I called her name, but she closed the door like she hadn't heard a word I said. I knew that she had, and as much as I liked her, I was starting to get sick of her childish behavior.

I was about to pull off, but my heart and conscience just wouldn't let me. There was something about her that captivated me, and it wasn't just her body. Childish behavior or not, she intrigued me like no other woman I'd ever met, including Anita. I knew if I drove away now, I would probably never see her again, and that just wasn't something I was willing to take a chance on. I opened my car door and called out to her again. This time she stopped, turning only her head toward me.

"What you want?" she huffed, sounding like I was grinding on her last nerve.

"I don't know why you're acting this way," I said boldly. "If you were any other woman, I would have let you go down on me!"

She whipped the rest of her body around, pointing her right index finger at me and placing her left hand on her hip. That's when I realized what I was trying to say hadn't come out the way I had wanted it to.

"What the fuck is that supposed to mean?"

"It was supposed to be a compliment," I answered, swallowing hard.

"It was?" She gave me a doubtful look as she raised her eyebrows. "Well, then let me apologize," she continued sarcastically, " 'cause I feel a lot better now knowing that you don't even think I'm good enough to suck your dick."

Oh, Lord, now she's blowing things all out of proportion. Damn, what is it about this girl? Can't she tell when a guy really likes her?

"I didn't mean it that way, Tanisha—"

She cut me off before I could explain. "Oh, yeah? What the fuck did you mean?"

When I didn't answer fast enough, she shook her head and turned toward her building. I stepped out of the car and sprinted toward her, trying to get my thoughts together so I could convey exactly what I really did mean into words. When I caught up to her, I stepped in front of her, hoping to give the respectful answer she deserved.

"Look, I don't know how this happened, and I admit at first I was just looking to have a good time, but after you showed up at the church the other night and we had a chance to talk, this stopped being a wham-bam-thank-you-ma'am thing for me. Like I said before, I like you, and for the first time in a long time I'm looking long-term. I don't want this to be about sex. I want this to be about us. So before we get intimate, I wanted to get to know you better. Is there something wrong with that? I thought that's what you women want."

She stared at me blankly, and for a second there I thought I saw a glimmer of hope, but slowly a smirk crept onto her face and she started clapping her hands. "Bravo! Bravo! You know, I really didn't think you had it in you. You really know how to run game, don't you? That was one hell of a performance," she told me, "but now that I've seen the show, there's no need for me to stay. Now can you get out my way so I can go upstairs?" She tried to push her way past me.

"Performance? You think I was acting?" I let out a frustrated laugh.

"Now I see why you're by yourself. That sounded like some corny-ass shit I read in a romance novel. I'm looking for a man, Dante, someone who's gonna keep it real like I do. Not some fake-ass Goody Two-shoes."

I couldn't believe what I was hearing. Here I was pouring my heart out to this woman and she thought it was a corny act. Well, I was about to act all right. I was about to act the fuck up!

"You know what, Tanisha?"

"What?" She smirked again. She was daring me to match her funky attitude, and I was about to take that dare. I didn't like to act this way, but I could when I was being pushed, and she was pushing me to that point.

I put my middle finger in her face. "Fuck you!"

"Fuck me?" She snapped her head back in disbelief like she wasn't sure the words had come out of my mouth.

"That's right. Fuck you! I pour my heart out to you, tell you how I feel and how much I respect you and that I don't wanna use you for your body, and then you treat me like this. You know what? I should've let you suck my dick, 'cause if you ain't got no respect for yourself, then why the fuck should I?"

"What you trying to say? You think I'm a ho or something?" All of a sudden she was on the defensive.

"Nope, I think you're a beautiful black sister with a fucked-up attitude who can't see a good thing when he's standing in front of you."

"You ain't all that." She showed me that damn smirk again.

I turned my head away from her then snapped it back, looking her dead in the eyes. She jumped a step back. I'll tell you this much—it was obvious she suddenly had more respect for me. My sister had always told me that women hate soft men, so from this point on, that Mr. Respectful shit was out the door.

"No, you're right. I'm not all that. But as far as me keeping it real, I was keeping it real. I'm a nice fucking guy, but baby, I ain't nobody to play with, especially when it come to my feelings." I stepped out of her way and started walking to my car. "I was really feeling you, Tanisha. We really could have had something special. It's too bad you couldn't see that."

12

Donna

It was Friday afternoon, and like most Fridays, I was looking forward to Saturday afternoon when I would hook up with Terrance. Things between us had been good this past week. Not only had we gone out to lunch twice, but we'd found some way to get in a quickie almost every day. Terrance kept to his word too. He hadn't brought up the anal sex thing once, though I have to admit it had been heavy on my mind. I was starting to feel guilty for not giving in to him. After all, he had tried to fulfill almost all of my fantasies, even if they were pretty tame compared to his. That's why I went to Brooklyn to see my best friend, RaShanda Wright. I was hoping she might have some answers to put an end to my sleepless nights.

When I knocked on RaShanda's door, I realized I hadn't visited her since a month before Terrance and I started dating. RaShanda and I were like Shorty and Dante—we'd known each other since elementary school. RaShanda's mom was one of my mother's best friends and one of the more powerful deaconesses in the church. RaShanda, on the other hand, was everything a church girl was not supposed to be. You know the type: scandalous, wild, and crazy. To be blunt, RaShanda was a slut, a straight-up freak, and everyone but her momma knew it until she got pregnant. That's when her mother kicked her out of the house in an attempt to hide the pregnancy from the people in the church.

Secretly, I believe every woman has a friend like RaShanda. I knew we were an unlikely pair, what with me just losing my virginity at the ripe old age of twenty, but RaShanda was still my best friend. She had been there for me through thick and thin, and I tried to be there for her even after she moved to Brooklyn from her mother's home. I think the reason I didn't judge her was because she had also provided me the opportunity to live vicariously through her freaky life. You see, RaShanda had participated in all the things I would have liked to try when we were kids but was too afraid to try.

"Who?"

"It's Donna, girl. Open the door."

RaShanda flung open the door, looking as divalicious as ever. She had the statuesque presence of an Amazon. As the men like to say, she was built like a brick house. It was late morning and she had on stilettos with a matching silk blouse and capri pants, both in the brightest shade of purple. She wore darkened designer shades although she was in the house. I could see she'd already had her weekly manicure and pedicure. Lord, that girl knew she was all that.

A quick glimpse around her place told me she was doing well and probably had a new boyfriend or two because she'd remodeled her apartment since my last visit.

"Hey, girl. Where you been?" RaShanda hugged me so tightly I had to catch my breath.

I hugged her back. "I been around. I tried to call before I came, but the operator said you changed your number. What's up with that?"

"Oh, I was gonna call you with the new number. I was messing with this crazy Jamaican brother and he found out I was seeing someone else. Lord, girl, I thought the nigga was gonna kill me. So I changed the number."

"I know that's right."

"Come in here, girl. You a sight for sore eyes. It has been a long time. What's up with that?"

"You know, with school, work, and *my man,* I'm busy." I waited for my words to register.

"Man! Looka here, looka here! The preacher's gal done got her a man? I knew there was something different about you." RaShanda lifted her shades then sniffed around me. A smile crept up on her face. "And you done messed around and got some too, didn't you?" She broke into a singsong then slapped her hands together. "Little Miss Donna the virgin done lost her cherry. Hot damn!"

"What are you, a psychic? How'd you know that?" I was shocked. Although I wanted to talk to her about the anal sex issue, I had planned to pretend it was an unnamed friend's problem. I meant to keep my new sexual liaison on the Q.T. for now, but my friend had already busted me.

"Girl, it's all in the way you carry yourself. You used to walk all stiff. Now you're walking with a little swerve in your hips. Turn around."

"For what?"

"Just do it. Damn."

I did as I was told, blushing the whole time.

"Damn, girl, you sure as hell been gettin' some, and I don't mean a little bit. Even your butt is bigger, and look at your titties. Somebody must be sucking on them puppies. Your shit is standing at attention. About time your horny ass went on and did it."

I waved my hand at her with a laugh. "You're crazy. You know that?"

"Maybe, but I can tell you doing your thing. You're absolutely glowing! I'm so proud of you." She pointed at the sofa and we sat. "How long you been doing it?"

"Couple months."

She glared at me. "And you just getting over here to tell me? I oughta slap you, girl."

"I'm sorry. I just been busy. It's hard work keeping a man happy."

"You think that's somethin', you should try keepin' three happy. But that's a whole 'nother story. Look, you protecting yourself? This AIDS is out here like a mother."

"Yeah. I been using condoms and we've both been tested. I insisted on it just in case the condom broke."

"That's good, but them condoms ain't enough. They can break. You get your ass down to the clinic too, and get you some pills or the shot for backup. You don't wanna be like me. Babies ain't no joke. By the way, how's my other baby doing?"

She was talking about Dante. RaShanda and him used to have a sex thing back in the day. I'm pretty sure she took his virginity.

"He's fine."

"Damn, why couldn't I have gotten pregnant by him? Now he's baby daddy material."

" 'Cause I would have kicked your ass."

"Oh, yeah, good point." She changed the subject. "So, now that you gettin' some, how is it? Is the dick good or what?"

I started laughing and covered my mouth.

"C'mon now, don't hold out on me. I been waitin' years to share sex stories with you." RaShanda wiggled her fingers like a loan shark. "Give it up."

"Some things are too personal."

"You ain't no good, Donna. You wrong now. As much as I done told your ass. You know secrets that I was planning to carry to my grave. Gimme the 411."

Placing her shades back on her eyes, RaShanda pulled out a cigarette, leaned back on the sofa cushion, and crossed her legs. I was silent for the longest time.

"Oh, all right," I finally said. "What you wanna know?"

"Who is it?"

"I can't tell you right now."

"Oh, Lord, don't tell me it's that cute little friend of Dante's. He been sniffing behind your ass for years."

"No! It's not Shorty," I replied quickly.

"Well, do I know him?" I smiled instead of giving her an answer. I think she got the hint so she continued her interrogation. "Well, tell me this. Does he satisfy you?"

I paused for dramatic effect and turned my head away, making her wait for my answer. "I didn't like it the first couple of times, but after that . . . Oh my God, it was the bomb! I have three or four orgasms every time. It's so good we've named it."

We both jumped up in the air and screamed with excitement as we high-fived. "Damn, now that's what I'm talking about! Sounds like you found a brother with some skills. Assuming he is a brother, now."

I nodded.

"What's your favorite position?"

I reluctantly answered her question. "I love it on top."

"Child, that's the number one position. You can ride that bad boy and break him like a bronco. Do you let him suck on your titties when you come?"

I shook my head. "RaShanda, you so nasty."

"Well, 'scuse me, Miss Just-Got-Some. I been telling you about all my conquests since we was damn near kids, and now you want to clam up on me."

"Okay. Yeah, I do."

"Do what?" She was something else.

"Like my breasts kissed."

"Oh, looka here at Miss Proper. Now, when you talkin' about lovemaking, you got to get funky." RaShanda stood, popping her fingers, and started dancing and singing, "We gonna have a funky good time." She stopped singing then high-fived me.

"Yeah. Don't that shit feel good?"

We screamed in laughter again. "Can you get yours when you're on the bottom?" she asked.

"Uh-huh. Why?"

"That mean whoever he is, he's big."

"How would I know the difference? This is my first and hopefully only man."

"Yeah, yeah, right." She was skeptical. "Well, let me tell you something. With those big ones, you getting that wall-to-wall carpeting. Men that are hung—well, especially if they know how to garden with that tool—they really know how to blow the dust off that thang. So, how big is he?" RaShanda held out her hands to show six inches, eight inches, or twelve inches.

I let out an exaggerated sigh. "Dang, don't you have any shame?"

"Ain't no shame in my game."

"I see. Well, that's for me to know and you to find out, Miss Thang."

"Oh, you gon' be dirty like that and not tell Mother everything. Girl, I'm the reason you gettin' your nuts already. It took me almost a year after my first time before I started reaching a climax. I have told you every good position and how to get to that G-spot and use that clit since we were fourteen."

I thought about the time when we were fourteen and RaShanda told me to go in the bathroom and use a mirror to look down at my pubic area so I would know where the clitoris was located. "Okay. Granted, you did make it easier for me to figure things out. Thanks. But I've come to you with a problem you never told me about."

"What's that?"

"What if a man asks you to do something you're uncomfortable with doing?"

"Like what? Suck his dick? Girl, you better give that man some head."

"No, I already do that." I paused. "My friend asked if I would let him have anal sex with me."

She laughed. Then she laughed harder.

"What's so funny?"

"Men. That's what's so funny." She continued to laugh and I started laughing right along with her without even knowing the joke. "I ain't met a man alive that didn't wanna fuck me in the ass, and that includes your brother."

I sat back in my chair, shocked. "Dante?"

"Yes, Dante. He ain't no different than the rest. He's a little more respectful and he doesn't kiss and tell, but when it comes down to it, he's just a man, and they all want the same thing. At first they want some pussy and some head. Then after a while they get bored with that and wanna fuck you in the ass."

"But why?"

"Because they're all secretly gay. Ain't you read that book by J. L. King, *On the Down Low*?"

"Really? So you think he's gay?" My eyes widened and my heart started pounding.

"No." She laughed. "I'm kidding. It's probably because it's taboo. He's probably just trying to see how freaky you are. Shit. I'm surprised he ain't asked you to have a threesome with another woman."

"He would never ask me to do that."

She smirked. "Yeah, right. Whatever you say. I bet you never thought he'd wanna fuck you in the ass."

I lowered my head. Damn, I hated it when she was right. "So have you ever tried anal?"

She sat back in her chair. "Yeah, but not often."

"Does it hurt?"

"Oh, it can definitely hurt, but if you're with the right brother, it can be fun. It's a feeling you have to get you used to, sort of an acquired taste."

We stared at each other in silence for a few seconds.

RaShanda finally spoke up. "Now, you know I'm no prude, but this isn't something you do with everybody. You gotta really love a brother to do that, and I don't mean puppy love. Do you love him?"

"Yeah, I do."

"This is the only word of advice I can give you. Don't do anything you feel uncomfortable about doing. But if you want, I can show you the best way to make it comfortable for you."

"Okay, but I still don't know if I'm gonna do it."

"Just the fact that you thinking 'bout it tells me this must be one special brother."

I smiled. "He is, and I'm going to marry him someday soon."

RaShanda smiled. "I bet you are."

13

Tanisha

At the end of my shift I walked into the back room at work. My friend Natasha, the head bartender who was about to start her shift, was sitting on one of the room's raggedy couches reading a *Jet* magazine. I gestured for her to give me a pull of the cigarette she was smoking. She handed it to me, and I took a long drag until my lungs couldn't hold any more. I wasn't really a smoker except when I drank, and I usually drank when I worked. So I was in the mood for a cigarette.

"You can have it," Natasha said without looking up from her copy of *Jet*.

"Thanks," I replied, taking another pull.

Natasha put down the magazine and looked up at me. "Where you been, girl? I ain't seen you in about three, four weeks."

"I been around. I just been trying to work days so I can watch my little brother at night. My mom is fuckin' up so bad I'm afraid somebody's gonna call CPS and they gonna take him away from me. Last night I found her passed out on the staircase of my building. Week before that she was letting dealers use our apartment as a crack house while I was at work."

"Damn, and here I am thinking you was with that guy from the church you was talking about so much. You know how you bitches get once y'all get a man. Y'all don't know how to call nobody."

"You mean Dante? Hmmph. Don't I wish. I ain't heard from him in almost a month." I sighed, wishing she hadn't brought him up. Not that I could forget him. He'd been on my mind ever since I watched his car pull away from my building four weeks ago.

"Uh-oh, what happened?" She patted the sofa cushion next to her, gesturing for me to sit.

I hesitated. I almost never trusted a woman enough to talk about a man. It had been a very long time since I'd done that, but this was different. This time my feelings were involved. I missed Dante more and more with each day that passed. When I'd get in from work, I would lie in bed and replay the evening of our first date over and over in my head like a broken record, trying to figure out just where I went wrong and how I could fix things. I'd been holding this in for almost a month, and I needed to get it off my chest. I sat next to Natasha on the couch.

"I thought you two straightened everything out that night you went to the church," she said.

"We did."

"Aw'ight, so what happened? He find out you was dancing?"

"Nah, it ain't had nothing to do with that," I glanced down at the floor, feeling ashamed. "I messed up, that's what happened, and he ain't called or come by since."

I explained the story to Natasha, from dinner at Umberto's to our time on the beach, from me being on my period to my offer to go down on Dante, from his rejection of my offer to my demand to go home. I also made it very clear that Dante tried his best to make things right when he brought me back to my house, but I wasn't having it and he ended up leaving mad. The more I explained, the more she shook her head, until finally she spoke.

"You're wrong," she told me. "You didn't mess up. You fucked up. Do you know how many sisters would kill for a man like that? Including me. Girl, you making us good sisters look bad."

"I know, my mother said the same thing, and she's a crackhead."

"Look, if I were you, I'd call him."

"I can't call him. I wouldn't know what to say."

"Shit, you better make something up. Tell him you're sorry and you wanna make it up to him. Ask him to dinner."

"I can't do that. He's gonna think I'm sweating him."

"You are, aren't you?" Natasha asked.

"No, I'm not."

"Yeah, you are. I mean shit, Tanisha, you wouldn't have chased him down in the supermarket or offered to suck his dick on the first date if you weren't sweating him. Stop putting your pride in front of your heart. If he's everything you say he is, you need to call him before somebody else does. Brothers like that don't come around but once in a lifetime."

The thought of Dante and that Anita woman from the church popped into my mind and a jealous knot developed in my stomach. Generally, I ain't got no problem blowing a guy off if it doesn't work out, but this time I just couldn't do it. Except for the humiliation at the end of the night, my date with Dante was the best one I'd ever been on.

I guess I had brought some of this on myself. It's just like that old saying about the word *assume*. I made an ass out of myself assuming he just wanted me for a booty-call or, even worse, a blow job. It had taken a long time, but the truth had finally hit me. Dante *did* just wanna get to know me before we hit the sheets. I'd never known a brother like him, and now I was too afraid to talk to him to make things right.

Natasha tapped my thigh. "Seriously, do you like him?"

I lifted my head and nodded as I spoke. "More than I've ever liked any other man in my life. I can't stop thinking about him. It's like he's invaded my head."

Natasha sat back. "You should call him."

"I can't, Natasha. I'm scared."

"Of what?"

"I'm scared he's not gonna wanna talk to me. And I can't deal with that type of rejection because I've never felt like this about any other dude."

She placed her hand over mine. "Well, if that's the case, then you have to call him." Natasha reached in her bag and pulled out her cell. "Call him."

I shook my head and refused.

"I said call him!" She shoved the phone in my face. "If you don't trust me, you're gonna regret it the rest of your life."

"Oh, all right." I took the phone from her hand and dialed Dante's number. I had it memorized.

As I listened to his phone ring, a chill ran down my spine. My heart was pounding and my palms were getting sweaty. After four rings, I was about to hang up. I didn't want to leave a message on his voice mail. Before I could hang up, though, Dante answered.

"Hello."

My heart skipped a beat at the sound of his voice. I almost hung up I was so nervous, but when I looked up at Natasha, she was pointing her fingers at the phone mouthing *Talk to him!*

Taking a deep breath, I finally spoke. "Hey, Dante," I said, my voice quavering. "What's crackin'?"

14

Dante

I was lying on the bed on top of the covers with all my clothes on. The TV was on but I wasn't really paying attention. I had other things on my mind because even I couldn't believe the situation I was in. My cell phone rang, interrupting the thoughts swirling around in my head.

"Hello."

"Hey, Dante. What's crackin'?" The voice was quiet and a little tentative but it seemed familiar.

"Who is this?" I asked.

"It's Tanisha." A smile crept up on my face and I sat up on the bed. I'd pretty much given up on her, yet she'd been on my mind just five minutes earlier.

"Tanisha," I repeated, glad she couldn't see my smile through the phone. "How've you been?"

"Fine, I guess . . ."

"So, what's poppin'? I didn't think you was ever gonna call me again." I was trying to keep my emotions in check.

"I don't know I just . . . I just . . ." She was obviously having a hard time expressing herself. "Dante, I just need to talk to you about how things ended between us. I know you weren't acting that night. I just got an attitude to hide my embarrassment, and—"

I cut her off. "Look, I can't talk right now. I'm a little busy, but you don't have to apologize. I understand. We're cool."

"Are we cool enough to start all over again? I really like you, Dante, and I'd like to make it up to you. Maybe I can take you to dinner. This time the treat's on me. I really wanna start over."

"I'd like that," I told her, and I think we both relaxed. "Just let me know where and when."

"I don't know yet. How about later tonight?"

"Give me a call in about half an hour. I just have to break a date with someone."

"I'll call you in an hour." She sounded as happy as I felt.

"I'll be looking forward to it." I closed my phone and looked up. I was surprised to see Anita standing in the threshold of the bathroom. We were at a local motel we had visited many times before she got married. I had promised myself when she came back to New York that she was out of my system and I wasn't going to mess with her, but here I was. After things fell apart with Tanisha, I had moped around for quite a while, and I think Anita sensed I was vulnerable. She caught me in my office at a weak moment and did everything she could to remind me of the skills she possessed. It didn't take much for me to give in, and before long we were in the Jet Motel just like old times.

Anita was more than ready for action. She even had a bag in her trunk full of lingerie, wineglasses, and other supplies she thought she might need for our little reunion. I didn't want to know how long she'd been carrying that bag around, but obviously she had been pretty confident from the start that eventually she would win me over. As cliché as it sounds, she had gone into the bathroom to slip into something a little more comfortable. That was when I lay on the bed slowly coming to my senses. She might have charmed me with promises of reliving the explosive sex we had shared in the past, but now I realized that couldn't happen. Back then I had loved this woman deeply, and that was part of what had made our sex so great. Now she had broken my heart and married another man. Things could never be what they were, especially since I had these feelings for Tanisha.

Before my phone rang, my big head was struggling with my little one. My body wanted to stay and get some action, but my heart knew I would only regret it later. Tanisha's phone call had made it much easier for me to come to a decision. Now I had to deal with telling Anita, who was in the bathroom doorway dressed in white stilettos and a sheer pink negligee, that I was leaving. From the look on her face, though, it was obvious she had heard my conversation and already knew what was up.

"Who was that?" she asked angrily as she walked out of the bathroom.

"A friend." I tried to sound casual.

"Male or female?"

"I don't think that's any of your business." I was now sitting on the edge of the bed searching for my shoes. Anita bent down and grabbed them before I could reach them. That's when I realized I'd made a bigger mistake than I thought.

"You going somewhere?" she taunted as she waved the shoes at me.

"I can't do this, Anita. I thought I could, but I can't."

"Why? Who was that on the phone? Don't tell me it was that hootchie who showed up at the church. I thought you said you were done with her."

"I was mistaken," I said tersely. I tried to remain calm as I approached her. "Now, can I have my shoes?"

"You're not getting anything until I get what I want." She gave me a wicked grin. "Take off your clothes." I could see fire in her eyes.

"Look, Anita, I'm sorry, but I can't do this."

"I don't wanna hear it, Dante." She pushed me backward. "I said take off your clothes!"

I was taken aback by her demand. I knew she was aggressive, but this was a side of Anita I was just learning about. "I'm not taking off my clothes. Now gimme my shoes." I sat up, reaching for my shoes.

"You want your shoes, you ungrateful son of a bitch? Well, take them!" She threw one of my shoes at me and it hit me in the side of the head. I felt a knot developing instantly.

"What the fuck is wrong with you?" I yelled, grabbing my head.

"You! You're what's wrong with me. All I wanna do is make love to you, you bastard. Why the fuck do you have to make things so complicated?" She threw my other shoe even harder than the first, but this time I ducked. Unfortunately, the mirror behind me didn't have that option and shattered into a thousand pieces.

"You're fucking crazy, Anita!"

"Now look what you made me do! I should just kill you and be done with you!" she cried out as she walked over to the broken mirror and picked up a jagged piece of glass. She didn't have to say that twice. That was my clue to get the hell outta there. I ran to the door, leaving my shoes and that crazy bitch behind.

"It's amazing the things you take for granted living in this city," I thought out loud as I surveyed the skyline. It had only been a few hours since I had left Anita in the motel. Luckily I had a pair of sneakers in the trunk of my car, so when Tanisha called, I was able to drive over and meet her. Now we were admiring the view from high above the city. "I've lived here all my life, and believe it or not, this is the first time I've ever been to the Empire State Building. It's so beautiful up here. What made you decide to pick this place anyway?"

Tanisha stepped up and smiled, obviously pleased with herself. It was her idea that we meet on the observation deck of the Empire State Building before having dinner. I think she wanted to clear the air before we moved forward with our relationship.

"This is my special place. The first place I can ever remember being truly happy. The only place in the world that I feel safe. Whenever I think things won't get better, I come here and somehow I find the strength to move on." She sounded serious.

"Oh yeah, why is that?"

"When we first moved up here from Virginia, I was about eleven or twelve. My mom had just gotten out of rehab for the first time. She had promised me the whole time she was away that when she got out she was gonna come get me and we were gonna go to New York to find my dad. She kept her promise too. As soon as the courts would let her, she came and got me from foster care. The next day the two of us were on a Greyhound headed to New York." Tanisha smiled at the memory.

"The first place we stopped when we got off the bus was the Empire State Building. When we got up here to the observation deck, she pointed to the horizon and said, 'Tanisha, your past and your future are out there. You just have to find it.'" She let out a lighthearted laugh, glancing out at the horizon. "I'm still looking for both."

"I don't know much about your past, but maybe your future is standing in front of you."

"Maybe." She turned back to me. "Can I ask you a question?"

"Sure. You can ask me anything you want."

"Are you serious about this getting to know me stuff?"

"Yeah. I am."

"Why me?"

"What do you mean? I don't understand."

"Why me? I see the way women look at you. You probably have women chasing after you all the time. Why do you wanna be with me?"

" 'Cause I like you. There's something about you that's special."

"But why? You don't know anything about me. I live in the projects. My mother's a crackhead. I work in a bar. I barely got a GED. I bet you got a college degree. What makes me so special? Why do you like me?"

I shrugged my shoulders. "I don't know. I just like you. It's not something I can explain. It's just something I feel. Something in here." I pointed at my heart. "When I'm with you, I feel like I can do anything. I've never felt a connection with anyone like I have with you, Tanisha."

"Does that include the Bingo lady?"

"Yes, that definitely includes Anita." I took her hand and massaged it with my fingers. She smiled. "Now, why do you like me?"

"At first it was because you were cute. Then after we talked at the church and at the restaurant, I realized you were the first guy who ever talked to me about stuff other than what we was gonna do after we ate dinner. You wasn't trying to impress me by how you was gonna fuck the shit out of me. You just kept it regular. Like we was friends. I like that. I never had a guy treat me like that."

"If you noticed that, why'd you wanna go home that night?"

Her voice got low. "Embarrassed, I guess. A little hurt too."

"Hurt? Why hurt?"

"It's not every day that you offer to go down on a guy and he tells you he ain't interested. It hurt a little. No, it hurt a lot. I thought I was doing you a favor. When you said no, it was like you was rejecting me. I don't deal well with rejection."

"Well, I'll tell you a little secret. Deep down I wanted to. I can't tell you how much I wanted to. But I also knew that I liked you, and if I had sex with you right away, I wouldn't have respected you. My father taught me a long time ago that if you like someone, the most important thing is that you respect them."

I reached out to touch her face then kissed her gently on the lips.

"Who are you, Dante? You go to church every Sunday, but you wear throwbacks and Tims. You kiss me like no dude I've ever met, yet you don't wanna have sex. Who the hell are you? I've never met a guy who acts like you."

"Maybe you just never met a guy who really likes you for you. And as for me going to church every Sunday, it's not by choice. If my father wasn't the pastor of the church, two of those four Sundays I'd be up in the bed getting some sleep."

"Your father's the pastor of that church on Merrick?"

"Yep, that's my dad, Bishop T.K. Wilson."

"Isn't he running for borough president? I seen those posters all over town."

"That's him. Why? Don't tell me you were planning to vote for someone else." He chuckled.

"No, to be honest, I'm not even registered to vote."

"Well, don't tell my father that when you meet him."

"You want me to meet your father?"

"Not right away, but someday. Him and my mother."

"Dante, I don't know. I don't do parents very well." She sounded worried.

I laughed. "Don't worry. My mother doesn't do girl-friends very well either."

"Girlfriend? I'm confused. So now I'm your girlfriend?" Uh-oh, she sounded nervous about that idea. Maybe I'd jumped the gun.

"Only if you wanna be," I replied cautiously.

"Yeah, I do." She smiled, although she sounded choked up. "I've just never been anyone's girlfriend before. As Wendy Williams calls it, I've always just been the *jump off*."

"Well, Miss Tanisha, things are about to change." I took her hand. "Now, come on. I'm hungry. Let's go get something to eat."

15

Donna

"What's up, girl?" RaShanda smiled as she slid into the booth across from me. "Sorry I'm late."

"It's aw'ight. I just got here myself." We leaned over the table and kissed cheeks.

"Good. Now, did you order yet? 'Cause I want me some cheesecake." She picked up a menu before flagging down a waitress. I'd asked RaShanda to meet me at Junior's famous cheesecake restaurant in Brooklyn because I wanted to talk to her about some of my concerns regarding Terrance.

It had been a while since I'd stopped by her place seeking advice, and I desperately needed it again. I'd been with Terrance almost six and a half months now and I was sick and tired of sneaking around. I wanted to tell my parents about our relationship, especially my mother. It might earn me some points if she knew I was with a man from the church, and Lord knows I could use help improving my mother's opinion of me.

I was also worried because Terrance was starting to do a lot of work-related travel. Maybe it was paranoia, but every time he left for a conference or a seminar, I started worrying he might be with someone else.

Once she'd ordered her cheesecake and some coffee, RaShanda turned to me. "What's this big problem that you didn't wanna talk about on the phone? You're not pregnant, are you?"

"Lawd, no! I'm not pregnant." RaShanda's words made my heart skip a beat. "My mother would kill me."

"I know that's right. She's got a bigger stick up her ass than my momma."

I gave her an ice-cold stare. I loved RaShanda but I hated the way she talked about my mother. "I done told you about talkin' 'bout my momma, RaShanda. She may be a bitch, but she's my bitch, okay? So don't talk about her."

"Damn. Aw'ight, calm down. I don't know why you always defending her. That lady treats you like shit."

"Well, that's my problem. She's my mom, and despite her shortcomings, I still got love for her."

"Aw'ight. Look, let's change the subject. Why'd you wanna meet down here anyway?"

I took a long, slow breath and closed my eyes momentarily. When I opened them, I told her, "I think I'm losing my man." I never called Terrance by name when we talked. I always called him "my man." The less RaShanda knew, the better. She was my girl and all, but she had a tendency to talk about other people's business when she was drinking. It was fine if she talked about me, but I did not want it to get out that I was dating Terrance until I—or rather he—was ready.

"Oh, Donna, I'm sorry," she said with sympathy as she reached across the table to caress my hand. "What happened? You seemed so happy when we talked last." She hesitated. "Don't tell me he still wants to do you in your butt."

"Nah, that's not it . . ." I had to pause and think about it for a second. "Well, at least I don't think that's it. He hasn't brought it up." Then again, maybe that was part of the problem.

"Then you think he's cheating?"

"I'm not sure. All I know is that things are different. He's different. I feel like I'm losing him, RaShanda, and I'm scared." RaShanda sat back in her chair with a curious look on her face.

"How's the sex been?"

"Good. That's never been a problem. He still can't keep his hands off me. We probably do it three or four times a week. And as far as I'm concerned, I enjoy it more and more each time we make love. It's after the sex that we have a problem. After we make love, he always seems a little distant. He turns away from me as soon as he comes, and this is when I want to cuddle. I put my arms around him anyhow, but he has his back to me. He never used to do that."

"He's getting used to the pussy. You gotta change shit up."

"What's that supposed to mean?"

"I'll explain it to you in a bit. I've got a few tricks that'll help, but eventually you might have to give him what he really wants. Make him think you care about his needs."

"Uh-uh." I shook my head. "I'm not giving him anal sex until he tells me he loves me."

"The question is, do you think he's ever gonna tell you that?" She folded her arms, waiting for my response.

"I don't know. He doesn't even want me to tell anybody about our relationship. Why should he tell me he loves me?" I was starting to feel depressed. That was the first time I admitted that to anyone including myself.

"What?" She jerked her head back. "Why would he wanna keep hiding things?"

"It's complicated."

"Can't be that complicated. I'm listening."

"RaShanda, if you tell anybody, I'll—" She cut me off with a glare.

"Who the hell am I gonna tell? You know how I get down. We friends to the end. Now, what's the problem? Is he married?" She leaned in like she was enjoying a soap opera.

"No! He's not married." I was insulted.

RaShanda lifted an eyebrow inquisitively. "Then who is he?"

She was relentless. I hesitated then looked up at her. "Oh, all right. Do you remember Terrance from church?"

"Terrance, Terrance," she repeated then smiled. "Oh, Terrance? Fine-ass Terrance with the green eyes?" She stared at me in disbelief as I nodded. "You lyin'! You ain't messing with him."

"Yes, I am." I pulled out a picture of him I had taken at the beach in the Hamptons. She looked down at the picture.

"Oh, my God, you bagged fine-ass Terrance? You know I must have really underestimated that virgin shit, 'cause I offered him some when he first came to the church and he blew me off. I thought he was gay."

That's comforting, I thought. All I would have needed was to find out RaShanda had slept with my man. God, I probably would have killed myself.

"Damn, girl. I'm not gonna lie. I'm jealous. He is one fine man."

"Thanks, but I think I'm gonna need your help to keep him."

"But why? You just told me y'all are still having sex three or four times a week. What in the world makes you think you're having a problem?"

"He always seems to be going away, and I don't know, sometimes I just worry that he's not really going to a convention."

"Girl, you just being paranoid. Isn't it your father who sends him on these trips?"

"Yeah."

"Aw'ight then. Why don't you just ask to go with him next time? I bet he says yes."

"I did." I sighed. "He's always promising he'll take me to the next one, but when the time comes, he starts talking about what would my parents say if they found out."

"Come on now. You know he's right about that one. What man would be in any kind of hurry to announce to the bishop and first lady that he wants to get with their daughter? Talk about pressure." She dug into her cheesecake.

I didn't say anything. I knew she made a good point, even though it was unfair. If I really thought about it, Terrance wasn't the first man to be intimidated by my family. Most of the boys who wanted to date me in high school were afraid to do anything more than think about it because they didn't have the guts to ask my father's permission. Back then it had bothered me, but with Terrance, I think it had gone from being annoying to making me paranoid about how he really felt about me.

"Look." RaShanda interrupted my thoughts. "If you really think you got something to worry about and you want him to confess his love, I got something for you."

"What?" I asked. I listened intently as my friend proceeded to give me some advice based on her years of experience in the art of pleasing men.

16

Tanisha

We'd just had dinner on City Island and on the way back Dante leaned over and gave me a very passionate kiss at a stoplight. I loved the way he kissed me and it seemed like he'd been kissing me all night. It was hard to believe, but we'd been seeing each other for over a month and nothing had gone wrong. He was different from any other guy I'd ever messed with, maybe even a little square by ghetto standards, but he kept me laughing and showed me things about life that I'd never seen before. I'd never had more fun with a guy in my entire life. He didn't crowd me or try to be in my face with that jealous shit like other brothers. And although we still hadn't had sex, now I understood why he was so reluctant to jump into bed too fast. It really gave us a chance to get to know each other, and believe it or not, it made me want him even more. I think we both knew it was about that time. It was just a matter of finding the right place.

When he pulled up in front of my building, I was shocked. A crowd had gathered around and pandemonium reigned. There had to be at least five police cars parked out there, and there were so many people I couldn't even see the entrance.

"Leave her alone. Let 'em go. Stop coming down here fuckin' with us, you racist bastards!" members of the crowd were shouting. I jumped out of Dante's car to find out what was going on, and I felt sick when I discovered it was my mother who was being arrested. Her clothes were dirty and she looked like something the cat had dragged home. She was kicking and screaming like a wild woman as five cops led her handcuffed out of the building. She was so high that foam was collecting in the corners of her mouth as she cursed the cops.

"Stoooooop! You motherfuckers! You're hurting me! This is police brutality. I'm calling Al Sharpton!" she screamed, only calming down slightly when she spotted me. "Tanisha, tell these motherfuckers to let me go. Let me go, damn it!"

"Leave her alone," I shouted as I stepped closer.

I was about to grab one of the cops' arms when another one stepped in front of me and said, "Miss, please back away or I'm going to arrest you for obstruction and interfering with a police investigation."

"Fuck that. I don't care. That's my mother!" My head rolled around on my shoulders and I was about to point my finger in his face when I felt someone take hold of my arm.

"Baby, you need to relax." Dante didn't know how close he was to getting the shit smacked out of him, but what he was saying did make sense. "We'll deal with them later. We need to find out about your brother. Wasn't he with your mother when we left?"

"Oh, my God! Aubrey!" I'd completely forgotten about him. My mother was going to have to wait until I found out where my little brother was. I ran up the stairs with Dante on my heels. "Where's my brother?" I began to scream the second I ran into my apartment.

My neighbor Cat was standing there with a policewoman. Aubrey was nowhere to be found. An angry thought came to my mind. *What the fuck is that bitch Cat doing in my house with the cops? Shit, she probably had something to do with this.*

"Cat, where's Aubrey? Where's my brother?" I would deal with Cat later if I found out she played any part in my mother's arrest.

"Girl, they done busted your momma and them no-good crackheads and Child Protective Services came and took your brother. You just missed them. I told them you would take your brother, but you weren't here, so they left. Here's the lady's card."

I took the card then yelled, "No! I ain't gonna let them put my brother in a foster home like they did to me." I broke down crying.

"Don't worry, Tanisha," Dante said. "We'll get him back. I'll go to court with you. You know they give relatives first priority."

"I hope you're right, baby. 'Cause if they keep Aubrey, I'm never going to forgive my mother."

I looked at my mother with disgust as she sat in the chair across the table. She reached for my hand and I pulled it back. I didn't want her to touch me. I was so damn mad at her I wanted to scream. Her preliminary hearing was set for the next day but I wasn't going. I would be at juvenile court trying to get my brother released into my custody.

"I told you this was gonna happen. You just couldn't stop smoking that shit, could you?"

"Baby, I'm so sorry," she whined.

"Sorry ain't good enough anymore, Momma. Sorry ain't good enough. You need some help. You really need some help." My voice was a cross between pleading and scolding, and I wasn't too far from shedding some tears.

"I know. I know that, baby, and Momma's gonna get some

help, I swear. But you gotta get me outta here. You know I can't get the help I need in here. Now, I know you have a little money stashed away, so can you bail me out? It's only a thousand dollars. Please, baby, you don't want me to be locked up in here, do you?" Her eyes continually twitched and she was scratching like she needed some Benadryl. She spoke so sincerely, though, I was almost compelled to take the little bit of money I had saved and bail her out just like I'd done countless times in the past. The vision of my little brother sitting in foster care stopped that. She didn't deserve to be free if he wasn't going to be.

"Momma, you've gotta be kidding me. I ain't got no money to bail you out," I lied. "Or did you forget you smoked up every dime I made last week when you went in my pocketbook?" I thought about all the things my mother had stolen from me over the years, including the TV, the radio, the microwave, the VCR, the Game Boy, and my money. It just made me angrier.

The truth is, I loved my mother. I always have, no matter what, but the thought of my brother being placed in foster care like I was when I was his age had tested my love to the limit. I was on the verge of hating her. The problem was that I also felt sorry for her. It seemed like she never really had a chance in life, so I was always trying to give her another one. Hell, maybe I'd even enabled her by not leaving when she stole from me, by bailing her out when she got busted, or by believing her when she swore she was going to get help.

When I was thirteen, I covered for her when Aubrey was born with cocaine in his system. When the social worker asked if I had ever witnessed my mother smoking crack, I said no, she'd never smoked. Momma was able to get the baby released to her because of my statement, and because she said she had been around other people who were smoking, and that's how she'd ingested cocaine just before she delivered. I could hardly go to school when Aubrey was a baby because I used to be the only one watching him while she would run the streets getting high. Thank God for the GED. Otherwise I wouldn't have had anything to fall back on.

A depression overcame me. The jail had the feel of a dark, dank dungeon. Suddenly, I thought I was going to throw up and I couldn't breathe.

"Mom, I'm getting ready to book."

"Are you gonna bail me out?"

Our eyes met in a cold stare as I refused.

She jumped back in her chair as if I'd just shot her.

"What do you mean no? I told you I'm gonna get help this time. I promise." A few tears escaped the corners of her eyes and rolled down her face. I knew if I didn't leave soon, she was going to wear me down and I would bail her out. "Please, baby, please. You don't know what it's like in here."

I stood up to leave. "I'm sorry, Mommy, but there's nothing I can do. I'm gonna put some money in your account."

"Baby, please don't do this. I swear on my momma's grave I'm gonna quit. You gotta believe me." Tears were now flowing down her face like a river.

"I wish I could."

"You can if you want to. I know you got the money." Now she was starting to look angry.

"Momma, I told you I ain't got the money."

"Well, then get it from Dante," she said desperately "He'll give it to you. That nigga loves you." She smiled as if Dante was the answer to all her problems.

"I'm not gonna ask him that. He's my boyfriend, not an ATM, Momma."

"And I'm your mother, bitch. Or have you forgotten that? If it wasn't for you, I wouldn't even be here."

"You're right, Momma, you wouldn't be here. You'd probably be dead. I'm going to see about Aubrey now. Good luck in court tomorrow." I stood holding my head up high.

"You ungrateful little bitch. You ain't all that. What's Dante gonna think when he finds out where you work, huh? Bet he won't be sending you flowers and candy then, will he?"

"Shut up, Momma!" I snapped.

"What's wrong? Afraid your secret's gonna get out?"

"Dante already knows my worst secret, Momma. He found that out the day he met you. I don't think anything can be worse than that. Have a good day in court." I walked away. I was just outside the door when I heard her yelling.

"Tanisha, I'm sorry, baby! I was just upset! Please don't leave me in here!"

When I left my mother, I had to get on a crowded orange-and-white city bus that took me over a bridge and off of Rikers Island. Dante was on the other side of the bridge waiting for me, and I couldn't wait until I was in his arms. I needed to be held, and when I stepped off the bus, he didn't disappoint. As we stood surrounded by people, he wrapped his arms around me and I felt all the tension melt from my body. He was such a good man, probably too good for me. Sometimes I wondered why he was even with someone like me.

"You okay?" he asked.

"Yeah." I nodded. "I'm okay."

"How's your mom?"

"She's mad at me 'cause I won't bail her out."

"If it's about money, I can bail her out if you want."

"No, she'll be all right. She's probably better off in there than she is out here. At least she won't get high."

"Yeah, but I thought you could get anything in there."

"Sure, if you got money, but I only left her fifteen dollars in her account. She sure as hell ain't gonna get high on that." He laughed and I joined in.

"What am I gonna do with you?" he asked with affection in his voice.

I looked in his eyes and smiled. "I ain't got nothing to do until nine o'clock tomorrow morning when I've got to be in court to see about my brother. So if you really wanna know, you can take me somewhere and make love to me."

"Sweetheart, there is nothing in this world that I'd like more."

17

Dante

I handed Tanisha one of the cups of coffee I'd gotten from the vending machine down the hall. We'd been in the family court building all morning and had come back for the afternoon session in hopes of getting her brother released into her custody. The halls were packed with families, most of them black or Hispanic. Babies were crying and children were running around like there wasn't any adult supervision to be found. Aubrey was in the section where they kept the children who were in the custody of the Department of Children and Family Services. Tanisha had a chance to visit with him about ten o'clock that morning.

I watched Tanisha yawn and rubbed her back with my free hand. She was tired. Hell, we were both tired. Who wouldn't be tired after being up all night making love? Not that I was complaining. I hadn't had sex like that since back in the Anita days. The only difference was that it didn't feel like regular sex. With Tanisha, there wasn't just a physical connection. For the first time in my life I think I was truly making love.

Finally, the bailiff stepped out of the courtroom.

"Aubrey Jones! Anyone here for the matter of Aubrey Jones?" Tanisha jumped up and the bailiff held the door open as we entered the courtroom.

The presiding judge was a black man. He seemed no-nonsense and straight to the point. He read over the petition for all those present in the room to hear. Charges of child endangerment, unsafe home environment, illegal substance possession, unclean and unfit home environment, mother testing positive for cocaine. The counts seemed endless. When he finished, he turned to the attorney appointed for Aubrey.

"It's obvious we can't place this child back in the home with his mother. Does the child have any family?"

"Yes, Your Honor. We have a family member, Tanisha Jones, willing to take custody. The only drawback is that the child would have to live in the same home. His mother is incarcerated at the time. She's taken a plea of six months on drug-related charges, so she would not be in the home with the child. But Ms. Jones is also unemployed and has no visible means of support."

I glanced at Tanisha and wondered what was going on. She had told me she worked at a bar. Why was this lawyer saying she was unemployed? And why wasn't Tanisha correcting him? Then it hit me. Being unemployed made her a much better candidate than working in a bar environment. That's when I got an idea.

"Excuse me, Your Honor, may I speak?"

Tanisha looked shocked that I had interrupted the judge.

"And who are you?"

"My name is Dante Wilson. I'm the director of church activities for First Jamaica Ministries on Merrick Boulevard in Jamaica Queens."

"Wait a minute. Is your father T.K. Wilson?"

"Yes, sir."

"Well, well. Small world. I know him. Fine man. What is it you want to say, son?"

"Ms. Jones has applied and been approved for one of our Help a Neighbor grants. I'm not sure if you're familiar with the program . . ."

"Yes, I'm familiar with the program. We have quite a few families who come in here and have been helped by that program."

"Well, with the grant and the foster care funds she should be eligible for, along with the fact that she will be home to care for her brother, I would think she'd be a great candidate for custody. As for the unclean and unfit home environment, now that her mother's out the house, I'm sure we can get some volunteers from First Jamaica Ministries to help with cleaning her place up."

The judge smiled. "You make a very convincing argument, Mr. Wilson. Have you ever thought of law school?"

His compliment took me off guard. Of course I had thought of law school. It was exactly where I wanted to be if I could just get up the nerve to stray from what my parents had planned for my life. "Yes, sir, I have. I'm in the process of filling out applications now."

"Good. Now, in the matter of Aubrey Jones, I'm going to issue Ms. Jones temporary custody pending a home evaluation and inspection. Good luck, Ms. Jones, and Mr. Wilson, tell your father I said hello."

"I'll do just that, Your Honor."

The bailiff handed Tanisha some paperwork and we walked out. The second the courtroom doors were closed, Tanisha jumped up in the air and began smothering me with kisses.

"Thank you!" Kiss. "Thank you!" Kiss. "Thank you!" Kiss. Thank you!" When she finally stopped kissing me, she was all grins. "Thank you, baby."

"You're welcome."

"You were better than the lawyer."

"You think?" I couldn't help but feel proud.

"Yeah, you were, and what is this Help a Neighbor grant? I never applied for a grant."

"You didn't? Well, you better fill out the paperwork. I've got it in the car. It's a good thing I'm the director of church activities and I can approve it on the spot."

"You'd do that for me?"

"You'd be surprised what I'd do for you."

"Not anymore I wouldn't." She kissed me. "You know, I think you're the best thing that ever happened to me."

18

Donna

My last class at C.W. Post University ended at 2:00, and by 2:05 I was in my car heading for the Long Island Expressway. I was on my way to catch Terrance before he left for the airport, and no one or nothing was going to stop me until I was in his arms. He was leaving that afternoon to go out of town to a conference. He'd been going away a lot lately and just the thought of him being gone for a week was driving me out of my mind. I'd been tempted to skip class altogether and meet up with him that morning, but as tempting as it was, I couldn't do it. I had a final exam in accounting that was fifty percent of my grade. I couldn't miss that, especially since my parents were paying for my education.

When I finally pulled into the parking lot outside of Terrance's office, I cursed under my breath. The lot was full and I couldn't find a space. I must have circled that lot for fifteen minutes before I finally just pulled into a handicapped space by the door. I rushed into the building and didn't stop until I was standing in front of the door to his office. The door was open, so I just stood there for a few seconds, admiring him as he read some papers on his desk. He really was the man of my dreams. It had never been more evident to me just how much I loved that man than right before he was about to leave me for a week. He must have felt my stare, because all of a sudden he lifted his head.

"Hey, pretty lady, what are you doing here?" His lips curled into a smile that made me blush. He really looked happy to see me, and that made all my rushing to get there worthwhile. "I thought you had a final."

"Did you really think you were gonna sneak out of town without seeing me?" I walked into his office and closed the door. I was about to do something I never dreamed of doing until I went to see RaShanda a month ago. I wanted to make sure he remembered what was waiting for him back here in New York while he was away. "What time does your flight leave?"

"Four o'clock. Why, what you got in mind?" He stood up and loosened his tie as I approached. He gave me the most devious smile. He knew exactly what I was up to.

I glanced at my watch. "I was thinking maybe I'd drive you to the airport and we'd stop by one of those short-stay motels before you leave, but it looks like we only have enough time for a quickie."

"What's wrong with a quickie?" He grinned, turning toward the window behind his desk and closing the blinds.

"Nothing, as long as you make every stroke count."

He turned back around, staring as I unbuttoned my blouse. "That's never been a problem before, has it?"

"Not once." I smiled naughtily, unhooking my skirt and letting it fall to the floor. His smile widened when he realized I wasn't wearing any panties. I thought that might get his attention, but I swear I could see his penis instantly expand in his pants.

"Is the door locked?"

"Uh-huh." I nodded.

With his right hand he pushed everything from his desk onto the floor, then he turned to me. I stepped closer in anticipation and I could feel myself getting moist. He took me into his arms and pressed his lips against mine. My entire body was becoming hot. I loved it when he was aggressive like this. He eased his tongue into my mouth and I sucked on it gently. His strong hands made me shudder as they slid down my backside until they held the firm, round melons of my ass. In one swift motion he lifted me onto the desk, and not once did either of us attempt to break our kiss. He held me on the edge of his desk. I reached between us and unbuckled his pants, then I slid them and his boxers down until his penis sprang free. I took hold of it, massaging it gently before guiding it to the entrance of its final destination.

"Wait, let me get a condom out of the drawer."

"No," I said, shaking my head and smiling. "We don't have to do that anymore. I went on the pill."

A huge grin crept onto his face. He kissed me as he pushed himself in. When he could go no farther, he broke our kiss and stared at me lovingly. Now I understood why RaShanda had recommended I go on the pill. Sex without a condom was amazing. And from the look on Terrance's face, he felt the same way.

"I love you, Donna," he whispered.

"What did you say?"

"I said . . . I love you, Donna." His words were shocking yet comforting. They were all that I had wanted to hear, and this was the first time he had actually spoken them.

"I love you, too, Terrance," I whispered back, kissing him gently.

"Good, because I just wanted you to know how I felt before I get on that plane. You never know what might happen tomorrow."

I pulled him closer to me. "Stop it, Terrance. You're scaring me. Why you acting like you might not come back?"

"I'm sorry. That wasn't my intention. I just wanted you to know how I felt."

He kissed me and we made love on his desk. For the very

first time, we climaxed together. It was amazing. I could feel his juices splashing inside me. I can't ever remember feeling that good or that close to anyone in my entire life. Unfortunately, it was all spoiled by a knock on the door. To make matters worse, the person knocking was my *father!* I had to bite my lip to keep from screaming in shock when I heard his voice. Both Terrance and I stared at each other, our eyes wide with fear. We were too afraid to move. I'm sure we both had the same thoughts. Did my father know I was there? Did he know what we were doing? Was that door definitely locked? Would the two of us survive his wrath?

"Reverend Reynolds? Reverend Reynolds? There's a cab outside waiting to take you to the airport," my father called through the door.

Terrance didn't even respond until I nudged him.

"I'll be right there, Bishop. I'm . . . on the phone."

"Okay, but you should hurry. That cab's been out there for a while. With all the extra security these days, you might end up missing your flight."

"No problem, Bishop. I'm hanging up now."

My father's fading footsteps eased my fear a little bit, allowing me to take a breath and gently push Terrance off of me. He got up without saying a word, looking like he was still in shock. His high-yellow skin was now pasty and his face was drenched in sweat that hadn't been there during our lovemaking.

"You okay, baby?" I pulled up my skirt as I waited for his response. He didn't answer so I walked over and placed my hand on his back. "You okay?"

"I can't believe we just did this. What is wrong with me?" He buckled his pants and walked away, bending over to pick up the stuff he'd knocked to the floor.

"I know. That was close. We could've been caught by my father." I tried to sound lighthearted.

Terrance turned to me and glared. "You just don't get it, do you? This is not about your father. This is about me. How can I call myself a man of God if I'm fornicating in the church?" You see, Terrance was the youth minister and assistant pastor for our church. That was one of the reasons he'd insisted we keep our relationship a secret.

"Come on, Terrance, we were just being spontaneous. That's what people in love do. God understands that. Granted, maybe we shouldn't have done it in the church, but we didn't get caught. Nobody knows."

"You don't understand, Donna. We shouldn't be doing this at all. And you're wrong. Somebody does know." He glanced at the crucifix hanging on his wall. "God knows, and I don't know if I can live with that." He actually looked upset.

"What are you saying?"

"I'm saying maybe this was a sign God doesn't want us to be together."

"Well, if that's the case, I'm not interested in what God has to say. I wanna know what you have to say. I thought you said you love me."

"I do love you, but this is not the way a minister conducts himself."

"Then let's tell my father. Let's tell him how we feel about each other, how much we love each other. He'll understand. We can get married."

He raised his eyebrows, looking shocked, but he gave a response that I'm sure he thought would keep me happy until he returned. "Let me think about it, okay?"

"What is there to think about, Terrance? We have to tell him sooner or later. I'm not going to sneak around for the rest of my life like some of these old maids around the church, so I much prefer sooner."

He avoided answering my question and got ready to leave. "We'll talk about it when I get back, Donna. Look, I gotta go. I have to catch a plane." He picked up a large suitcase. "Can you straighten this place out for me?"

"Yeah, I'll clean up," I told him as he hurried toward the door. "But I want you to know something."

"What is it?" He stopped and turned to me, doing a poor job of concealing an exasperated look.

"I'm getting tired of you running out of town every other weekend. Saturday used to be our day. Now, if you're not going to talk to my father about cutting back your schedule, then I will."

Terrance's face hardened for a second, then a soft look eased onto it. "Donna, I won't have to do it too much longer. I only have two more conferences and a wedding to attend in South Carolina, then I'll be around every weekend, okay?"

"All right," I answered, feeling slightly better that things would change soon. An idea came to me. "How about you take me with you to the wedding? I'll tell my parents I'm going to see a friend in the Hamptons."

"I can't," he said. "There will be people there who know your father." He ignored my pout as he said, "Look, let me go before your father comes back knocking on this door again."

I was disappointed, but I didn't want my father back any more than he did. "Fine." I sighed. "Do you want me to pick you up from the airport?"

He hesitated for a moment before he nodded and said, "Yeah, sure, that would be nice. I'll call you and let you know what time my flight gets in." He put his hand on the doorknob then gave me a sad smile. "I love you, Donna. Always remember that."

19

Tanisha

Things were looking up for me and my brother. Once the home evaluation was completed by the Department of Social Services, Aubrey came back home. I was relieved to have him out of foster care, and determined to keep him out. I even quit my job at the club just in case some caseworker decided that my place of employment was a good enough reason to send him away again.

I had learned my lesson. From now on I would be even more careful to do whatever it took to protect Aubrey, but I was still furious with my mother for everything he had already been through. I decided that I wouldn't visit her or contact her while she was at Rikers Island. It was time for me to let her know that I wasn't always going to forgive her. Dante tried to convince me not to cut her off, but I had had enough. I did let him talk me into attending his father's church one Sunday, though. Maybe he thought I would feel the spirit and open my heart to my mother again. I didn't hold out much hope for that, but he'd been so helpful in getting Aubrey out of foster care, I didn't want to disappoint him by refusing to attend. So I got Aubrey dressed in his nicest clothes and we headed to the church.

When Aubrey and I showed up at the church, we were a good twenty-five minutes late. I was tempted to not even go in, but I had promised Dante I'd be there as long as he didn't embarrass me by trying to introduce me to his friends and family. Anyhow, the church was so huge it looked like a cathedral. That first night I was there, I was so confused about Dante I hadn't paid any attention to how big this place was. There were so many cars in the parking lot it looked like one of those used car superstore lots. I was starting to think that maybe Jesus really was in there, not in spirit but in the flesh.

We entered the church and an usher directed us upstairs and handed us a nicely designed program. I couldn't remember the last time I'd been to church, but they sure didn't have a glossy, full-color program like this. I took Aubrey by the hand and we tiptoed up to the balcony, where it seemed like thousands of people were seated. A few of them smiled at us. I wondered if I'd ever become a frequent visitor to this church if Dante and I worked out. The thought brought a smile to my face. The girls in the club sure wouldn't believe that.

I looked around for Dante but didn't see him. Peering down at the congregation, I looked into the pulpit. The choir sat in the back. To the right sat an attractive woman who I recognized as Dante's mother from a picture he'd shown me. I could tell by the way she carried herself that she was a woman of class and wasn't to be played with. I was going to have to tread lightly around her. A tall, gray-bearded man who I assumed was Dante's father sat next to her. They looked like an African king and queen. When he stood up, the entire congregation became quiet.

Dante's father began his sermon, announcing the scripture he would be preaching about. Because I saw the members do it, I picked up the Bible in front of me. It was placed on the back of the pew before our row. I decided to try to follow along. To tell the truth, holding a Bible in my hands was a strange feeling. We didn't even own one in our house. I'm not big into scripture and church, but Dante's father sure knew how to preach. He had everyone in the building, including me, rocking and clapping and screaming "Amen!"

I was having a good time and I think Aubrey was too, until I was distracted by a woman in a green hat staring at me. I couldn't see her face; every time I looked in her direction, she'd turn away. Finally I ignored her and turned my attention back to the bishop's sermon.

After a while I decided to find the restroom. I took Aubrey with me.

"You go in the men's restroom then wait outside for me," I told him as I walked into the women's room.

When I walked into the restroom, I drew in my breath. It was so pretty, decorated in a soft peach and green wallpaper. The furniture in the lounge area looked better than the furniture in my apartment. I just wanted to sit in those chairs for a minute. But before I could put my purse down, without warning, the solid oak door opened and the woman in the green hat came flying in.

"I thought that was you," she said, snatching her hat from her head. Her eyes looked wild and her teeth were bared like an animal's. She glanced quickly into the lavatory, and when she was sure no one else was around, she actually got in my face. "I'm not gonna tell you this but once, you little ignorant heifer. Stay away from my man."

"Excuse me? Do I know you?" I was trying to be cool and act like she was a stranger to me, but I knew exactly who she was—she was Dante's ex, the woman with the one-armed husband, and if she didn't get out my face, she was going to lose one of her arms.

"You know who I am," she hissed. "We met a while back at Bingo."

"Oh, yeah, now I remember you," I said in an exaggerated tone while striking a pose, "but I don't want your man. It takes two hands to handle a woman like me, and your husband only has one."

I know I was wrong but I just felt like it was the right thing to say. I could see the frustration in her face. "I'm talking about Dante."

"Dante?" I laughed sarcastically. "He's not your man. A woman your age couldn't handle a young stud like him."

"Hmmph, I'll have you know I handle it quite well. Much better than you, I'm sure."

"Oh, yeah, then why does he find his way to my house every night?" I taunted this desperate woman.

She looked like she was going to burst as she put her finger in my face. "Stay away from him. I'm not going to tell you again."

"Look, Dante don't want you. And if you don't get your finger out my face, I'm gonna break it off." I was trying to stay calm since I was in the church, but she wasn't making it easy, especially when she got personal.

"You're nothing but a loose skank ho, and Dante is too good for you."

I bit my lip because I could feel my temper rising. "First of all, who you callin' a ho? And secondly, it takes one to know one, bee-itch."

"Aw, no, you didn't call me no bitch." She stepped closer to me, her hands clenched into tight fists.

"Oh yes I did, and if you don't get out my face, I'm gonna whoop your ass."

"You ain't gonna do nothing." She took a swing at me and I ducked, coming back at her with an open palm that knocked her ass to the floor. If there was one thing I could do, it was fight. I had to, with people talking about my mother all the time and with me working in the clubs. I hadn't meant to come to church and do this, but she really gave me no choice. I was about to finish what I started when another woman rushed in just in the nick of time. She was a big sister, and I was afraid that she might be the other woman's friend. I glanced over at the sink for my bag. I was gonna need my blade to take both these bitches down.

"What's going on in here, Anita?" the tall sister demanded. She glanced down at Anita then at me.

"This crazy bitch attacked me, Donna. Call the police. I wanna press charges." Oh, Lord, that was all I needed. Dante would never forgive me if I'd gotten arrested in his father's church.

"Oh, please, Anita," the tall sister snapped. "Ain't nobody callin' the police. You know you started this shit. I watched you follow her in here."

"Donna, I was just trying to protect your brother. Do you want him messing with a slut like this?"

"No, you didn't just call her a slut when you trying to mess with my brother and got a husband. Only thing you was trying to protect was your own interest." She laughed. "You must be Dante's new girlfriend." She extended her hand to me. "Hi, I'm Donna. Dante's sister. He thought something like this might happen so he asked me to keep an eye on Anita. He's downstairs doing collections. He told me to tell you to meet him at his car after the service."

Her friendliness melted some of my hostility. I shook her hand. "Hi. Tanisha."

Donna turned to the Bingo lady. "Anita, you know the bishop ain't gon' have all this carrying on in his church. Now, Dante's made his choice, so I suggest you get on out of here before I tell your husband on you."

Anita looked from Donna to me, then threw her nose in the air and stalked out of the restroom, but not before she told me, "This ain't over."

After my near fistfight with Anita, Donna came and sat with me and Aubrey for the rest of the service. As quickly as I had almost risen to violence, I calmed down. I had grown up in a violent environment, and no matter how I tried to hide it, it came as second nature to me.

Meanwhile, Donna pointed out Dante below on the first floor. My eyes beelined to where he stood passing the collection plate. He was working with the ushers. That boy was too *foine*. He knew he was wearing that suit. No wonder that old hag wanted to fight over him.

After church let out, Donna led me to Dante's car. He was surrounded by a group of young teens, but he smiled as soon as he saw me and broke away from the crowd. "So you and Aubrey came?" he said as if that wasn't an obvious fact.

"A promise is a promise."

"I like a woman who keeps her word. How about us going to Coney Island for the afternoon? Then maybe we'll shoot over to my house and you can meet my parents."

"Coney Island sounds nice, but I told you before. I don't do parents."

He ignored me and turned to my brother. "What do you think, Aubrey? You wanna go to Coney Island?"

"Yeah," Aubrey cheered.

Later, I was so glad we went. I had never seen Aubrey laugh so much in his twelve years. For the first time, he looked like a child instead of a worried old man in a child's body.

We stuffed ourselves with hot dogs covered in chili with onions, cotton candy, and popcorn. We rode on the rides together and screamed and hollered in joy on the roller coaster. Dante even won me a large teddy bear on one of the toss games.

Most of all, I enjoyed how Dante seemed so patient with Aubrey. I'd never seen my little brother open up like this with any of my other men friends. It had been a long while since I'd had a friend, too, because of that fact. After the last one, I had said I'd stop bringing my men around Aubrey. He was so hungry for male attention, so whenever I'd break up with a man, Aubrey would be depressed. See, he had never known his father, and the truth of it is, I don't think my mother knew who his biological father was either. She was really hanging out there when she got pregnant with Aubrey.

"Dante, can we go down by the boardwalk?" Aubrey asked. He'd only been there a few times in his life, when his school took him on field trips.

"Sure, Aubrey. Let's go. Race you."

As I watched the two of them race toward the ocean, I looked at their shadows and a strange feeling came over me. What if we could have a life together? I guessed the only way to find out was to meet his parents.

20

Dante

After weeks of prodding, I'd finally convinced Tanisha to come to our house for Sunday dinner, only now that we were pulling into my driveway, I was having serious reservations. To be honest, I'd been having second thoughts since the moment I picked her up and saw what she was wearing. Don't get me wrong, she looked good. Damn good. I would have been proud to have her on my arm if we were going to a club or a party, but to meet my parents she looked totally inappropriate. To start with, her scarlet dress was way too short, not to mention too tight. She wasn't leaving anything to the imagination with that bad boy. I tried to be open minded. I mean hell, lots of people wear short skirts on Sundays, but already I could imagine her dress filtering through my mother's eyes and I cringed inwardly.

I didn't have the heart to tell her that her dress was inappropriate and would not pass my mother's litmus test. Tanisha was already looking for an excuse to back out of meeting my parents, and I didn't want to give her any reasons. Hopefully she'd make up for her dress's shortcomings with her personality.

"You live here?" she asked in amazement as we stepped out of my truck and headed hand in hand up the walkway.

"Yeah, why? Is something wrong?" I looked around playfully.

"Nah, but your people must be rich. Your garage is bigger than my whole apartment."

I squeezed her hand. "As my father would say, the Lord has been good to us."

"I'll say."

When I opened the door, we were immediately greeted by Donna, who offered her hand to Tanisha.

"Hey, Tanisha." She smiled, glancing momentarily down at Tanisha's outfit then at me. There was no doubt in my mind that she was thinking the same thing I thought when I saw the outfit: *Trouble!* Tanisha, who was clueless to my sister's and my silent communication, smiled back at Donna. It was obvious she was relieved to see a familiar face. "Look, girl, Dante is my mother's favorite, so don't take nothin' personal that goes on tonight 'cause she be trippin'."

Tanisha looked nervous. "I'll try not to."

"Where's the first lady and the bishop?" I asked.

"They're in the dining room, setting the table."

"They alone or is Reverend Reynolds with them?"

"He's out of town."

I drew a deep breath and asked, "Well, sweetheart, you ready to meet my parents?"

"Not really, but I'm here, so let's do it."

We walked through the living room and into the dining room, where we found the bishop and the first lady sitting at the table in their Sunday attire. Of course, the bishop smiled the second he saw Tanisha. My mother, on the other hand, stared at her, stone faced.

"Ma, Bishop, this is Tanisha. Tanisha, these are my parents, Bishop T.K. Wilson and my mother, First Lady Charlene Wilson."

"Nice to meet you, Bishop Wilson, and you, First Lady Wilson."

"Just call me Bishop," my father replied, offering his hand. Tanisha shook it then reached out to my mother, who ignored her. She didn't even speak to Tanisha, which was her blatant message of disapproval. She merely eyed her up and down then, acting miffed, threw her nose in the air.

"It's time for dinner," she said with irritation.

"Yes, it is, isn't it?" the bishop said, glancing at his watch.

We all sat down, and after my father delivered the blessing, which somehow felt more like a eulogy, we all began to eat in silence.

Finally, the bishop spoke up. "Well, Tanisha, where are you from?"

Tanisha paused before she spoke. "I'm from the Forty Projects."

The bishop's facial muscles twitched subtly then shifted downward as he glanced at my mother, who was sighing loudly. Trying his best to cover up his disappointment, he smiled at Tanisha. "We have quite a few parishioners from Forty Projects. Do you know Sister Wilma Johnson?"

"No, sir, I can't say I do."

"What about Sister Charlotte Dumpson?"

Tanisha shook her head.

"Too bad. Now, that sister can cook some fish." The bishop smiled at the thought.

My mother fired a couple of questions at Tanisha.

"Is that a tattoo on your arm?"

"Yes, ma'am. I have three of them," Tanisha said proudly. "I have one on my arm, one on my shoulder, and one on my—" She stopped herself when she realized my mother wasn't impressed.

"In my day, the only women who had tattoos were Jezebels."

Everyone fell silent. I was terrified of what might come

out of my mother's mouth next, but mercifully my father spoke first, changing the subject.

"So, Tanisha, what church do you belong to?"

"I don't really belong to a church, although after hearing you preach last month, I'm thinking about joining First Jamaica Ministries. You were very inspiring."

The bishop smiled. "Why, thank you, young lady. It's always good to know the young people are listening. I hope you know the doors of First Jamaica Ministries are always open to you."

"Well, the Lord knows I need to make use of them," Tanisha replied.

"Now, that's the first intelligent thing I've heard all night. You look like you could use some soul cleansing," my mother snapped.

"Charlene," the bishop scolded. "May those without sin throw the first stone."

I was proud of Tanisha. It looked like she'd won over my father.

"So, Tanisha . . . did Dante tell you he would be starting at Howard's Divinity School in the fall?" my mother interjected. "And that he plans to be a minister?"

"A minister?" Tanisha turned to me. "I thought you told me you wanted to be a lawyer."

"A lawyer? Heavens no!" My mother's eyes were on me like a laser beam. "Dante, what is she talking about?"

I sputtered, "Well, Ma, I'm thinking—maybe I don't wanna be a—"

Before I could finish a thought, my mother spoke. Her voice was filled with even more venom than I expected. "That's just it. You're not thinking. So I'm going to think for you. Now, you're going to Howard's Divinity School and that's final. I don't know what's gotten into you. Maybe it's this tramp you brought home, but I thought at least one of my children had his head on straight."

"Charlene," the bishop tried to interject but my mother raised her hand and kept on talking.

"I'm ashamed of you, Dante. You know that? We have all these nice girls in the congregation but no! You have to bring home this . . . this tramp."

"Ma!" was all I could manage to shout before Tanisha stood up slowly and calmly and placed her napkin on the table.

"Well, I guess I'll just bounce my trampy self up out of here, then." She pushed her chair in then spoke politely. "Donna, it was nice seeing you again. Bishop Wilson, thank you for dinner. Mrs. Wilson, you have a lovely home. I'm sorry we didn't get to know each other better because we have something very special in common. We both love your son."

She turned to me. I was still frozen in my seat. "Don't worry about getting up, boo. Finish dinner with your family. I'll catch a cab." Then she marched out of the room with her head held high. I'd never seen anything classier in my entire life.

When I finally regained my composure, I turned to my mother. "Ma, I can't believe you. How the hell can you call yourself a Christian acting like that?" I demanded to know.

"Don't you dare talk to me like that, young man. I am still your mother, and you live under my roof."

Infuriated, I saw red. I pushed my chair out and stood quickly, causing it to fall over with a bang. "I might live under your roof now, Ma, but that's about to change." I called out, "Tanisha, wait!"

I heard the bishop speak as I bolted from the room. "Charlene, that was uncalled for."

"I can't believe he chose her over us. I thought one of my children would do right," was her snide reply.

I found Tanisha at the end of our block, using her cell phone. Apparently, she was trying to call a cab. I tried to talk her out of it, but she was determined not to take a ride home from me. Finally, when she had waited a half hour, she realized no cab was coming. She reluctantly settled into my car, but she refused to speak to me during the drive.

The night had been a total disaster, and I was blaming myself. Maybe if I had prepared Tanisha better for my mother's attitude, or if I had asked her to put on a different dress, then none of this would have happened. But as I looked over at Tanisha in the passenger seat, I realized I didn't want her to change—not for my mother or for anyone else. I thought she was perfect just the way she was.

21

Donna

I'd been sitting in my car crying for the better part of twenty minutes before I decided to wipe my tears and go inside. If there was ever a day that I wished Terrance was home, it was today. He'd gone away to a wedding in South Carolina and I needed him. I needed him bad and I couldn't wait until he returned, 'cause this was quite possibly the worst day of my life.

The light shining in the living room told me my parents were waiting up, and my day was probably only going to get worse. I really didn't wanna hear my mother's mouth about me coming in so late. It was only a little past midnight, but there was no doubt in my mind that she and the bishop would be sitting in there waiting for me to come through the door.

God, did I hate my mother's double standards. She never treated Dante like this. Ever since he was sixteen years old, he could come and go as he pleased and she wouldn't say a word. But if I walked into the house even one minute after eleven on a weekday or a second after midnight on a weekend without a decent excuse, she'd have a fit. I swear I would have paid good money if I could have found someone to make her understand that I was twenty years old and no longer needed her to babysit my virtue. Didn't she realize that anything she wanted to stop me from doing after midnight I could just as easily do before?

When I walked into the house, just as I expected, both my mother and father were sitting in the living room waiting for me. My father was still in his suit, reading his Bible as he sat in a high-back chair. My mother was sprawled across the sofa in her silk housecoat, looking distraught. She sat up immediately when I entered the house. I knew what she was going to say before she even opened her mouth.

"Mother, I'm sorry I'm late, but—"

She stopped me before I could explain. "Sit down!" her shrill voice demanded as she pointed to the love seat.

I reluctantly did as I was told, mentally preparing for her lecture on how a responsible Christian lady conducts herself. This was a lecture I'd heard a million times before, though I couldn't figure out why. It wasn't like I had given my mother a whole bunch of reasons to lecture me on virtue. Before Terrance, I was pretty well behaved as far as teenagers go. Even now, I came in late a few times and forgot about Bingo, but it wasn't like I was presenting myself as a hootchie or something. Nevertheless, my mother always found something to nag me about, and tonight would be no exception.

She had been staring at my red eyes, so I was sure she was about to falsely accuse me of some type of drug use. My mother had always been our household disciplinarian, and even though she'd stopped using a switch a few years back, if you weren't prepared for her tongue-lashings, you could get your feelings hurt. That's why I was both surprised and relieved when my father started to speak.

"Is everything all right, princess? You look a little upset. Is there anything you wanna tell us?" His voice was low and filled with concern. He must have spotted my red eyes, too.

"Everything's fine, Bishop. I—"

My mother cut me off again. "Stop beating around the bush, T.K., and ask her. This isn't a time for games. This is our family's reputation on the line. Now, you ask her or I will."

"Ask me what?" I turned to the bishop for an answer but the question came out of my mother's mouth.

"Donna, are you pregnant?"

"Huh?" was the only response I could manage. My mouth hung open as I stared at my mother in bug-eyed disbelief. I couldn't believe what she had just asked me. Especially since her question sounded more like a statement. I turned to the bishop, who was now sitting on the edge of his chair waiting for my response. The concern in his face was even deeper than before.

"Madonna Marie Wilson! I asked you a question. Are you pregnant?" my mother snarled in her holier-than-thou voice.

I was still speechless. Where was this coming from? Was she on a fishing expedition, or had she been searching my room again? Dammit, I knew I should have hidden those condoms in a better place than my dresser drawer.

"She's pregnant, T.K. There's no doubt in my mind," she snapped with certainty.

My head was spinning. *How the hell could she know that I'm pregnant?* I asked myself. *Damn, I only found out myself this morning.*

I glanced back and forth between my parents, trying not to look into my father's eyes. Suddenly, all my questions were answered when my mother started to wave the small plastic applicator from the home pregnancy test I had taken that morning. As I suspected, my mother had violated my privacy once again, this time by going through my bedroom wastebasket, looking for anything she could nag me about. And unfortunately for me, this time she'd found more than even she probably expected.

"Charlene, calm down. You're not giving her a chance to

speak," the bishop admonished. He shot my mother a look, letting her know that he was taking control of our conversation, and she reluctantly sat back on the sofa. My mother might have been the disciplinarian in our house, but there was no doubt my father was the king of his castle. He turned his attention to me. "Are you, princess? Are you pregnant?"

I couldn't lie to my father, although I wanted to. So, ashamedly I lowered my head and whispered, "Yes, Bishop, I'm pregnant."

He inhaled loudly, clutching his Bible as he sat back in his chair. He actually remained pretty calm, but I was sure he wasn't pleased with the fact that his little princess, as he called me, was pregnant. Instead of speaking, he just stared at the floor. I could almost feel the hurt and disappointment he must have been feeling.

Tears sprang to his eyes and mine as I whispered, "I'm sorry, Daddy."

He didn't say a word. He just lifted his head, and when our eyes met, I knew I was forgiven and that everything would be all right. He opened his arms and I sprang into them, weeping like I was a five-year-old child. Even at twenty I was still his little princess, and that meant the world to me.

My father was the sweetest, kindest, and gentlest man I'd ever met, and to be honest, it was him that I hated to disappoint, not my mother. She'd made it clear years ago that there was room for only one woman in our house, and that was her. So either I was gonna stay a little girl under her thumb or I was gonna have to go.

"I can't believe this. Now what are we gonna do? I told you we needed to keep a closer eye on her, T.K.," my mother snapped sarcastically, sounding as if my news had just proven every negative thing she'd ever said about me. "But nooooo, you didn't wanna invade her privacy. You trusted her. Do you trust her now?" My mother was now back in control and staring at me with a sinister look. "Lord, why couldn't you have given us another son instead of a hot-to-trot daughter?"

"Charlene!" my father shouted sharply. "I know you're upset, but Donna isn't perfect and neither are you."

"Upset is an understatement, T.K. I'm way past upset. I'm pissed off. How could you do this to us, Donna?" The look she gave me was as cold as they come.

"It . . . it was an ac-accident," I sobbed.

"An accident?" My mother's voice went into hysterics. "Did you accidentally pull down your britches and let some man do his business? Please, I know you can do better than that."

"Charlene, you need to calm down. What's done is done. All we can do now is try to help Donna."

"Help her?" My mother laughed. "Seems to me, T.K., that's all I've ever tried to do for her. I've done everything in my power to make this girl become a good Christian woman and prevent this from happening. Without your help, I might add. But now she's on her own. I want her out! I want her outta my house!"

"Charlene, where do you expect her to go?" my father reasoned.

"She can move down South with your sister and have her baby, but she's not staying here to embarrass this family or me. Now pack your shit, Donna, and get out my house!" She pointed at the door. This was no heat-of-the-moment speech from my mother. She was serious; she honestly wanted me to leave.

"Daddy," I whined.

"Don't worry, princess. You're not going anywhere." He turned to my mother. "Charlene, I'd like a word with you in private if you don't mind."

"I don't care what you say, T.K. That ungrateful wench is not staying in my house."

"I'd like a word in private, Charlene," my father repeated

sternly. My mother immediately but reluctantly got up from her chair. "Excuse us, princess."

I let go of my father and he stood and walked toward the kitchen. My mother followed him with her arms folded across her chest and a huge scowl across her face. She refused to make eye contact as she passed by me.

A few seconds later I could hear them arguing. I couldn't quite make out what they were saying, but my mother was yelling from the very start. To my surprise, my father began to yell even louder. That was something I couldn't ever remember happening before, and from the look on my mother's face when they returned, neither could she.

"Okay, Donna." My mother took a deep breath then sat down next to me, placing her arm stiffly around my shoulder. I couldn't be sure, but I think she was even holding back a few tears. "Maybe I was a little too hard on you. If I was, I'm sorry. I know this can't be easy on you. It's just that you're my only daughter and I love you. I just want what's best for you. You haven't even finished college." I'd never heard my mother speak with such concern. "Well, what's done is done. How far along are you?"

I wiped away a few tears. "I'm not sure. Two, maybe three months. I missed two periods."

She exhaled, her voice still filled with newfound concern. "Well, that's good. At least you won't be showing at your wedding."

I froze for about three seconds then sat up straight as a board. "Wedding? Who said anything about a wedding?"

"I just assumed the baby's father *is* going to marry you."

Marry me? I thought. *He doesn't even know he's a daddy yet.*

"Once again, you assumed wrong, Mother."

She moved away from me, pulling her arm off my shoulder, looking at my father. I know she was dying to tell him, "I told you so."

"B-but why? Why wouldn't he wanna marry you?" my father stuttered.

I looked at my dad knowing he wanted an answer, but I doubted he would want to hear that I was pregnant by his good friend and right-hand man, the Reverend Terrance Reynolds. So I kept quiet.

"Listen, princess, maybe your mother and I should have a talk with him."

"No, Daddy!" I replied desperately. "Leave him be. Leave him alone!"

"Leave him alone? What do you mean leave him alone?" my mother demanded. "He got you pregnant! That makes him responsible. He has a responsibility to you and his baby to make this right."

I gathered all my strength then replied, "I said no, Mother! I'm not having any shotgun wedding. Did you ever think that I might be the one who doesn't wanna get married?"

All expression left my father's face. "But princess, why? Why wouldn't you wanna get married?"

"Probably because he's ghetto!" my mother accused. "She's always been a attracted to ghetto people, T.K., just like you." I wanted to slap my mother for saying that, and I guess my father could see it.

"Charlene! You're not helping matters." My father glared at my mother and she sat back in her chair with a pout. "Donna." My father's voice was as serious as it had been all night. "I need you to tell me who this young man is and where I can find him. I'd like to have a man-to-man talk with him."

"I can't do that, Bishop," I replied defiantly.

My father gave me a disappointed look. "Why not?"

"Because, because—" I was about to admit that I hadn't told Terrance yet, but my mother cut me off.

"Because she don't know who the father is. Do you?"

I was so hurt by my mother's accusation that tears exploded from my eyes. All I wanted to do was hurt her back, so I lashed out at her in a nasty sneer, not really caring how it might affect my father.

"And what if I don't know who the father is, Mother?" I shouted hysterically. "What do you want me to do, give you a list of the five most likely candidates so you can decide which one you want to be your son-in-law?"

Both my parents sat back speechless in their chairs. My mother looked like she wanted to hit me, and my father, well, he was in shock.

"How could you do this to us? You tramp. Look at your father. He just announced to the world that he's running for borough president, and he might've had a good chance before you went and did this. Now he doesn't have a chance running on a family values platform!"

She looked at my father and tried to bring him into her campaign to crush what was left of my self-esteem. Granted, there wasn't much left for her to do considering how bad I already felt about this, but she was going to try just the same. I wanted to just disappear at that moment.

"Leave her be, Charlene," my father said softly.

"No, T.K. Can't you see she's done this to hurt us? To hurt me. She ain't nothing but a tramp who didn't have the common sense to use protection. Jesus, I can just hear Lillian Wright and the other deaconesses now. 'Did you hear about the bishop's daughter? That heathenous wench done gone and got herself knocked up and she don't even know who the father is.' "

My father, as always, was there to protect my feelings from my mother's harsh words. "Charlene, you're wrong. Donna is human and she made a mistake. She didn't do it to hurt us. Really, this is between Donna and God. It has very little to do with us."

"How naive can you get, T.K.? This has everything to do with us as long as you're the bishop of the church and I'm the first lady. You're never gonna be elected to borough president now, and you might have a tough time keeping your job as pastor once the deacons board finds out. Lord, how could I have one child that's so good and another that's so bad?"

There she went again, throwing Dante up in my face. I loved my brother, but it always hurt when my mother tried to compare me to him. He was nowhere near being a saint, but in her eyes, compared to him, I always ended up looking like yesterday's garbage. Sure, I'd messed up big-time and I knew that, but this was by far not the first time she'd compared me to Dante. Even when I did small things, like spill a drink on the kitchen floor, my mother would rant about how stupid I was, how clumsy I was, how I should try to be more like Dante. Now that I'd gotten pregnant, I doubted I'd ever hear the end of her insults.

"You know what, Mother? If I'm such a bad child and I'm gonna ruin everything for Daddy, then maybe I should just go down to the clinic and have an abortion. I wouldn't wanna have a baby who might turn out like me." I didn't look at my father after that. I just got up and ran up the stairs, not stopping until I was lying on my bed with my head buried in my pillow.

I wasn't sure who it was standing outside my bedroom but I could feel a presence before there was a knock on the door. I was hoping it was my brother Dante, 'cause I wasn't ready to face my father again, and the Lord knows I wasn't ready to deal with my mother's crap.

I hesitated for a second before answering. I sat up, sniffling back tears and wiping my eyes. It had been close to a half hour since I left my parents in the living room with the thought that I might have an abortion. I was actually surprised that neither of them had come upstairs to talk me out of it. They were both staunch pro-life advocates in our community and just the thought that I might have an abortion was as bad as the reality of me being pregnant. Then again, knowing my father, he was probably just waiting for cooler heads to prevail or perhaps for Dante to come home so we could discuss the whole situation as a family. Now that I thought about it, I wouldn't be surprised if all three of them were standing outside my bedroom door.

Once I had gotten myself together, I turned toward the door and hollered, "Who is it?"

No one replied, but the door opened and my mother stepped into the room. She was alone and her face was still wearing the same evil scowl she had earlier when she and my father confronted me downstairs in the living room. She closed the door behind her and started to pace back and forth in front of my bed. The way she was staring at me made me feel like a wounded antelope about to be pounced on by a hungry lion.

"You just couldn't keep your damn legs closed, could you?" she finally snarled.

I didn't answer, so she continued her outburst. This time, though, she pointed her finger in my face at the end of every sentence to drive home her point. "How many times did I tell you to stay away from them boys? How many times did I tell you that if you didn't stay away from them boys, you were gonna end up getting knocked up?"

She paused and took a deep breath, but there was no relief in sight. She was no longer acting like the first lady of the church that everyone knew and respected. She was now acting like her true self. She was acting like a bitch. She scrunched up her face evilly as she continued her finger-pointing tirade.

"But nooooo, you just wouldn't listen to me, would you? You swore up and down that you weren't doing anything. That you wasn't having sex. That you was gonna wait till you got married. Well, you're pregnant now, and I wanna know when the hell you got married, 'cause I sure wasn't invited to the wedding."

And you won't be in the future if I have anything to do with it, I thought.

"Now, I wanna know who this baby's father is, and I wanna know now." Her index finger hit the bridge of my nose and it took everything I had not to grab it and break it off her hand. "Look at you. Look at you! You've been with so many damn men you *really* don't know who the father is. Do you?" She looked like she was about to explode.

"Mother, I've only been with—"

"Shut up!" she snapped. "I don't wanna hear it. All I wanna know is what fool you let knock your hot ass up. Give me a name, Donna."

Again I was silent, but I wanted to say something to shut her up. I wanted to tell her that despite her cock-blocking efforts, my baby's father was the Reverend Terrance Reynolds, the most sought-after and respected man in the church. But I knew it wasn't fair to tell her before I told him. I was just going to have to take her abuse until he came home in two days. But once Terrance came home, not only was she going to know he was my baby's father, but so was the entire congregation.

She looked down at my belly as she shook her head in disgust. "So, are you going to tell me who the father is?"

I shook my head and I could see her entire body tense like she was about to slap the shit out of me. I braced myself for the blow, but it didn't come. It was a good thing for her that she took a deep breath and held her anger, because I was sick of her shit and I hated to think of what I might have done if she had hit me.

"All right. Let me ask you a question. Do you still want to live in this house?"

I nodded, but this time she wasn't accepting any gestures.

"I asked you a question, and I'd appreciate an answer." She was back to her finger pointing.

"Yes, Mother, I want to stay in the house." I tried to keep

myself under control but I was starting to get a little attitude in my voice.

"Well, if you're gonna live in my house, you're going to live by my rules." She tilted her head. "Do I make myself clear?"

I really didn't have a choice. I was about to nod, but she gave me that don't-go-there look.

"Loud and clear, Mother," I replied coldly.

"Good." She reached into her robe and tossed something on my bed. I looked down and realized that it was a roll of money held together by a rubber band.

"What's this for?" I'm sure my face showed my confusion.

"It's for your abortion," she said just as calm as if she were handing me a glass of water instead of money to get rid of an unborn child.

"An abortion?" I barely got the words out of my mouth. "You *want* me to have an abortion?" I was shocked.

"Rule number one: There is only one woman in this house who is allowed to have a baby, and that woman is me. Now, I just went through the change, so I'm not having any more children. Either you get rid of that baby or you get out my house."

"I don't believe this. You're serious? You really want me to have an abortion?"

"I want whatever's best for your father and this family, and you having a baby out of wedlock is not what's best for this family. You said you wanted to have an abortion. Well, now you have the money. Just don't do it in Queens or any of the other five boroughs. Go out to Long Island or New Jersey. We wouldn't want anybody from around here to recognize you."

I looked down at the money again and then looked back up at my mother. The look on her face told me she was serious, dead serious. I had made the abortion threat downstairs, and now she was calling my bluff.

"Mother, I'm not—"

She cut me off. "You're not what?" She was back to pointing her finger in my face. "You're not going to mess up this election for your father, Donna. Do you understand me? I won't allow it. It's too important to m—him. Now you either tell me who the father of this baby is so we can arrange for him to marry you, or take your ass to an abortion clinic. The choice is up to you." She walked over to my closet and pulled out my overnight bag. She placed it at the edge of my bed.

"What's that for?"

"You're not staying in this house until this problem is fixed. And if you know what I know, you won't tell anyone outside this family that you're pregnant."

"Does Daddy know about this? Does he want me to have an abortion?"

"Sometimes your father doesn't know what's best for him, so I make those decisions. I wouldn't tell him about this if I were you. Who do you think he's going to believe, you who lies all the time, or me, his loving wife?" She pushed the suitcase closer to me.

"Aren't you going to come with me?" I asked in disbelief.

"I wasn't there when you conceived it, so why should I be there when you get rid of it? That's your problem. Just don't come back here pregnant."

I could feel the tears begin to well up in my eyes again.

"Mother, why are you doing this?"

"I didn't do anything to you. You did this to yourself. Now get out my house and don't come back unless you have a husband or an abortion."

22

Dante

When I pulled up to my house, I could sense something was wrong inside. It was half past midnight and it seemed like every light in the house was on, which meant my parents were awake. That in itself was strange, because they were usually in bed right after the eleven o'clock news unless there was a church function, which there hadn't been that night.

"Son, could you come here for a minute?" the bishop called just as I walked into the house. His voice seemed agitated and I tried to run through my mind what I might have done to have him waiting up for me so late. He was probably upset because I spent the last couple of nights over Tanisha's place.

I turned toward the living room and my earlier concerns of trouble were confirmed. My father was sitting in his chair, the high-backed one he always sat in after dinner, holding his Bible in one hand and a glass of J&B in the other. This was a definite sign that something was troubling him and it wasn't something small. My father was a social drinker at best, and he hardly ever drank hard liquor.

"It's a little late to be drinking, isn't it, Bishop?" I pointed at the half-empty bottle of J&B on the coffee table. Sitting there like that, he reminded me of a guy I'd seen on TV, with an angel on one shoulder and the devil on the other, both of them giving him advice. For the bishop, his Bible represented the angel and the liquor represented the devil. My only concern was which one he was listening to.

"Yeah, I guess it is a little late to be drinking, isn't it, son? But after the news your sister just gave us, I need something to calm down my nerves." He finished off his drink and placed the glass on the coffee table, gesturing for me to have a seat. I sat down on the love seat across from him, curious about what my sister had done this time.

"What'd Donna do now? Wreck her car again?" I asked.

"No, nothing like that." He frowned.

Whatever was going on had to be serious, because he picked up the bottle and poured himself another drink.

"What is it, Bishop? What's wrong with Donna?" I felt myself starting to panic. I'd never seen the bishop so hesitant. The only thing going through my mind was that Donna might be sick or dying.

He picked up his glass, took a long swig of the J&B, then cleared his throat before speaking solemnly. "Dante, your sister's pregnant."

"What?" My eyes shot wide open. I sat back in my chair with a frown, then I smiled, almost laughed. My father had almost scared me to death, and for what? To tell me some crap about Donna being pregnant. I swear if he were anyone else, I would have slapped the shit outta him for wasting my time and lying on my sister, but instead I chuckled. I knew it wasn't true. It couldn't be true. I hadn't spoken to Donna all day, but we were close. Much closer than she was with my parents, so there was no doubt in my mind that she'd tell me she was pregnant before telling them.

"Stop playing, Bishop. That isn't funny." I waved my hand as if to dismiss his joke.

"I'm not playing, Dante," he snapped in frustration. "I wouldn't play about something like this. I saw the results of her pregnancy test with my own eyes."

I sat there speechless, contemplating his words.

"You're serious, aren't you?" I tilted my head and studied his face.

"Yes." He lowered his eyes. "I'm serious. Your sister is pregnant."

"Oh, boy." I ran my hands across my face. "I'm sorry, Bishop, but this is kinda hard to believe. Donna wouldn't get pregnant."

"Son, an hour ago you would've been preaching to the choir," he replied, gulping down half his drink. "Hell, I thought she was a virgin. But the truth of the matter is she's not a virgin. She's going to have a baby."

He took another swig of his drink and I wanted to reach over and take a shot myself. Now I understood why he was drinking. It must have been devastating for him finding out that the daughter he thought was perfect had not only lost her virginity but was pregnant, too.

"Did she tell you who the father is?" I asked curiously. My first and only thought was that it had to be her mystery man.

He shook his head. "No, I was hoping you might be able to answer that for me. She wouldn't tell me or your mother."

His eyes shifted to my face and I shook my head.

"I know she'd been seeing someone the past few months, but I don't have a clue who he is," I replied honestly.

The bishop hung his head and mumbled to himself just loud enough for me to hear. "Dear Lord, where did I go wrong?"

He finished off his drink then solemnly placed his glass on the table. When he lifted his head, tears ran down his cheeks. I got off the love seat and placed an arm around his shoulder. I'd never seen him so emotional. His sad face almost brought tears to my eyes.

"You all right, Bishop?"

"You know, Dante, ever since I got saved, I've tried to be a good man, a good Christian, and a good minister. I just don't understand how I became such a horrible father. How could I fail you kids like this? I wanted to be there for you and your sister."

"You were there for us, Bishop," I said. "And you are a good father. But Donna and I aren't kids anymore. You and Mom taught us everything we need to be good, upstanding adults. The rest is up to us. I'm not your little boy and Donna's not a little girl anymore."

"She's my little girl, Dante. I don't care what age she is. She is always going to be my little girl, and you're always gonna be my little man. No one will ever convince me I shouldn't have seen this coming." He took off his collar and set it down on his Bible next to the bottle of J&B, then picked up the bottle and poured himself another drink. "Look, why don't you go talk to your sister? She's going to need a lot of support now, and I don't think your mother and I are up to it quite yet. We're still dealing with our own demons."

He sat back in his chair and took another long swig of his drink then closed his eyes as if he were trying to make everything go away.

"Hey, Bishop?"

He opened his eyes. "Yes."

"If you still wanna do right by Donna, there's a way."

"What's that, son?"

"Accept your grandchild."

He smiled sadly. "I already have, son. It's your mother I'm worried about."

"Me too."

That subject was too much for either one of us to think about yet, so he changed it to something lighter.

"How are things going with you and Tanisha?"

"Good," I answered then admitted, "I really like her, Bishop. She makes me feel alive."

He winked at me. "I'm happy for you, son. There is nothing like being with a woman you really care about. When this mess with your sister is over, I think you, me, and your mother need to sit down and talk about your future. What do you think?"

"I'll look forward to it."

He sat back in his chair and finished off his drink, closing his eyes as he held the empty glass in his hand. I took that as a sign that he wanted to be left alone. I headed toward the staircase to see my sister and hear her side of the story. That's when I heard my mother calling me from the kitchen.

"Dante?"

"Yeah, Ma," I replied as I stepped into the kitchen. My mother was sitting at the kitchen table eating cheesecake. Although she was a slim woman who watched her figure and usually ate like a bird, there was always a cheesecake in the house just in case she got upset or angry. She used cheesecake as a coping mechanism whenever she was upset. Judging by the small amount left in the pie tin and on her plate, my sister's pregnancy had her very upset.

"Did your father tell you about your sister?"

I took a deep breath then released it as I pulled out a chair. "Yeah, he told me. I was just going upstairs to talk to her." I sat down.

"Don't bother. She's not upstairs. I heard her car leave about fifteen minutes ago."

"I can't believe she's pregnant."

"Believe it, son. Your sister's just plain stupid. She doesn't care about anybody or anything but herself." She lifted her fork to finish what was left of her cheesecake. The way she stabbed it, I felt sorry for the cheesecake.

"Ma, you sound like you think she got pregnant on purpose."

"I wouldn't put it past her. Your sister is nothing like you, Dante. She's always been a bad seed, despite my efforts to keep her in line." I was happy to see I was once again her favorite.

"I don't know, Ma. She's only human. She's gonna make mistakes."

My mother rolled her eyes. "Well, this mistake might cause your father to lose the election. Do you know how much that means to us?" She let go of the fork then pushed away her plate with disgust.

I hadn't even thought about the election, and after my conversation with the bishop, I doubt he was thinking about it either. "You think this could lose him the election? But why? The bishop didn't get pregnant, Donna did. One shouldn't have anything to do with the other."

"Dante, Dante, Dante." She sighed, patting my hand. "You know you remind me more and more of your father every day. The both of you have such good hearts, but you're so naive." She explained, "Your father is running for office on a family values platform. In order to do that, he would want to have his own family in order. The minute the word gets out that your sister's carrying a bastard child, your father's career in politics is over, and perhaps his job as pastor of the church as well."

I hadn't thought of it that way, but the scary thing was, what she had said made sense.

"Is there anything I can do?" I asked.

"Don't worry, dear. Despite your sister's efforts, Momma has everything under control." She reached across the table and patted my hand.

23

Donna

The sun hadn't come up yet when I opened my eyes, and the only thing illuminating the room was the bathroom light that crept under the door. Like the night before, I hadn't been able to sleep more than an hour or two. I tried to move, but his arm was laid across my side, his hand resting on my belly. I didn't know if he was trying to be cute or not, but I immediately removed it. The last thing I wanted him to do was to touch my belly and remind me that I was pregnant.

We'd been lying on his bed since sometime late the night before, and I'd fallen asleep with all my clothes on, my back to his front. Spoon position, I think they call it. It was nice, maybe even comforting, but it wasn't what I wanted. What I wanted was to be in my house, in my bed, without the burden of this pregnancy.

I still couldn't believe I was carrying a child, and even worse that my mother had kicked me out the house and told me not to return until I had an abortion. If I knew her, she was probably praying she'd never see me again. I was sure, though, that Dante and my father were worried sick. I just hoped they didn't go to the police and file a missing person's report. Maybe after I got up and went to the bathroom, I'd turn my cell phone back on and give Dante a call. I'd turned it off when I left the house two days ago and hadn't even touched it to check my messages since, so I was sure by now my voice mailbox was full.

"Donna?" he whispered, breaking my thoughts.

I turned over and looked at him. His face was full of concern. I'm sure he'd had less sleep than I had, considering every time I opened my eyes throughout the night, he was staring at me. He must have really hated me for being pregnant.

"Yeah," I replied.

"Donna . . . Donna, will you marry me?"

I sat up straight as a board then bit my lip to make sure I wasn't dreaming. The sharp pain I felt told me it wasn't a dream but possibly his way of making a cruel joke.

"What did you say?" I leaned toward him.

He grasped my hand as he cleared his throat and looked deeply into my eyes. Goose bumps began to crawl up and down my arm and I felt short of breath.

"I asked you to marry me."

"Are you serious?" I still couldn't believe what I was hearing.

"Yeah, of course I'm serious. I love you, Donna, and I want you to be my wife." He gave me a tentative smile. Obviously he wasn't confident about what my answer would be. If I didn't know it before, I knew now; he really was in love with me and I was starting to think he was actually happy about me being pregnant. "I want you to marry me, Donna, so I can take care of you and the baby."

Marry me. I never dreamed I'd hear those words come out of his mouth. I must admit, though, they were the most touching words that anyone had ever said to me. It was too bad I couldn't give him the answer he wanted. It was too bad he wasn't the man I wanted to hear those words from. I pulled my hand free from his.

"I'm sorry, Shorty, but I can't marry you."

His tentative smile became a disappointed frown, and his voice was sad enough to make you wanna cry. "Why not?"

"Because I'm not in love with you, Shorty. I'm in love with someone else. I thought I explained that to you last night."

I swung my feet off the bed, took my cell off the night table, and turned it on as I walked toward the bathroom. I knew I was being harsh on Shorty, especially after how kind he'd been to let me stay at his apartment the past few nights, but I was under so much pressure. The last thing I needed was for him to complicate things by offering to marry me.

I'd come to Shorty's house the night my mother kicked me out. I had no intention of even stopping by his place that night, and I definitely didn't have any intention of spending the next few nights with him. I was actually headed to the church parsonage, where Terrance stayed. I knew where he kept his spare key and was planning on waiting there for him until he returned home Monday morning. However, my plans were changed when I had an accident with my car. I was so emotional about being pregnant and having my mother kicking me out that I got distracted and hit a pole.

Thank God for airbags, because although I was shaken up, I didn't have a scratch on me. Not that it mattered to the paramedics, though. Once I told them I was pregnant, they insisted that I go to the emergency room to get checked out, then the hospital wouldn't discharge me unless someone was there to pick me up. There was no way I was calling my parents or even Dante, and since Shorty's apartment was only two blocks away, I had the nurse call him. He was there within five minutes and insisted on taking me to his place when I refused to go home.

Shorty was following behind me toward the bathroom. "You did explain, but—"

I stopped in my tracks and turned to him. "There are no buts, Shorty," I said sternly. "Now, I appreciate you coming to get me from the hospital and letting me stay here the last few nights, but don't get it twisted. We are just friends."

"Yo, that can change. And you can learn to love me, Donna. The baby's gonna need a daddy." I stepped into the bathroom and turned to him before I closed the door.

"Let's get something straight, Shorty. My baby already has a daddy."

"Oh yeah? Well, where is he, then? Why'd you call me and not him? Your baby ain't got a daddy, Donna. He's a sperm donor. Can't you see that? The baby's father is using you." Shorty's face was serious and he spoke as if he was preaching the Gospel.

"He's not fuckin' using me, Shorty!" I cursed angrily. "He loves me. And get your facts straight; the reason I called you instead of him was because he was out of town. Now I suggest you keep your jealous comments to yourself, 'cause you don't know nothin' about him."

I slammed the bathroom door in his face and he had the audacity to knock on the door and shout, "Oh, I know a thing or two about him, Donna! That's why I know he's not gonna want this baby and you gonna have to raise it on your own."

I swung the door open. It was time for me to leave. Coming to Shorty's house had been a mistake. A big mistake. Thank God Terrance was coming home later that morning. "Shut up, Shorty! I'm sick of your jealous shit. You don't even know him."

"Yeah, I do," he said with sadness in his voice. I couldn't believe he thought he should feel sorry for me. But that wasn't anywhere near as shocking as when he said, "Donna, I know Reverend Reynolds very well, and he's not gonna marry you. Trust me on that."

I held my breath for what seemed like an eternity. I couldn't believe it. How the hell did he know about Terrance and me? We'd been so careful except for that day in his office last week when my father almost busted us. Dear God, if Shorty knew, did that mean Dante knew also? And if he did, had he told my parents?

"How . . . how did you know?"

"That day at the Soul Café. I saw Reverend Reynolds walk in when I was walking out. After that it wasn't hard to put things together. Especially after you just said your baby's father was out of town. Everyone knows Reverend Reynolds is out of town."

"Does Dante know about Terrance and me?"

He shook his head and I let out a sigh of relief. "Nah, he don't know. And it's a good thing too, 'cause he'd probably kill that bastard."

"No, he wouldn't. Dante likes Terrance, and the bishop does too." I smiled confidently.

"Let's see how much they like him when they find out his ass got you pregnant," Shorty said in his most condescending voice yet.

"They'll get over it."

"Maybe, but I doubt it. Reverend Reynolds is not what he appears to be."

He was starting to get on my last nerve with this shit. "Then what is he, Shorty?"

Shorty looked like he wanted to cradle me in his arms. I didn't want his pity at this point. "Donna, he's a player. A straight womanizer. That man—"

I let out a laugh. "You know what, Shorty? You need help. Are you that obsessed with me that you would lie on a man of God?"

"What you call obsession I call love, Donna. And I'm not lying."

"Uh-huh. Sure you're not." I cut my eyes at him.

"Puh-lease, Donna. That man's screwed half the congregation. You were just the last one left. If you don't believe me, ask Dante."

"I'm not going to ask Dante anything, Shorty, 'cause I know it's not true." I couldn't take it anymore. I was about to slam that bathroom door in his face again, but just then my phone rang and we both fell silent, staring at it. I checked the caller ID and the number came up unknown. Fed up with the conversation I was having with Shorty, I flipped the phone open and pushed the talk button.

"Hello."

"Donna?"

A huge grin came to my face. It was Terrance.

"Yes, baby. It's me. Where are you?" I glanced over at Shorty and smirked.

"I'm in Charlotte at the airport."

"At the airport!" My grin was even wider. "Are you coming home, baby?" I asked with excitement. "Please tell me you're coming home. I miss you and I really need to talk to you."

"I really need to talk to you, too. Have you spoken to your father this morning?"

"No. That's part of what I wanted to talk to you about."

"Look, Donna, I think you need to avoid your mother and father till we get a chance to speak, all right? There's something I need to tell you but I don't wanna do it by phone."

"You don't have to worry about that. I've been staying with a friend the last few nights," I replied. "So are you coming home, Terrance?"

"Yeah. I'm waiting for the plane to load now."

"Good!" I felt like I was going to burst. "What time does your flight get in? I'll pick you up."

There was hesitation on the line then he said, "Don't worry about that. I've already made other arrangements."

"You've already made arrangements?"

"Yeah. I tried to get ahold of you last night but your phone went straight to voice mail and your box was full."

I let out a frustrated breath. "I'm sorry. I forgot I turned off my phone."

"Listen, why don't we meet at Bronx BBQ over by Green Acres Mall around noon? We have a lot to talk about."

"All right. I'll see you there. I love you, Terrance."

"Yeah, me too," he said as we both hung up.

"Why didn't you tell him about the baby?" Shorty demanded as soon as I closed the phone.

"I want to tell him to his face."

"Don't expect him to be jumpin' up and down about the news, Donna."

"I know he's going to be a little surprised, but when he thinks about it, he'll be happy." I was nervous about telling Terrance, but I was confident he'd be there for me.

"Aw'ight, Donna. If that's what you wanna do, then go ahead. But don't say I didn't warn you." Shorty turned around and walked toward the bed. I knew he was upset, but like my brother and father, he'd get over it. If he didn't, that was his problem, because by that night I was planning to be staring my mother in the face with my baby's daddy on my arm.

I was one pissed-off sistah when I stepped out into the sunlight to search for Shorty's car. I was actually surprised and relieved to find that he was still there. I'd been sitting at the bar inside the Bronx BBQ restaurant waiting for Terrance for almost an hour, and he never showed up or even called. Thank God Shorty had insisted on sticking around after he dropped me off. I told him that I was going to be leaving with Terrance but he insisted on waiting just in case I was stood up. My God, it was like he was psychic or something.

"Well? What happened? Was he there?" Shorty asked. He actually looked a little surprised to see me when I got into his car. "I didn't see him go in. Was he already in there or did he stand you up?"

I was too embarrassed to even look at him. I just lifted my left hand like I was trying to stop traffic. "Don't. Okay, Shorty? Just don't. I'm really not in the mood right now."

This wasn't like Terrance at all, and at first I wanted to give him the benefit of the doubt. Maybe his plane was canceled or delayed. But when I called the airports, they said all flights coming from down South were on time. I started to get upset. It wasn't like he didn't have my cell phone number. Besides he always called when he was going to be late.

I took out my cell and started to dial a number, but I was so upset it took three times to get the number straight.

"First Jamaica Ministries," the secretary answered.

"Anita, this is Donna. Have you seen Terran—Reverend Reynolds?"

"Yes, he's downstairs with—"

I didn't even give her a chance to finish before I hung up. I had no idea why Terrance was still at the church, but I was about to find out.

"Shorty, take me to the church."

When the car didn't move, I turned my head toward him. He was staring at me tight-lipped, his eyes full of concern. "Donna, what's going on?"

I tried to hold back tears. "I'm not really sure yet, Shorty. That's why I need to go to the church."

He nodded his head as he put his foot on the gas.

24

Shorty

I needed to have my head examined. When Donna and I rolled into the reserved parking lot of the church, it looked more like a Sunday morning than a Monday afternoon. The lot was packed, and with all the luxury vehicles parked in the spaces, it looked like everyone who was someone was inside the church. That included Donna's mother and father, my boy Dante, and that snake in the grass Reverend Reynolds. Whatever was going on must have been pretty damn important to bring this many big shots to the church on an early Monday afternoon. I didn't mention it to Donna, but there was no doubt in my mind that this was the reason why Reverend Reynolds had stood her up. I just wondered what the hell was going on. Was it possible they were kicking the bishop out because of Donna's pregnancy? If so, how the hell did they find out?

"Pull into that handicapped space right in front of the church," Donna ordered, pointing at the parking space as if I was blind. I did as I was told, but I hadn't even placed the car in park before she jumped out and headed down the stairs to the church basement.

"Donna, wait!"

I wanted to tell her to be careful, and that I didn't have a good feeling about this, but she kept going, paying me no mind. I loved Donna, there was no question about that. And despite what she might or might not have believed, deep down I wanted her to be happy, even if it was with Reverend Reynolds. Still, my street intuition told me this was not a good time to be rolling into the church to confront him about his illegitimate child. I was tempted to sit this one out and stay in the car like I did at the restaurant. Reverend Reynolds was one thing but Bishop Wilson, First Lady Wilson, and Dante were another, and when it came to the Wilson clan, whenever the shit hit the fan, I was usually the one it blew back on. However, I was curious and perhaps even hopeful that once Reverend Reynolds found out he was going to be a dad, he'd start denying shit and push Donna right into my arms. Against my better judgment, I let my heart be my guide and got out of the car, following Donna into the church.

When I walked into the building, Donna was standing at the bottom of the stairs in the small corridor outside the Bingo hall/recreation room. The door was closed, but even from where I was standing, I could hear the people inside. Donna no longer had that determined look she had when she jumped out of my car. She was staring at the door looking tentative, perhaps even scared, and I couldn't blame her one bit. Once she walked through that door, the moment of truth was at hand. Not only was Reverend Reynolds in there, but so were her parents and brother, who were probably going to be pretty upset since they hadn't seen or heard from her in days. I walked up behind her and placed my hand on her shoulder. She turned around and lowered her head onto my shoulder. My selfishness disappeared, and the only thing I could think of was protecting her.

"You sure you wanna do this now?" I asked. "Your parents are probably in there, and this could get ugly."

"I know. That's why I haven't gone in yet, Shorty. I'm not sure about anything anymore." It was a little awkward because she was taller than me, but I wrapped my arms around her and pulled her in as close as I could.

"Look, maybe we should get out of here before anyone sees us. You can always talk to him later, in private."

She looked at me and nodded, but before we could head toward the exit, the door opened and Dante walked out.

"Donna, Shorty!" he greeted us as he stepped into the hallway.

"Dante," Donna and I replied in unison. Our hands immediately dropped to our sides but there was no doubt that he thought something was up. A question flickered in his eyes as he grabbed his sister and wrapped his arms around her in a tight, brotherly bear hug. There had always been a very special bond between Dante and Donna and it was never more evident than now as I watched him embrace her like they'd been separated for years.

"Girl, where have you been? I was worried sick about you," Dante scolded. "I've been looking all over for you. Why didn't you answer my calls?"

"I'm sorry, Dante. I just needed some time to myself."

"I hear you," he said in a low, sympathetic voice. He looked around to see if we were the only ones in the corridor then continued. "Mom and the bishop told me you were pregnant." He was talking to his sister but his eyes were on me.

"Dear ol' Mom," Donna repeated, rolling her eyes. "Did Mommy tell you she kicked me out and told me not to come back until I had an abortion?"

Dante looked dumbfounded. "Nah, she left that out."

"Where was I gonna go?" I could hear the hurt in Donna's voice as Dante's eyes traveled to me.

"If she said that, Donna, she was probably just upset. She didn't mean it. The next day she probably expected you to come home."

Donna looked at her brother and shook her head. I think she was about to get him straight but she stayed silent when the door opened again and a couple walked out and headed for the exit.

"Look, Dante, it's a long story, and this is neither the time nor the place."

"Aw'ight. We'll talk about it later," Dante said reluctantly. "But we are gonna talk." He released her then gave me a glance.

"What's up, Shorty?" he asked, sounding far from sincere as he offered me his hand. I took it, letting him pull me in close. "I guess you don't know how to call a brother back either, huh? I been trying to get in touch with you ever since Donna turned up missing. Figured you might wanna help me find her."

"Sorry 'bout that, D. I got a little caught up in something."

"I bet you did, *friend*," he whispered coldly, patting me on the back. We both slowly backed away, and when our eyes met, he said, "For your sake, you better not be too caught up in it. You know what I mean?"

There was no need for anything else to be said. We both knew what he was talking about. He turned his attention back to his sister.

"So, you're coming home tonight, right? I don't care what Mom said, Donna, I want you home and so does the bishop."

Donna smiled a real smile for the first time since I'd picked her up two nights before.

"I know, and I want to come home, but it all depends. I have a few things I have to deal with before I can face the bishop again."

She glanced toward the recreation room and asked, "What's going on in there?"

Dante let out a laugh. "Oh, that's right. You don't know. Reverend Reynolds messed around and got married last weekend."

"Married!" Donna and I shouted in unison, although my shout was more out of glee than hers.

"Yeah, that son of a gun had a fiancée. They been engaged for the past two and a half years. Can you believe he managed to keep that a secret?" Dante continued to laugh, but I was concerned about Donna, whose olive complexion seemed to be getting paler by the second. She was also starting to sway and I was afraid she was gonna pass out.

25

Donna

"Married!" I shouted once, but the word kept repeating itself over and over in my mind. *Terrance can't be married. He's supposed to marry me.*

"Donna, you aw'ight?"

I could hear Shorty talking, but I could barely comprehend what he was saying. I was so dazed by what I'd just heard. My brother had just unknowingly informed me that my boyfriend, the love of my life and the father of my unborn child, who had gone down South for a wedding last week, had actually returned as the groom. I was in such a state of shock that I couldn't think straight. My entire body was numb. To make matters worse, it was just a matter of seconds before my legs would give out from under me and I'd be sprawled out on the floor. Thank God Shorty was behind me and grabbed my arm to hold me up.

"Hey, little sister, you okay?" This time it was Dante's voice I heard, but I still couldn't fully understand what he was saying. My thoughts were too cluttered and preoccupied with the fact that Terrance had gotten married. I felt like I was dying and my mind and spirit were moving further and further from my body. I'd heard people say that they'd seen their life flash before them when they thought they were going to die. Well, I might not have been physically dead, but my life with Terrance was, and I'd just seen the last six months of my life flash before me.

How could he do this? How the hell could he do this to me? I wondered as my legs finally gave out on me. *He said he loved me.*

"Oh my God, Donna! Donna! Go get the bishop!" Dante screamed at Shorty, and like smelling salts, the mention of my father's name gave life to my wobbly legs and snapped me out of my fog.

"No, Shorty," I said sternly, placing my hand on Dante's shoulder as I struggled to maintain my balance. "I'm, I'm all right."

"No you're not. Look at you. You're as white as a ghost. I'm taking you to the emergency room." He took hold of my other arm and tried to guide me toward the door but I resisted.

"I said no, Dante. I'm just a little weak. It's probably just morning sickness," I lied.

"You sure you're all right?" Shorty still had his hand on my other arm.

"I'm fine," I told them, pulling my arms free from their grasp. I was still wobbly but I tried to put on the best front that I could, sucking in a deep breath as I stepped in the direction of the recreation room.

"Where you going?" Shorty asked. His voice was full of panic and I'm sure it was not because he thought I was going to pass out. He thought I was going to confront Terrance, and he was absolutely right. "I thought you wanted to leave."

"I do, but didn't you hear Dante? He said Reverend Reynolds just got married." My voice was dripping with sarcasm. "I can't leave without paying my proper respects."

"Donna, I don't think that's such a—"

I pushed the recreation room door open before Shorty

could finish his sentence. I really didn't give a damn what he or Dante thought at this point. I no longer felt numb or helpless. The only emotion I felt was anger, and I was going to make sure that bastard Terrance and the bitch he married knew exactly how angry I was. At least that was the plan I had when I stepped into the crowded recreation room and scanned for Terrance.

I completely froze when I spotted him in the back of the room standing next to my parents, shaking hands and kissing cheeks. Next to him was a woman about my height who I assumed was the woman he married because of the arm she occasionally rested on his shoulder. Her back was turned to me so I couldn't see her face. It was killing me because I desperately wanted to see if she was prettier than me.

"Donna, you don't have to do this. He's not worth it." Shorty had just walked up next to me. Dante was coming through the door when a member of the congregation stopped to chat with him.

"I can't let him get away with this, Shorty," I whispered. I was trying to hold back tears. "I'm carrying his child, and if I have to have an abortion or raise this baby alone, I'm going to make sure he, his wife, and the whole church knows he's the father."

"Donna? What the hell is going on?" Dante asked. He had just stepped into listening range so I doubted he heard what Shorty and I had been talking about, which was good. I wanted him to hear it at the same time as everyone else.

"You really wanna know, big brother? Then follow me."

I began a purposeful stride toward Terrance. Each step was more painful than the last, and the closer I got, the angrier I became until I was only a few feet away and realized I was about to make a fool out of myself. Sure, I could embarrass Terrance and the dumb-ass bitch he married, but in the end I was the one who was going to look stupid because I was the one who was pregnant by a married man.

I decided to leave and seek my revenge in other ways. The

only problem was I'd just been seen by my parents. My mother was eyeing me like she was a sniper and I was caught in her crosshairs. The bishop actually called my name, which of course made Terrance and everyone else in the vicinity turn my way.

Funny thing is, when we made eye contact, I had to admit to myself he was still the best-looking man I'd ever seen, and I loved him. Somehow in my anger I expected him to be ugly or look less attractive to me, but when I saw him, that was so far from the truth, it hurt even more. He looked better than ever and had the nerve to be wearing the same blue suit he was wearing the last time we made love in his office.

"Donna. How are you?" Terrance tried to act as if he weren't surprised. I'm sure nobody but Shorty and I were even paying attention, but the look on his face as we stood eye to eye told me inside he was terrified that I was going to blow up his spot. Somehow I took satisfaction in that.

"I'm fine, Reverend Reynolds. I hear congratulations are in order. My brother tells me you just got married." I turned my head to the woman standing next to him. One thing was for sure, she was not prettier than me. She was what my grandmother would call a handsome woman. But along with that came confusion. Why would he choose her when he could have had me? Was she better in bed than me? Did she give him anal sex? What the hell was it this manly looking heifer had that I didn't?

"Ah, yes." I could tell he was nervous, but he managed to say, "Donna, this is my wife, Shawna. Shawna, this is Donna Wilson, Bishop Wilson and First Lady Wilson's daughter."

"Pleased to meet you, Donna." She offered her hand and I reluctantly took it.

"The pleasure is all mine, Shawna. I hope we can become friends. We probably have a lot in common." I glanced at Terrance with a smirk.

"Oh, I would just love that. I used to live around here, but

I've been gone so long that I don't have any friends in New York anymore." She was so clueless it was sickening.

"You don't? Well, you just consider me your new best friend. I'd love to show you around New York." I turned toward Terrance. "You don't mind if I hang out with your wife, do you, Reverend?"

My father smiled, obviously proud of his daughter's kind offer. Terrance, on the other hand, didn't appreciate my sarcastic suggestion, and he shot back with a jab of his own. "No, I don't mind at all. But it's too bad you're single because we'll probably be spending most of our free time with other couples. Isn't that right, honey?"

"Well, isn't that a coincidence? Me and my fiancé are looking for another couple to hang out with. I guess we're going to be spending a lot more time together than you thought, huh, Reverend?"

"Fiancé?" Terrance snapped. He managed to regain his composure quickly, though, so I was probably the only one who noticed that my announcement had upset him.

"Yes. Fiancé." I grinned. "I'm getting married."

"You are?" Terrance was the one who asked the question, but I could hear gasps from the other people around me, including my father and Shorty.

"Yep, in a few weeks. You're not the only one who can get married, Reverend." I tried to make it sound like a joke to the other people around, but Terrance knew my words were meant to wound him.

"Who are you marrying?" Terrance asked with feigned interest, but I could hear the anger in his question and it was exactly what I had hoped he would feel.

"Yes, who are you marrying?" the bishop finally interjected when his initial shock wore off enough for him to speak.

I turned to my father then reached out and took Shorty's arm, smiling at my mother smugly. "I'm marrying Shorty."

26

Shorty

Donna and I had been summoned into the bishop's office right after she made the stunning announcement that the two of us were getting married. Her news had gotten her the desired effect—it made Reverend Reynolds take notice, but now we were the ones in the spotlight. Donna's announcement had not only shocked her family, it had surprised the hell out of me, too, since she'd been so adamantly against the idea of marrying me when I brought it up that morning. Not that I was complaining. I'd been in love with her for as long as I could remember. I just didn't know whether to jump for joy or to expect somebody to tap me on the shoulder and holler "April Fools!" Of course I was hopeful when it came to Donna, but I wasn't stupid. I knew this whole marriage thing was probably just some desperate scheme for her to get back at Reverend Reynolds, but I loved her. If there was any chance of us being together, I was willing to take the risk. I'd just forgotten that dealing with her family was part of that risk.

"Shorty, are you the father of Donna's baby?" Bishop Wilson asked, glaring across his mahogany desk with contempt. I'm not gonna lie. The way he was staring at me made me more than a little nervous. This was a man who had been more like a father figure to me than a religious figure, and here he was thinking I'd impregnated his daughter. If I were him, I would've jumped over that desk to strangle me already.

I glanced at Donna. She reached over from the chair next to me and grabbed my hand, squeezing it tight. I knew she wanted me to say I was the baby's father, but I just wasn't quite sure I could do it. The bishop had practically raised me. On more than one occasion he'd called me his second son. He'd been there for me ever since I was a kid, and that meant a lot to me, especially since my pops walked out on us when I was a kid. If it weren't for the bishop looking out for me, I'd probably be in jail or maybe even worse. Hell, he even helped me get my new job working for the Sanitation Department as a garbageman. He really showed me what being a man was about, so the last thing I wanted to do was just straight up lie to his face, even for the woman I loved.

"Shorty—" I'm sure he was about to ask me the question again, but Donna cut him off, answering for me.

"Yes, Bishop, he's the father." Donna said it so convincingly that if I didn't know better, I might have believed her myself.

"Dear Lord. God, why are you torturing us so?" First Lady Wilson, always the dramatic one, cried out from her place beside the bishop. It was obvious she had a much bigger problem with us than he did.

"No one is torturing you, Mother. I'm the one who's going to marry him, not you. Why can't you be happy for us?" Donna's words actually made me feel good. For the first time since her announcement, I felt a glimmer of hope that our marriage was a real possibility.

"Because he's trifling!" First Lady Wilson shouted. "I can barely tolerate him as your brother's friend. I will not have him as a son-in-law. He will not humiliate me with his tri-fling behavior and neither will you."

She was talking as if I weren't even in the room. In truth, I wished I was somewhere else, because I hated the fact that I couldn't defend myself.

Donna let go of my hand and stood. "It's always gotta be about you, doesn't it, Mother? Well, here's a little news flash: it's too late. You said you wanted me to marry my baby's father." She pointed at me. "Well, here he is, and we're engaged to be married. Or would you rather I had an abortion? It don't much matter to me."

The room fell silent as Donna looked at her mother then her father and back to her mother. The two women stared at each other, neither one saying a word. The tension was heavy in the air. Things were about to get personal, real personal.

"You do not want to go there," the first lady said coldly as she shook her head.

"No, Mother. *You* don't wanna go there." Donna's words sounded strangely like a threat. "Now, I'm marrying Shorty whether you like it or not. You better get used to it, because the two of us are gonna be at the Sunday dinner table humiliating you for years to come."

"Who are you talking to? I know you're not talking to me. I brought you into this world and the Lord knows I will take you and that trifling son of a—"

She stopped herself before she started cursing like a rapper. She looked like she was going to bust a gasket as she glared at Donna, then at me. She finally looked like she might calm down when the bishop reached up and took hold of her hand, patting it gently.

"Relax, Charlene. Shorty and Donna are going to have enough problems trying to raise a family and go to school. They don't need our insults. They need our support."

The bishop stood and brushed his suit off then came out

from around his desk. He smiled gently at Donna. That smile melted a lot of the tension in the room. "Is this what you want? Is this what you really want, to marry Shorty?" he asked.

Donna hesitated, then nodded.

The bishop turned and said to me, "Well, Shorty, it looks like you and Donna have put us all in quite a situation."

"Yes, sir, and I'm sorry about that. But I want you all to know that I love Donna. I always have."

"Well, now's your chance to prove it. Welcome to the family." He stuck out his hand and I grasped it. We stared at each other. I tried to read his expression, but I guess years as a public figure had taught him to keep his emotions concealed. Finally, he wrapped one arm around my back and hugged me.

"Be good to her, young man," he told me in a misty voice. "She's the only baby girl I've got."

"I will, Bishop. I promise."

He released me with a nod and returned to his seat. I turned to the first lady and offered my hand but she ignored me, putting hers on the bishop's back instead.

"If we're going to do this, we'd better do it soon," the first lady interjected, emotionless. "The last thing we want is for Donna to start showing before the wedding. It could lose you the election, T.K."

The bishop looked at the large calendar on the west wall of his office. "I can have Reverend Reynolds marry you in two weeks. It looks like the church's calendar is clear. Is that okay with you two?" Donna's face was almost white. I could just imagine what she was thinking because the last person either of us wanted to be marrying us was Reverend Reynolds.

"Why can't you marry us, Daddy?" She was using this little girl voice.

"Because I have to give you away, princess."

"Well, then I prefer to have Reverend Tate marry us. After

all, he is my godfather." The bishop glanced at the first lady then back at us. I'm sure he sensed something was afoot but he left it alone.

"Okay, Donna, I'll give Reverend Tate a call. How's that?"

Donna glanced at me and I nodded. "That's fine, Bishop."

"It's not fine with me," the first lady protested. "That's not enough time for me to plan a wedding. Why, I've got to get caterers, flowers, music, dresses, and the invitations made. And what about clergy from out of town? My God, where is the reception going to be held?" She threw her hand to her forehead in a dramatic gesture.

"Charlene, I'm sure you'll rise to the occasion," the bishop said quietly.

"Contrary to popular belief, I'm not a miracle worker, T.K."

"Well, if we have to, we can have the reception in the church recreation hall," he suggested.

"My daughter is not having some cheap reception in the church hall. Do you know how that will look? It's bad enough she's marrying him."

She gestured toward me again. Donna didn't show any reaction to her mother's statements, and I certainly wasn't about to open my mouth. Bishop Wilson finally defused the situation.

"Okay, Charlene. Obviously you have a lot of planning to do, but maybe we all need a day to get over the shock of Donna's announcement before we start worrying about these details. Why don't we leave this discussion until tomorrow, after we've had a chance to get used to the idea of a wedding?"

She was pouting, but the first lady agreed to his suggestion, and Donna and I were mercifully dismissed from the room. Both of us were too stunned to even speak after we left the room, though she did hold my hand as we walked toward the parking lot. The people who had been congratulating Reverend Reynolds and his wife were now outside in the church parking lot. A few of them pointed our way and started whispering, no doubt gossiping about our just announced engagement. I cringed at the thought of how their conversations probably included me as the bad guy in all this.

"I'm going home. I have to get out of these clothes. I've been wearing them the past three days," Donna mumbled.

"Jump in. I'll give you a ride." It was all I could manage to say as I climbed into my truck to leave, though we still had so much more to talk about.

"No, I'm gonna walk to the cab stand. I need to be alone."

"Aw'ight, but you should come over later. We need to talk."

"Mm-hmm, just not tonight, Shorty. Tomorrow, okay?" Donna answered, avoiding eye contact.

"Donna, before I go, I just need to know. Do you really wanna get married?"

She touched her belly as she glanced over at the church parsonage where Reverend Reynolds and his new bride were entering with some members of the congregation. "I don't think I have a choice."

27

Donna

After a long, drawn-out conversation with my parents about my wedding plans, my mother had decided we were going to have a small wedding. Her idea of small, though, was somewhere in the neighborhood of one hundred and seventy-five people. Instead of a guest list representing both the bride and groom equally, my mother informed me that she couldn't possibly reduce her number any lower than one hundred and twenty-five. She was, after all, the first lady of First Jamaica Ministries, a position she sometimes imagined to be as prestigious as first lady of the United States. If this weren't a shotgun wedding that needed to be expedited, I'm sure my mother would have tried to stretch her list to well over five hundred people.

Even though her list was small by her standards, I felt like it was a slap in the face to Shorty and his family. They were left with only fifty spaces for their guests, and my mother didn't seem to see anything wrong with that. By this time I knew there wasn't any use fighting with my mother over this. She had made her decision, and if I dared to question it, she would be sure to make me feel even guiltier about the fact that I was shaming the family with my pregnancy. Who was I to hold an opinion about my own wedding? There would be no need for one if I had just kept my pants on. Yes, my mother had spent years cultivating this type of guilt in me, so I could already anticipate what she would say to shut me up and get her way. Instead, I kept silent and let her make all the decisions, knowing that I would be left with the unfortunate task of informing Shorty that his family was only one-third as important as the first lady's.

Surprisingly Shorty didn't protest at all when I went to his apartment to tell him. I think he was just so happy we were getting married he would have accepted any number, as long as I was going to be walking down that aisle to marry him. Shorty didn't care if there were no guests besides the two witnesses required by law. Well, that wasn't exactly true. He did make it very clear that it was important to him for Dante to be there. Shorty loved Dante like his own brother, and he really wanted him to be his best man. The only problem was that Dante wasn't taking this whole thing very well. My brother had already let my mother know that if he thought she would let him get away with it, he wouldn't be at the wedding at all. Of course that wouldn't happen. How would it look for the bishop's son to stay away from his own sister's wedding? People would surely gossip about that, and my mother was determined to make this wedding appear as normal as possible.

Shorty knew Dante was angry. Dante had refused to speak to him ever since my surprise announcement, so now Shorty was afraid to ask him to be the best man. After I promised to ask Dante for him, I told Shorty I had done enough talking about the wedding. It was just too much stress. We sat on the sofa watching Donald Trump's *The Apprentice 2*. It's not that I liked the show that much, but it was comforting to have a distraction from my own reality, even for a little while. Shorty, on the other hand, didn't seem to want to let the subject go.

"You sure you wanna get married?" he asked me for the fifth time in five minutes. I guess he still couldn't believe that we were getting married. Neither could I, for that matter.

"Yes, Shorty, I want to get married." I didn't bother to conceal my exasperation with his constant questioning.

"And you want the baby to have my last name?"

"Uh-huh." I didn't take my eyes off the television as I answered.

He reached out and took my hand, staring at me until I was forced to take my eyes off Donald Trump's bad hair and look at him. He was smiling ear to ear. "How we gonna deal with the reverend? You know he's going to suspect the baby is his."

The mention of Terrance made my stomach lurch. I was still hurting deeply over his betrayal, but I didn't want to admit it. I put on a brave face, hoping if I just kept saying I didn't care about him, I might eventually believe myself. It hadn't work so far.

"Don't worry, Shorty. I got that. He doesn't even know I'm pregnant, and when he does find out, I'm going to make it very clear to him it's not his baby."

I could see my words comforted him when I looked into his eyes.

"Donna, you know I love you, right?"

"If I didn't before, Shorty, I sure do now." I squeezed his hand and he turned to me with affection in his eyes.

Shorty kissed me for the first time in over a year. The kiss was nice, but—I hated to admit it—it just wasn't Terrance. We kissed for a while, and as time went on, I noticed his breathing was growing heavy and harsh. As I sat there mourning the loss of what I thought I had with Terrance, Shorty was becoming overjoyed at what he saw as a new beginning for us.

"Donna, you don't know how long I've dreamed about this day," he murmured as he kissed my neck and massaged my shoulders and arms. His roaming hands and body lan-

guage told me that he was way more aroused than I was. I
grew tense as I realized what was happening. He wanted to
take our relationship to the next level. For a moment, I didn't
say anything; I just let him continue, hoping he'd stop. Then
his hand slid down toward my thigh and began to creep up
under my dress.

Without delay, I jumped up. "Stop, Shorty. What do you
think you're doing?"

He stared at me like a contestant on a game show who
didn't know the answer to the million-dollar question. "I
thought now that we're engaged we were going to . . . you
know."

"Look, I know we're getting married, but I've already
made one mistake giving it up before I went down the aisle.
I'm not going to make that mistake twice. I'm not going to
sleep with you until after we're married. I hope you can respect that."

It was obvious he wasn't happy about things, but he
sucked it up and smiled at me. I guess he decided that he'd
waited this long, what was another week or two? Still, he did
decide to remind me of how much I owed him.

"I hope you're not trying to play me for Reverend Reynolds, Donna, 'cause I went out on a limb for you. I'm not
the one who announced to the world that we were getting
married. You did."

I felt like I was about to lose my mind. After spending all
afternoon with my mother making me feel guilty about getting pregnant, here was Shorty laying another guilt trip on
me. In some ways I could understand. He did go above and
beyond the call of duty when he let me tell everyone he was
the father of my baby. Still, I was so tired of feeling guilty
and pressured by everyone. It seemed like I was the last one
anyone was concerned about. My mother was only interested in saving the family reputation so that the bishop could
get elected, and Shorty suddenly seemed to think I owed him
sex for what he'd done for me. Well, I'd had enough. As

much as I appreciated Shorty, he was just gonna have to wait.

"Shorty, believe me, I know you went out on a limb for me, and I am not trying to play you. Once we get married, I'm going to be the best wife I can be for you. I will meet all your needs. I promise. Please just give me some time." Mercifully, he accepted my words with a smile.

"You can take all the time you need because I'm gonna be the best husband and father you could ever imagine. I swear you're never gonna regret this."

I wasn't about to tell him, but I was starting to have regrets already. Shorty was a good man. I couldn't think of anyone else who would marry a woman who was pregnant when he knew it wasn't his child. Still, as good a man as he was, he wasn't the man I loved. He wasn't Terrance and he never would be, and after next Saturday I was going to have to deal with that the rest of my life.

28

Donna

"Please, Dante. It would mean the world to us."

"I'm not going to be in the wedding, Donna, so I damn sure ain't gonna be his best man. Not after the way you two played me. The bishop and the first lady still don't believe I didn't know what was going on between you two." I was sitting in Dante's office trying to convince him to be Shorty's best man in my wedding.

"I'm sorry, Dante. This is all my fault. Shorty wanted to tell you, but I knew you wouldn't have approved. I made him promise to keep our relationship a secret." That old cliché about telling one lie always leading to another is true. I'd probably told more lies trying to cover up the fact that Shorty wasn't my baby's father than I'd told in my entire life.

"You darn right I wouldn't have approved. I would have stopped it and you wouldn't be knocked up by my best friend." He sneered. "And don't by any means think that I don't blame you in this, little sister."

Dante sounded so hurt. I was tempted to tell my brother the truth to make him feel better, but before I could say anything, there was a knock at the door.

"Come in!" Dante shouted then looked at me and spoke softly before the door opened. "I'm going to be at your wedding because the bishop wants me to be there, but I'm not going to be in your wedding party."

The door opened. "Dante, have you seen your sister? Oh, there you are."

My back was facing the door. When I turned around, my heart, which I thought had started to heal the past few days, felt ready to crumble at the sight of Terrance.

He'd been keeping a pretty low profile since the day he showed up back in town with his new wife. As much as I wanted to hate him, my body betrayed me now, because I still felt that magnetic physical attraction to him. That man looked so good in his designer suit he was making my nipples stand at attention. Thank goodness for padded bras. My face, of course, stayed expressionless, as if carved out of stone.

"Donna, is it possible for me to speak to you in private?"

"About what?" Though I wanted to scream, I tried to keep my tone even since Dante was in the room.

"Your father wanted me to speak to you and Shorty about your premarriage counseling. Do you have a minute?"

This cannot be happening to me, I thought. Of all the people to be counseling me and Shorty on our marriage.

"Look, I've got a meeting with Deacon Black. Why don't you two use my office?" Dante sounded more than happy to hand me over to Terrance so he wouldn't have to deal with me himself. I wanted to cry and beg my brother to stay, but in reality, I didn't want to be with either one of these men right now. At one time they had been two of the most important men in my life, but now they were both making me feel like shit.

Dante left and Terrance and I stared at each other for what was probably only a few seconds but seemed like eternity. Finally, he stepped inside and closed the door behind him. "Donna, we've got to talk." He spoke barely above a whisper.

"Talk? What is there to talk about? We don't have anything to talk about. By the way, how's your wife?" My tone was cold and my voice sounded so hollow that it didn't even sound like my voice anymore. It sounded dead, just like I felt.

Terrance got right to the point. "You can't marry Shorty. I won't allow it."

"Won't allow it?" I was shocked by his arrogance. "How you gonna stop it? *Why* would you stop it? You're a married man."

"For starters, you don't love him. You love me."

"Ha! What's love got to do with it?"

He stepped closer, reaching for me, and I threw up my hands. "Don't touch me. Do you understand? Don't you dare touch me."

He stepped back. "Donna, baby, please. I know you're upset, but don't do something you'll regret the rest of your life. You don't want to marry that man."

I wanted to smack him, and I'm sure my expression told him that. "Who the hell are you to say that to me? You're the man who ruined my life. I loved you, Terrance. I didn't deserve this. You didn't even have the decency to tell me. You had me sitting in a restaurant you knew you weren't coming to so you could show that heifer off to *my friends and family.*"

He turned away from me. "I know, and I'm sorry. I just didn't want you to make a scene."

"You're pathetic, you know that, Terrance." I was crying now. "But what I wanna know is what did I do wrong? Is it because I wouldn't fulfill your sexual fantasy? I was planning on doing that the night you came home. What did I do, Terrance?"

"You didn't do anything wrong, Donna. It was me. I should have told you about Shawna in the beginning."

I stopped my sobbing long enough to ask, "Do you love her?"

"We have a lot in common. We're a good team. She

knows a lot of powerful people. She can help me get my own church. I want my own church, Donna."

"Is that what this is about? We were a good team too, you know. If you had married me, you could have been the pastor of this place someday. Dante doesn't want it."

"I didn't know."

"Obviously. I still wanna know why, Terrance. Why would you cheat on me?"

He hesitated and I could tell what he was about to say was a struggle. "I wasn't cheating on you. I was cheating on her. I'd been with her since before I came to New York. She was overseas studying in Jerusalem when you and I got together. She just came back a few months ago."

"How could you do this to me? I gave you the only thing I had left. I gave you my virginity."

"Donna, I'm sorry."

"Will you stop saying that? All I want to know is, do you love her?"

"I did until I fell in love with you."

"If you loved me, why didn't you tell her about us?"

"She knows your mother and father. She'd asked your mother to keep an eye on me."

"So that's why my mother tried to keep me away from you. She knew you were a bastard, engaged to one woman and up here enjoying the attention of all the women of this church."

He ignored my statement and changed the subject. "Donna, I need to know something."

"What?" I just wanted him to leave.

"Your father told me you were pregnant. Is that true?"

I felt the slightest satisfaction knowing that he cared enough to even ask. "Why?"

"I want to know if it's my baby."

"What do you think?" I wasn't about to make this easy for him.

"I don't think, I *know* it's my baby."

"What makes you so sure?" I crossed my arms and hated him for being so damn confident.

"I know you didn't fool around. I just don't know how this happened. I thought you were on the pill."

"I was on the pill, but obviously it didn't work."

"Oh, Donna, please forgive me."

I rolled my eyes at him. That simple apology didn't come anywhere near what I felt he owed me.

"We could have been so happy, Terrance."

I saw tears fill his eyes. The way his eyes crinkled in the corners reminded me of the way they used to when we were laughing together. It reminded me of how much I loved him. For a moment my heart softened, but suddenly, the last week of my life replayed in my mind. I saw a flashback of myself crying in the car when I found out I was pregnant. I thought about how my mother put me out of her house like a stepchild. And as if that weren't bad enough, I remembered how shocked I was to find out that Terrance was married to someone else. No, my heart couldn't take any more pain. I would never let a man hurt me again. Just like that, I felt my heart turning to stone.

Terrance's words interrupted my thoughts. "What are we going to do? I love you, Donna."

"No, you don't love me. If you did, you would never have married her."

"I had to marry her. Besides, your father never would have allowed you to be with me. He knew I was with her."

"I could have taken care of my father. I still can. If you really love me, why don't you divorce her and marry me so you can raise your child?"

"You know I can't do that." He said it as if he was expecting me to be reasonable after he had ripped my heart out.

"Why not?"

"Because I made a vow before God. I can't go back on that."

"But why did you start seeing me at all if you knew you were engaged?"

"I'm a man. Men make mistakes."

"Men ain't shit. That's why women are always left holding the bag, Terrance. Or should I say holding the baby? Thank God for Shorty."

"Donna, you can't marry him. I can't live with the thought of another man raising my child. I'll take care of the baby. Just don't get married. Don't marry that man."

"Are you crazy? I can't be an unwed mother, Terrance. You know what that would do to the bishop's political carrier? To my family?"

He wasn't giving up. "Please, Donna, don't marry Shorty."

"You have no right to ask me for anything, Terrance. You led me on when you knew you had a fiancée. How could you do this to me? I hate you, Terrance. I hate how you've destroyed my life. You, you—" I lunged toward him, my fingernails bared, ready to claw his eyeballs out.

Before I could attack him, though, Terrance grabbed me, pulled me into his arms, and gave me a deep, passionate kiss. For a moment, I felt the old sap rising, the strong feelings coming back, but then I thought about his new wife and pulled away from him. I reared back and slapped him with all my might. His hand flew up to his face in shock and he remained speechless. For the first time, I saw him for the coward that he was.

"Don't you ever put your hands on me again. I'm going to marry Shorty and that's that. He's a good man, and he'll be a good father to my baby."

"Oh, yeah? Well, don't be surprised if you find me interrupting your wedding."

"Is that a threat?"

"No, it's a promise," he said then turned and walked out the door.

29

Shorty

"Yo, Shorty, can I see you for a moment?"

I was surprised to see Dante standing above me. I was sitting in the vestibule of the church, waiting for Donna, who had gone into his office to ask him about being the best man at our wedding. I definitely hadn't expected him to be the one to come out and talk to me. He hadn't spoken to me since Donna had made the announcement that we were getting married and that I was the father of her baby.

I'd seen Dante upset before, but now there was an iciness about him, a threatening look in his eyes. Before now I hadn't realized how tall and menacing he could appear. Obviously Donna's conversation with him in his office hadn't gone so well.

"Sure, bro, what's up?" I asked, wishing things hadn't become so tense between us. I had actually been hopeful he would agree to Donna's suggestion to be my best man, but now I saw the way he was looking at me, and I knew that wasn't going to happen.

"Why don't we step into the choir rehearsal room? This ain't for everyone's ears, if you know what I mean," he said.

I stood up without taking my eyes off Dante. We went into the empty choir rehearsal room. I wondered if there were something I could say to defuse the situation, but then I looked at Dante. His nostrils were flared, and it looked like steam would come out of his ears any second. This was the time for me to keep quiet and let him say his piece. I loved Donna, and I knew I was doing right by her, but I had to remember that Dante believed I deserved his anger. As far as he was concerned, I was the man who had gotten his sister pregnant. If he were anyone else and we were in any other building, I would have been expecting a fight. I considered myself lucky that it was Dante I was dealing with. He was usually pretty good at controlling his anger, so at worst I was expecting to get cursed out. What hurt more than any punch ever could, though, was knowing that I was probably about to lose my best friend.

"Did your sister ask you about being my best man?" I was hoping we could talk instead of shout at each other.

"Yeah, she asked me, and I told her no." His eyes looked shiny, like he might be about to cry or something. "How could you, man? You s'posed to be my boy."

"Dante—" I started to speak, but he wasn't interested in listening.

He got in my face. "How could you do my sister? How could you do my sister behind my back? You played me!"

I wanted to tell him the truth: that I hadn't slept with Donna, that I was marrying her to protect his family name and honor. But he wouldn't have believed me, so what was the use?

"It's not what it looks like, bro. I swear it's not what it looks like. You know you've always been my boy. I would never hurt you."

"Oh, no? So why do I feel so hurt? Of all the pussy you could want, why'd it have to be my sister?"

"Dante, you know I've loved Donna for a long time."

"Love her? Shorty, you knocked her up! And I'm not sure

you didn't do it on purpose." Spittle had gathered in the corner of Dante's mouth. His eyes were moving wildly in his head, and his arms were flailing about as he paced.

"Look, we're getting married, Dante. I'm trying to do the right thing by her."

"That's all you can say? That you're trying to do right by her? What about doing right by me? I've had you in my home since we were kids. I trusted you, man, and so did my parents."

"Dante, I'm sor—"

Before I could get the words out of my mouth, he hauled off and hit me. I saw stars. The next thing I knew, I was lying on the floor, holding my jaw.

"Get up, punk."

I shook my head and held my hand up in surrender. "I'm not gonna fight you, man. I love you too much for that."

"Well, ain't no love here. I'll never forgive you," Dante said. He gave me one final kick, then left me huddled on the floor

"Dante, it's not what you think!" I yelled after him, but he was gone.

All I could do was shake my head. Lord, I didn't want to lose my best friend. He was like a brother to me, but I didn't want to lose Donna either. And if she was going to be my wife, my first loyalty was to her. I had to respect her wishes. I would never let Dante know that I hadn't slept with Donna. I would never admit that his new niece or nephew was not my baby until Donna said it was okay.

30

Donna

"What? What is it, Mother?" I asked.

My mother and I were in Pilar's Dress Shop on Hillside Avenue in Queens Village. Ever since she figured out that I was not going to fight her on any of the details of the wedding, there was an uneasy truce between us. As long as I didn't question any of her decisions, she had stopped obsessing over the issue of my pregnancy. I was no longer made to feel like I was going to be the downfall of my father's political career. Though things still hadn't turned out the way she would have wanted, with me marrying some distinguished church member and getting pregnant *after* the wedding, she was no longer reminding me of this fact every time I happened to be in the same room with her. Occasionally I would still catch a glimpse of the disappointment in her eyes, but this was a far cry better than being wounded by her words every day.

Among the many wedding details I had allowed my mother to control, I let her choose my gown. I know most brides consider the gown choice to be practically sacred and would never dream of letting someone else do it for them, but I was having such mixed feelings about even getting married that it didn't matter to me one bit. I could have worn a pair of faded Levi's and a stained T-shirt for all I cared. My mother obviously cared about it much more than I did, so I was more than happy to let her find a dress for me. She had picked out an eggshell white wedding gown earlier in the week, and I was trying it on in front in the floor-length mirror when her reflection caught my eye. She was staring at me with a handkerchief in her hand, wiping away tears. To tell the truth, it spooked me. I've never seen my mother cry except at funerals. She was definitely not one of those mothers who shed tears of pride and joy for their children's accomplishments. You know the type. The ones who sniffle and wipe their eyes when little Johnny gets a trophy for peewee soccer. That was definitely not my mother. She'd always seemed like she was made of steel, which was why I had no idea what to do when I saw tears now.

"Are you okay, Ma?" I asked uneasily.

"Oh my Lord, Donna, you look so beautiful." She wiped her face again.

"Really?" I smiled at the unexpected compliment, trying to conceal my shock.

She nodded. "Just beautiful."

I was trying to hold back tears of my own, but it was no use. Within seconds I was crying too, overwhelmed by all that was happening to me. I was pregnant by a man who had crushed my heart, engaged to a man who didn't have my heart, and now my mother was starting to look like she actually had a heart. I turned to my mother and hugged her with an affection I hadn't felt for her since I was a child. All my life I'd wanted my mother's approval, just an eensy-weensy-teensy bit of her attention, and now, here I was almost three months pregnant and rushing into a shotgun wedding, and out of nowhere she tells me I'm beautiful. I had never heard her say those words to me, not in my twenty years on this earth. I wished I had a tape recorder, because moments like these are what life is all about.

"You are going to make such a beautiful bride." She sniffed back her tears.

"I owe it all to you. I know I haven't been everything you wanted me to be, but I couldn't have done this without you, Mom. Thanks." This time she reached out and hugged me.

If folks only knew how many details she had pulled together in one week's time, they'd have the first lady open up a wedding planning service for church members. In the past seven days, my mother had picked out my gown as well as five bridesmaids' gowns, and had them altered individually from size 20s down to the petite size 6 that RaShanda wore. She also made favors out of miniature elegant shoes, filled with birdseed and covered with tulle. Before now I had assumed all the details were only important because she was worried what people would think about her, but now I wasn't so sure. Maybe beneath her harsh exterior my mother had been trying to make a beautiful day for me, even in these less than perfect circumstances.

"How are you ladies coming?" Mrs. Pilar, the owner, stuck her head into the dressing room.

"We're fine," my mother replied, releasing me from her embrace. "We'll take this dress. Can you let it out a little more in the hips? We Wilsons have rather large backsides."

"Sure," Mrs. Pilar replied, pulling out a measuring tape and some tailor's chalk. She did what she had to do then smiled at me and left the room so I could get out of the gown.

Once Mrs. Pilar was gone, I broached the subject that had been on my mind all day. "Mother, can I ask you something?"

"Ask away," she said, standing behind me as she unzipped the gown.

"Mother, do you really hate Shorty?"

She stopped unzipping for a second to think, then answered me. "No, I don't hate him, Donna. You don't hate someone who you've allowed to spend as much time in your house as I have Shorty. I think the best way to say it is he rubs me the wrong way. I also just think Dante could have done better finding a friend."

"What do you mean by that?"

"I just don't think Shorty is in Dante's class. I don't think he's in your class, either, but we're going to have to make do."

I suddenly decided to reveal my true feelings to my mother. The tenderness she had revealed to me moments before gave me a sense that I could trust her with the truth. It didn't take long to discover just how wrong I was.

"Well, what if I told you I don't know if I wanna marry him?"

She looked at me through the mirror, and just like that the steel wall was back up around her heart. Her teary eyes were replaced with the stern gaze I was so accustomed to seeing from her. That magic moment of closeness between us had vanished as quickly as it had appeared.

"I'd say tough. You made this bed with Shorty; now it's time for you to lie in it."

"What if I'm not happy?"

She spun me around, hands firmly gripping my shoulders. "And just who told you life was supposed to be happy? I know I didn't. Happiness is what you make it." She dropped her arms to her sides, but the tension in her body was still obvious. "Now you listen to me, Madonna. You put our family in this situation, and you are going to marry Shorty. He's got a decent job as a garbageman, and even more importantly, he's the father of your child. I don't want to hear anything different."

"I understand that, Mother, but I don't love him."

I wished she could understand how scared I was about the decisions I had been making in my life recently. Things had spiraled out of control ever since I fell for Terrance, and there was not one person I felt I could talk to about it. Terrance had forbidden me to reveal our relationship, and I had allowed him to control me. Of course, now I knew why he wanted it kept secret, but at the time I was just doing what I was so accustomed to doing: following directions. My parents had raised me to follow the laws of the Bible, and to follow the laws of their household, and I had been such a good little girl, always doing what I was told, trying to please everyone else and gain their approval. Even now, I was marrying Shorty to please others. I knew it would please my parents, at least to some extent, and of course, it would please Shorty, who I felt I had to repay for his help. But there was a small voice inside me that was finally starting to protest, reminding me that I mattered, too, that I shouldn't forget about doing what pleased me. My mother, though, wasn't interested in what that small voice might have to say.

"You don't love him? So what? In time, you will learn to love him. Besides, you should have thought about that before you lay down with him. I bet you thought you loved him then, didn't you?"

I almost slipped and told her that I had never "lay down" with Shorty, as she called it, but I caught myself. I silenced that little voice inside and fell back into doing what I did best.

"You're right. I will learn to love him," I said, defeated. "I just wish I could be like you and Daddy. You've always loved the bishop."

A strange look passed over my mother's face. She started to say something then stopped, only to start once again. "Men like the bishop don't come around very often, Donna."

"I know, Mother." I sighed and ignored the faint echo of protests from my inner voice. "I guess you're right. I could do much worse than Shorty. Now help me get out of this dress so we can go home. I'm feeling very tired all of a sudden."

31

Tanisha

Dante had just come to pick me up, and I was putting on one of the new outfits he had bought me when we went shopping for clothes for his sister Donna's rehearsal dinner and wedding. After much pleading on Dante's part and plenty of complaining on mine, I had finally agreed to go with him to the dinner. After the way his mother treated me at their house, I had vowed never to go near that woman, but now here I was getting ready to face her again.

Aside from my own issues with Dante's mother, there was plenty of other drama surrounding this dinner and the upcoming wedding. Dante didn't want to have anything to do with it because he still couldn't get over the fact that his best friend had knocked his sister up. And his parents? Forget it. His mother had disliked this guy Shorty from way back, so you know it was just killing her that he was getting ready to become a part of the family. Secretly I was loving that part. That stuck-up woman deserved to be humbled, and maybe this was just the thing to put her in her place, to make her understand that there was nothing special about her. I did feel bad for the bishop, though. He seemed like such a nice man, and I know it was probably really hurting him that his daughter had gotten pregnant.

When Dante first asked me to go, I had flat out refused. There was no way in hell I was going to expose myself to that woman's insults again. But the more Dante and I talked, the more I realized it wasn't all about that. Because of the issues he was going through over his sister's pregnancy, he said he really needed me there for support. He was asking me to set aside my pride and be there for him. After all Dante had done for me and my family, how could I say no to this request? So I agreed to go with him to the rehearsal dinner. We had also bought an outfit for me to wear to the wedding, depending on how well behaved his mother was at the rehearsal.

It was kinda cute, because he insisted on choosing the outfits I was going to wear to both events. I knew Dante liked the champagne suit I was wearing for the rehearsal dinner because when I walked out of the bathroom, I caught his approving stare. I have to admit that the outfits weren't exactly my style, but I still liked them, especially since Dante had picked them.

"Baby, you look good," Dante told me with a wink. "No, you look better than good. You look so . . . so classy."

He smiled and I laughed. I'd never heard my style of dress described as classy. Tight, maybe; sexy, definitely; revealing, most of the time; but never classy.

"Just as long as I don't look trampy. You know how bad things turned out last time I had dinner with your family. You sure you even want me to go?"

"Of course I want you to go. And you look fine." He directed me to the full-length mirror on the door. I almost didn't recognize the woman in the reflection. If you didn't know me, you might think I worked in the city as a businesswoman with my brown pumps and conservative suit. I did look classy. Over the past few weeks, I guess I had changed without knowing it. It seemed like being with Dante was smoothing out some of my rough edges. I wasn't even cursing as much as I used to.

"Tanisha, everything will be fine. I love you. I love my family, and I'm sure in time they will come to love you, too. But if they don't, that's their problem, because I wanna be with you for the rest of my life."

"Do you really mean that? 'Cause that's how I feel about you. Baby, I'll walk through walls for you."

He smiled and kissed me.

"Well, why don't you walk your pretty little behind over to that bed and take off your clothes?"

I smiled seductively. "I'd love to, but aren't we going to be late for your sister's dinner? I don't think your mother's going to appreciate that."

He frowned. "Good point, but when we get back, you owe me."

"Don't worry. You know I always pay my debts."

On the way to meet the family, Dante filled me in on the events of the wedding rehearsal he had just come from. It was a tense situation for everyone there, but they had gotten through it without any major blowups. His mother had managed to control her tongue, and Dante had managed to control his fists, so considering what could have happened, it was a successful rehearsal.

The rehearsal dinner was being held at Peter Luger's, a fancy steak house in the city. One of the things I liked about Dante and his family was that they sure knew how to live in style. When I stepped into the restaurant, I could almost feel the first-class service that would be provided. I was glad I'd let Dante choose my outfit, too. I looked just as classy as the other women in the restaurant, and though I was dressed conservatively, the admiring glances from several men in the restaurant told me I still had it going on. Dante held my arm and walked proudly as we approached his family and their guests. He made me feel so good. Right away, he began to introduce me to everyone. I'd never met so many ministers, reverends, deacons, and deaconesses in my entire life.

The thing that made me feel the best was Dante's father, who gave me a huge hug. "I noticed I've been seeing you in the pews almost every Sunday. I'm very proud of you, young lady. Hopefully we'll be having one of these dinners for you and Dante one day." He gave Dante a wink then smiled at me.

Believe it or not, even the first lady eyed me up and down with an approving look on her face. She complimented me, too. Well, sorta. "You're looking very ladylike today," she said. Her mouth twisted a bit in the corner, but I was still willing to think of her words as a strange brand of acceptance. "I love your suit. Let me guess. Dante picked it out, didn't he?"

"Yes, he did. He has wonderful taste in clothes. Don't you think?" I was determined to maintain an attitude to match my classy attire.

"Yes, he does, but the jury is still out on his taste in women." So much for thinking this woman had the potential to be human.

"Mother, are you still harassing her?" Donna slipped past her mother and wrapped her arms around me. "Tanisha, I'm so glad you came. Dante told me you weren't going to be here."

"Thanks for inviting me." I wanted to thank her for saving me from the wicked witch, aka her mother, but I bit my tongue. The first lady would not goad me into showing my ass tonight. "Congratulations on your wedding, Donna."

"Thanks," she replied quickly then turned and beckoned to a short, stocky man who was standing in the background. "Let me introduce you to my fiancé. Shorty, come over here. Meet Tanisha, Dante's new friend."

As soon as I saw Shorty, my heart started to race. I had known him as John, but this was definitely the man who used to be a regular at the club. He'd seen me dance before. Matter of fact, I'd given him a few lap dances. One of the girls at the club used to make a lot of money off of him, and it didn't seem like too long ago that she mentioned he had just kind of disappeared. Now I knew why he hadn't been around. Donna probably wouldn't be too happy with a fiancé who frequented a bar full of naked women, so he had stopped coming.

"Tanisha, this is Shorty," Donna said.

"Nice to meet you," I told him, wishing I could crawl into a hole somewhere far, far away. I was praying that he wouldn't recognize me with my conservative clothes on. My only other hope was that if he did recognize me, he would want to keep his mouth shut. It wouldn't be the easiest thing in the world to explain how he knew me.

Shorty's eyes widened when they met mine, so I knew I was busted. He shook my hand coldly. I didn't know if I was safe, but I know I nearly fainted when I saw Dante approaching us. Luckily, the two of them had their own issues to work through at the moment, so Shorty didn't say anything about me. My job would remain a secret for the time being. Now I would spend the rest of the night walking on eggshells around Shorty. I knew I had to tell Dante the truth, but I wanted to do it when I felt the time was right.

"Hey, man. Glad you could make it." Shorty held out his hand to Dante, who just looked at it, keeping his own hand in his pocket.

"I didn't come here for you. I came to support my sister," he muttered. Quickly directing Dante away from him, I made a mental note to try to speak to Shorty later in private. The last thing I needed was for him to blow up my spot before I could tell Dante about my past employment.

As we sat down to eat, Dante held out my chair, always the perfect gentleman. I felt like a queen, and though I was still distracted by Shorty's occasional glances, the rest of the evening went pretty well. I felt eyes on us, but not in a negative way. People at the table obviously loved the bishop and his family, so it was natural that they were curious about who his son had chosen.

I was determined to make a good impression on these people, so when they brought wine to the table, I politely declined. I was not about to make a fool out of myself if I had a little too much to drink. Dante's mother actually smiled at him when she heard me tell the waiter, "No, thank you." Dante patted my knee under the table, and I knew I had just scored a few brownie points with the first lady. It was going to be a hard battle, but maybe there was some hope yet. In fact, things went so well that a few people even asked Dante if we would be the next couple headed to the altar. I didn't know if that was definitely in our future, but if I could just convince Shorty to keep my secret, it might be possible. At the very least, I knew I would be attending the wedding with Dante tomorrow.

32

Donna

"Do you, John Tyrone Jefferson, take this woman, Madonna Marie Wilson, as your lawfully wedded wife? To have and to hold, to love and to cherish, until death do you part?" Reverend Tate asked Shorty.

"I do," Shorty replied, his voice quivering with emotion. His eyes, brimming with tears, never left mine.

"And do you, Madonna Marie Wilson, take this man, John Tyrone Jefferson, to be your lawfully wedded husband? To have and to hold, to love and to cherish, until death do you part?" My knees almost gave out on me as my brain tried to get the words "I do" out of my mouth. I tried again, but my mouth was listening to my heart, which was telling me to hold off for just a few more seconds, that Terrance was on his way to stop the wedding just like he'd promised.

"Madonna," Reverend Tate whispered.

I didn't look his way. I was staring at Shorty. Poor, sweet Shorty who was willing to marry me even though I didn't love him. *Come on, Terrance,* I thought, willing him to arrive. *You promised you would be here.*

I could feel RaShanda, my matron of honor, poking me in

the back, encouraging me to speak. I didn't even want to look at my parents, who were probably mortified by my hesitation. *Please, Terrance, if you're gonna come, you have to come now.* To my surprise, and the surprise of the nearly two hundred guests, a cry came from the back of the church.

"Stop the wedding! Stop the wedding!" When I turned to see who it was, my heart leaped. It was Terrance, just as he'd promised that day in Dante's office, and he was coming toward us in a hurry. "Stop the wedding, Reverend Tate!" he repeated as he climbed onto the altar. I could barely hold myself back. I wanted to jump right into his arms. He'd come for me, like this was a fairy tale.

The bishop rose from his seat and shouted, "Reynolds, what's going on here?"

"I love your daughter, Bishop, and the baby she's carrying is mine. Not his." He pointed at Shorty and there was a collective gasp from the crowd.

"Do you know what you're saying, man?" My father looked mortified.

Terrance reached for my hand. "Yes, I do. I'm saying that your daughter should be marrying me instead of him."

"But you're a married man," my mother protested. She looked like she was about to faint.

"Not anymore. I had my marriage annulled." He turned to me. "That's why it took so long for me to get down here. I was waiting for this FedEx envelope." He handed the bishop some papers.

"Dear Lord. You did have your wedding annulled," my father said as he examined the papers.

"Bishop, I love your daughter more than I love life itself. I want her to be my wife, so I'm asking you for her hand."

My father looked at me. "Is this what you want?"

"More than anything in the world, Daddy."

"Then who am I to stop you?" he said, and I immediately hugged him tightly. "We're going to have to wait a few more days for the license, but if Reverend Tate doesn't mind, we can still have the ceremony."

"What about me, Donna?" I'd completely forgotten about Shorty and his family. "Do you think I'm just gonna stand here while you marry him?"

"Shorty, I'm sorry." What else could I say?

"So am I," he said, turning toward Terrance. Shorty's neck muscles were bulging and I was sure there was going to be a fight. But out of nowhere Shorty turned back toward me and his hardened features softened into a forgiving smile. "I told you once before that if I really love you, then I'd want you to be happy above everything else. So if this is what will make you happy, then I won't stop you."

He was being so understanding. I bent down and gave him a kiss. "I love you, too, Shorty, as a brother."

"Donna! Donna! Wake your ass up!"

I could feel someone shaking me. I opened my eyes and saw RaShanda standing in front of me. Reality set in. It was a dream. It was only a damn dream. I was still getting married to Shorty, and Terrance wasn't coming.

"Girl, you better get up and get your dress on. The limo is here." I wiped my eyes, trying not to smudge my makeup.

"I was knocked out."

"Girl, I ain't never seen no one take a nap before their wedding."

"RaShanda, I just had the best dream." Just thinking about it made me smile.

"Well, stand up and tell me while you get into this dress. I told you not to take this thing off when the photographer left." She lifted my dress off the hanger and held it up so I could step into it.

I told her about my dream. "I was just about to say 'I do' when Terrance busted into the church and stopped the wedding."

"Stopped the wedding? What the hell'd he do that for?"

I stepped into the dress. "Because he loves me. What do you think?"

RaShanda pulled the dress up and stopped three-quarters of the way. "I hope you're not expecting that to happen today, 'cause if you do, you just wasting your time, on account of it ain't gonna happen."

I sighed. "I know, but it was a nice dream to think about. I hate that man and I love him at the same time."

"What about Shorty?"

"He's nice, but he's not what I want."

"Look, girl, you already said you were having second thoughts about getting married. If you don't wanna marry Shorty, then fuck it, don't. You know I got your back. My car's parked right out back. We can be in the wind in fifteen minutes."

It was scary, but I was actually contemplating RaShanda's offer. I liked Shorty, but I knew I didn't love him, and as long as I could remember, I always thought marriage was about love. I would have liked to think that it still was.

There was a knock on the door, interrupting my conversation with RaShanda.

"Yes?"

"Princess, it's me. Can I come in?"

"Just a minute, Bishop." I gestured for RaShanda to help me finish pulling up my dress and zipping me up. Then she opened the door for my father.

"Your mother and the other bridesmaids are already in the ca—" He stopped himself and stood motionless as he stared at me. "My, my, my, aren't you the prettiest sight I've ever seen."

"Daddy, are you just gonna stare at me or is there a reason you're here?"

"I'm here to tell you I love you." His eyes glistened with tears. "Today, I'm the proudest man on the face of the earth. And Shorty is the luckiest." He wrapped his arms around me, and right then and there I knew I was going to marry Shorty.

33

The First Lady

The sound of silverware clinking against glasses signaled another call for the bride and groom to share a newlywed kiss. I had been standing in the corner, watching our guests enjoying the reception, and I saw Shorty lean over to kiss Donna with such tenderness that I smiled in spite of the fact that I still couldn't believe I was now going to be calling him my son-in-law. Actually, I had been surprised by my own reactions throughout much of the day. For so many years I had seen him as nothing more than an annoying nuisance, poised to get Dante into trouble, but during the ceremony even my eyes got misty when I realized just how much Shorty clearly loved Donna.

When I first learned of Donna's engagement, it was devastating to think she had sunk so low as to actually be involved with someone of Shorty's caliber. I had always envisioned her falling in love and marrying the son of some distinguished member of the clergy or a high-powered member of the church. But in the two weeks between their announcement and the wedding, I had a chance to witness Shorty in a different light. When it came to Donna, he was so gentle and attentive. In many ways, he reminded me of the way T.K. had treated me when I was pregnant with Dante, and that memory warmed my heart. I had started to get a little worried at the dress shop when Donna confessed to having jitters. To be quite frank, I thought she was going to back out of the wedding, but now my mother's intuition told me that, with Shorty's love and a new baby, they'd have enough to hold them together until Donna realized she had a good man. And of course, I'd be there just in case she needed a nudge in the right direction.

Perhaps Shorty was not destined to greatness, perhaps he would always be working for the Department of Sanitation, but I was starting to think that, for Donna and her unborn child, love was a good place to start.

"Hey, Ma," Dante said as he approached me. "Look at you over here grinning. Proud of yourself, aren't you?" I didn't answer, but my smile widened as he leaned down and kissed my cheek. "You did a great job with this wedding, Ma. You should be proud."

"Thank you, son. The circumstances may not have been the best, but as your father said, we all had to rise to the occasion. I just hope one day Donna appreciates it."

Dante squeezed my hand. "She might not say it, but I know Donna really appreciated the work you did to make this all happen. She loves you, Ma."

"You think so?" I was touched by the thought.

"Ma, I know so." He rubbed my shoulders and pulled me closer to him.

My eyes misted over again and I tried to hide my face. "Now, stop it, Dante, before you make me ruin my makeup. I know your sister and I might not always see eye to eye, but that's only because I want the best for both of you."

"I know you do, Ma, and I love you for that." He leaned down and kissed my forehead. "Hey, see you in a little bit. I'm going to run to the bathroom and then see if I can find Tanisha in the lobby. I think she's a little overwhelmed by all the attention. You know some of these people in here can get a little too nosy."

"Who you telling? Sister Dunbar has already asked me when we planned on having your wedding. It seems that Miss Tanisha has made quite an impression on a few folks tonight. Tell her to keep up the good work. If she wants to spend time with this family, she's going to have to keep up appearances."

Dante raised his eyebrows; he looked shocked. It was understandable, though. I certainly hadn't been kind to Tanisha the first night we met, so I'm sure he was waiting for some more harsh words about her now.

"Why are you staring at me like that?" I asked with mock insult.

He smiled. "You're starting to like her, aren't you?"

I gave him a half smile then looked in the opposite direction. "I might be changing my opinion of her just as long as she doesn't try and stop you from going to seminary. People are entitled to change their opinions, aren't they?"

"Yes, they are." He continued to stare at me. "It's just that I'm not used to seeing you do it. It's weird enough to see you accepting Shorty, but now to hear that you're changing your opinion of Tanisha, I'm not sure what's going on. You're not drunk, are you? How much champagne have you had tonight, anyway?" he teased.

"Be quiet, boy." I pushed him away from me playfully then smoothed my skirt and put on my best first lady face. "Stop teasing your mother and go to the bathroom so you can find your date. Tomorrow at church I don't wanna hear about her being seen spending time with someone else. That would probably change my opinion of her again."

"Okay, Ma, but don't forget to save me a dance. I'll be back." He kissed me again and left.

I watched him cross the room. He glanced at Shorty and Donna, and I was happy to see his face didn't fold into a frown. Ever since he had found out that Shorty was the father of Donna's baby, he hadn't been able to even be in the same room with him. I guess he had felt as betrayed as I had felt disappointed. Perhaps he was seeing the same thing I was now—Shorty's devotion to Donna.

I noticed that I wasn't the only one whose eyes were on my handsome son as he went toward the lobby. Quiet a few of the young ladies in attendance were watching him, too. Dante had always been popular among the young women of the church, and even many of their mothers, who would be more than happy to marry their daughters off to the son of the bishop. But there was one woman in particular watching him who had no business staring at my son at all. Anita Emerson was a married woman, yet she was eyeing Dante like he was a glass of cool water and she'd been lost in the desert and needed a drink. When she got up from the table and gave her husband a peck on the cheek before making her own way to the lobby, I had seen enough.

I crossed the reception hall and went straight to the lobby to check on things myself. There were several guests standing around in the lobby, but I didn't see Dante, Tanisha, or Anita anywhere. I decided to check outside. Some of the guests were stepping out to enjoy the cool evening air. Maybe Dante had gone out there to look for Tanisha.

When I exited the hotel, I didn't see Dante, but I spotted Tanisha right away. She was standing at the other end of the building, and it looked like she was in a heated conversation with Anita. I wasn't close enough to hear what they were saying, but it wasn't hard to read their body language and know that this was no polite banter between my son's girlfriend and the deacon's wife. I headed toward them.

As I got closer, I heard Anita saying, "You better think about what I'm saying. Don't nobody want you here. I heard the first lady tell the bishop she wanted your ass outta here, so if I was you, I would get to steppin' before you embarrass yourself and Dante."

Oh no, she didn't, I thought. Nobody speaks for me but me, and I was about to let her know it.

"I'm not going anywhe—" I placed my hand on Tanisha's shoulder, greeting her with a smile.

"Excuse me, Tanisha. Do you think I could speak to Sister Emerson alone for a minute? It's church business."

Both of them looked shocked to see me, but I also saw a look of relief pass across Tanisha's face.

"No problem, First Lady Wilson. Anita and I were just finishing our conversation. Weren't we, Anita?" Anita didn't say a word.

"Oh, by the way, Tanisha, you don't have a problem with Dante going to seminary, do you?"

"No, ma'am, that's between him and God."

"Good, I think Dante's looking for you. He said something about wanting to dance."

"Oh, okay, thanks. I'll go find him right away." She smirked at Anita. "Have . . . a nice night, Anita. I know I will."

Once Tanisha was far enough away, I said, "Why don't we step over here around the corner, Sister Emerson?"

"Actually, First Lady, it's getting a little breezy out here. Maybe we should talk inside?" She couldn't hide the fear in her eyes, and I wanted to laugh. She knew I had heard her threatening Tanisha, and she knew there was no way out now. She tried to walk past me. I put my arm up to stop her.

"No, I think you'll prefer to be out here where no one can hear us."

She looked toward the entrance as if someone might be there to rescue her, but we were alone. She sighed and followed me around the side of the building. I wasted no time putting her in her place.

"Anita, I'm going to say something I should have told you a long time ago." I delivered the words slowly and clearly, so there would be no mistaking the seriousness of my message. "Stay away from my son and his girlfriend."

She still had the nerve to try to play dumb.

"I don't understand, First Lady. We were just talking." She gave a nervous laugh.

"What's not to understand? I said stay away from my son and his girlfriend." I took a step closer and got in her face. "Do you understand now?"

"Yes, First Lady, but I'm not the one you should be concerned with. That girl is. You don't know her background. She's not good for Dante and she's not good for the church." I'm sure the second she mentioned the church, she expected me to back off.

"And I guess you and him are better for the church?"

"Well, yes . . . I mean no . . . I mean . . . I'm a married woman. I don't want you to get the wrong idea. Me and Dante, we're just good friends. I don't wanna see him get hurt."

"Is that right? So, were you just good friends all those times you were in his office with the door locked? What about those times before he had a car and you used to drop him off at the house at three and four o'clock in the morning?"

"I . . ." Her mouth opened and she tried to speak, but after the first word she froze.

"That's right, Anita. I know about you and Dante, so don't bother to try and lie your way out of this one. Did you really think that you could have an affair with my son for two years and I wouldn't know about it? I'm the first lady, Anita. You of all people should have known that nothing happens inside that church without my knowledge. And I mean nothing."

"You knew?" she asked, sounding both embarrassed and horrified.

"Of course I knew. I also knew that Dante was becoming a man, and I wasn't going to be able to stop him from sowing his oats. I figured that at least with you I wouldn't have to worry as much. Some of these young girls out here will get pregnant in a heartbeat to trap a man, but I figured you wouldn't do that. You had too much to lose, seeing as how you were the bishop's secretary and so much older than Dante. You would have been thrown out of the church in the blink of an eye."

She still had nothing to say, so I continued.

"You do know I pushed the deacon to ask you to marry him, don't you? And you were so predictable. I just knew you wouldn't be able to resist his money and you couldn't, could you? You don't know how relieved I was when you got married and moved to Florida, putting an end to your little fling with Dante."

I must have struck a nerve, because she finally spoke, sounding indignant. "It wasn't just a fling!"

"Wasn't it? What else would you call something you had to hide? But it doesn't matter now anyway, does it, because you're going to leave him alone. My son isn't interested in you anymore, Anita. He's moved on, and I suggest you do the same."

"Oh, please," she spat. "You can't possibly approve of that, that . . . relationship."

"Whether I do or not, it's none of your business, Anita."

"Oh, I think you might be happy that I made it my business when I tell you what I found out about that girl. The girl's a tramp. Don't let that cheap suit fool you. That little hood rat is a—"

I put my hand up to stop her. "You let me worry about Tanisha. She's my problem, not yours. But let's put it this way: Whatever she is, I approve of her a lot more than I approve of you. Besides, you've got bigger things to worry about, like what you're going to do if I tell Deacon Emerson about your obsession with my son. Did you know he still keeps your naked pictures with his old baseball cards? Wouldn't Deacon Emerson love to see them?"

"You wouldn't dare," she said angrily.

"I wouldn't? Actually, Anita, you have no idea what I'm capable of, do you? I've ruined much better people's lives than yours. But I will tell you this—I will do whatever it takes to protect my son, and that includes whipping your ass with my own two hands if necessary. Do I make myself clear?" I reached up and took off one earring then the other. The look of shock followed by the look of defeat on her face was just what I had intended.

"You're making a big mistake. When you find out the truth about Tanisha, you'll *wish* Dante had stayed with me," she said before storming off.

I put my earrings back on before I came around the side of the building and headed back to the reception. I didn't want to be seen walking back into the hotel anywhere near Anita. The look on her face was enough to get even the most pious church members gossiping.

I was satisfied that Anita had gotten my message when I entered the lobby and saw Deacon Emerson waiting at the coat check area.

"Deacon," I said as I approached him. "Leaving already?"

"Yes, I'm afraid Anita isn't feeling well. Once she comes out of the ladies' room, I'm taking her home."

"Oh, I'm sorry to hear that." I gave him a sympathetic gaze, though I wanted to laugh. "Well, thank you so much for coming. I'll see you tomorrow at church."

"I sure hope so. It all depends on how well Anita feels in the morning."

"Of course," I answered as I patted his hand. "You take care now, Deacon." I waited until I turned my back to him before I allowed myself to smile. I was sure Anita would not be feeling well enough to attend services in the morning. And she'd be feeling even worse once I figured out a way to convince T.K. that she needed to be removed from her job as his secretary. Like I said, I would do anything for my son.

34

Shorty

It was almost one o'clock in the morning when I struggled to carry Donna over the threshold of our honeymoon suite at the Long Island Marriott. Somehow we had gotten through the two weeks since she'd announced our engagement, and we'd made it to the wedding. Poor Donna had been so stressed that at times I wondered if she was really going to meet me at the altar, but she kept reassuring me that she was fine. She told me that her mood swings were related to the pregnancy, and the nervousness was just because of the pressure she was feeling to get married so quickly.

At the time I worried that she was really still harboring feelings for Reverend Reynolds. After all, it wasn't even a month ago that she was in my house telling me how certain she was that he would marry her once he found out about the baby. Again, she was reassuring, telling me that she was over him and ready to move on. All I could do was hope she was telling me the truth and show her in as many ways as possible that I loved her with all my heart. Apparently she was starting to believe it, because she held my arm tightly and rolled her eyes at that piece of shit Reverend Reynolds when he and his wife came up to congratulate us at the reception. He really had some nerve showing up at all.

Now that the stress of the ceremony and the reception was over, I was happy to get back to the room with Donna. As strange as the circumstances of our marriage were, I couldn't wait to spend a lifetime with her. Tonight was our first night together as husband and wife, and I was hoping that Donna would be more relaxed now that the wedding was behind us. Of course, I was also looking forward to consummating the marriage. Ooh, I couldn't wait. I figured I wouldn't have to use a condom since she was already pregnant, and we were both HIV negative when we did the blood tests for the marriage license.

After I carried Donna across the threshold, she sat on the bed and started to slip her wedding gown off her shoulders. She seemed limp with exhaustion. I was pretty darn tired, too. Getting married was a lot more stressful than you would think. I had already ordered a bottle of sparkling cider instead of champagne for the room since Donna couldn't have alcohol while she was pregnant. I wanted to share a toast to our wedding night before we made love for the very first time.

I was a little funky from all the dancing, so I decided to jump in the shower real quick before we got down to business. I soaped my body down in the shower, whistling the whole time. This had to be the happiest day of my life. After years of wanting her, I was finally going to make love to Donna. I knew I had to be careful with her being pregnant and all, so I decided I would take it slow. That was going to be hard, seeing as how I'd fantasized about this moment since we were teens.

I dried off with the thick towels the hotel provided, then eased into the bedroom part of our suite, the towel wrapped around my waist. Donna was stretched out across the silk comforter, snoring loudly. I noticed she was still wearing her slip. The little bulge beneath her navel warmed my heart.

"Our baby," I said out loud to get used to the sound, then I nudged her gently.

"Baby, wake up."

Donna mumbled sleepily, "Ten more minutes, Ma. I promise I'll get up in ten more minutes."

"Honey, it's me. Shorty."

She opened her eyes halfway. "Shorty, what you want? I'm tired."

"I want you. Wake up. It's our wedding night." I ran my hand across her body.

"Stop." She slapped my hand away.

"Come on, Donna. Wake up. I'll be gentle."

"No, Shorty, I'm pooped. This has been a long day."

"I know. I'll make it quick." I was reduced to pleading. This wasn't exactly the romantic wedding night I had imagined.

"No, I'm tired." She rolled over.

"Donna, you promised."

"Let's do it tomorrow," she whined, half asleep.

I shook my head and smiled at my bride. "Okay, slide under the covers."

I tucked her in, and she was back to sleep as soon as her head hit the pillow. I smiled at my sleeping beauty, then kissed her on the forehead. As much as I hated to wait one more day to make love to Donna, I was elated at the thought that I had the rest of my life to be with her.

Tomorrow, it was on. Only what was I gonna do now? After a shower and the anticipation of getting some, I was now wide awake. I decided I would go down to the hotel lounge and have a drink by myself. As soon as I entered the lounge, I spotted Dante. I hesitated to greet him at first, seeing as how we had just fought a couple of days before the wedding. I must admit, though, he did act cordial all throughout the wedding events. I headed for the bar, thinking maybe I would speak to him after a while. To my surprise, he rose, strolled over, and met me at the bar.

"I think we should talk," he said.

"Look, Dante, I'm not trying to fight with you. It's my wedding day. Last time you wanted to talk, you punched me in the eye."

"I'm sorry, Shorty. Things got a little out of hand. Let me buy you a drink and make it up to you."

"Aw'ight," I said tentatively. I wasn't sure what he was up to. After last week I'd learned not to assume Dante would control himself, even if we were in a public place.

"Man, I really hated you at first, but after seeing how happy you were today, I think I was wrong. You really love my sister, don't you?"

"Yeah, I really do, man."

"You know, I'm starting to believe you." We did the brother handshake followed by a hug. "You're not just my friend anymore, Shorty. You're my brother now."

"D, man, I feel the same way."

I couldn't find the words to tell him how thankful I was that we were friends again, but I could tell by the look on his face that he already knew.

I felt relieved to know I now had Dante's blessings. I ordered a shot of cognac.

"Where's Donna, man?"

"She's upstairs 'sleep. With the baby and everything, she's exhausted. I tucked her in and she was calling the hogs before I could leave the room. I thought I'd just come down and have a drink before I go to bed."

Dante stood to leave. "Yeah, I probably should get upstairs myself. My parents think I brought Tanisha home, but she's up in my room waiting for me. I better get up there before she falls asleep. Yo, I'm in Room 1206. Come check me in the morning. We can all have breakfast."

"Aw'ight. I'm right down the hall in 1276, the honeymoon suite." He started to walk away. "Hey, Dante, you really like her, don't you?"

I had been wrestling with my conscience ever since I'd

met Tanisha at the rehearsal dinner. Dante obviously cared a lot about this woman, and I didn't know if it was my place to tell him what I knew about her. On the one hand, I knew she wasn't exactly the kind of woman his parents would approve of. Maybe it would be best for me to tell him so he could decide what to do about it before the news somehow got to his parents. On the other hand, maybe he wouldn't care what his parents thought. After all, he had remained a true friend to me no matter how many times his mother tried to convince him how bad I was. Maybe I was better off staying out of it, especially since our friendship was more than a little fragile right now. Unfortunately, he must have sensed something in my body language or the way I asked my question, because now he knew something was wrong.

"Yeah, I do. Why?" he asked with suspicion.

It felt too late to turn back now. I had to tell him and just hope that I wasn't breaking the very fine threads that were holding together our friendship at the moment.

"As your brother, I have something I think you need to know."

The grimace that came across his face told me that he was thinking the worst. He asked, "You slept with her, didn't you?"

"No, but I've seen her naked."

Suddenly his chest seemed to inflate and he wore the same expression I'd seen before he hit me last week.

"What the fuck is that supposed to mean?"

"She's a stripper, Dante. I seen her working at Scandalous." My body tensed as I prepared for him to hit me. The blow never came.

"Shorty, what are you saying? Are you sure it's her and not someone who looks like her?"

"Yeah, I'm sure. I wish I wasn't. I don't go there anymore now that I'm with Donna, but I've had my share of lap dances with her. She recognized me, too, the night of the rehearsal dinner. I would have told you sooner, but we weren't exactly on the best terms lately."

Dante looked crushed. "Shorty, I was going to ask her to marry me tonight."

I wished I could take back the news I had given him. At the very least I wanted to think of some words that might ease the pain he was obviously feeling. Instead, I felt power-less to do anything but watch as he jumped out of his seat and announced, "I gotta go, Shorty."

"You gonna be okay?"

"I don't know, but I know things aren't gonna be the same between me and Tanisha if what you said is true." He strode out of the bar like a man on a mission.

35

Tanisha

I'd been waiting anxiously for Dante to come upstairs from the bar, where he had gone to talk to a few of his friends after Donna and Shorty's reception. Before he left the room, I reminded him that he might want to hurry back so I could show him how much I appreciated him taking me to the wedding. Things had gone pretty smoothly as far as I was concerned, and now that I thought about it, it made sense. This was Donna's day, so the first lady was much too wrapped up in the details of the wedding and the reception to have time to scrutinize me. For that I was thankful, and hopeful that things could only get better between us. Who knows? Someday she might actually come to accept me enough to treat me like a person worthy of being in her presence.

Shorty, of course, was much too caught up in his new bride to give me any thought. I stood in line to congratulate the new couple, and though his greeting was chilly, he left me alone after that. In fact, I don't think I noticed him looking my way one time. He was too busy gazing adoringly at Donna.

As an added bonus, Anita and her husband were seated far away from me, at the deacon's table on the other side of the reception hall. Though she glared at me every chance she got, I made sure to never head to the ladies' room alone. When I needed to go, I just waited for one of the other women at the table to excuse herself, and then I followed. I figured that as long as I wasn't alone, Anita wouldn't dare confront me. She had a lot to lose if her obsession with Dante became public knowledge. She had a husband and a job to hold on to, and though she was a huge pain in my ass, Anita was not stupid. So while she sat at her table and sulked in silence every time she watched Dante kiss me, I had a great time.

The ceremony was beautiful, and Shorty was so obviously in love with Donna. His face glowed every time he looked at her. I don't know, maybe I was wrong, but Donna didn't seem quite as overjoyed. When they kissed after the minister said, "You may now kiss the bride," I noticed Donna seemed a little hesitant. She was the first to pull away from their embrace. Oh well, she was pregnant, and pregnant women can be moody. Still, if it were me up there getting married to Dante, they would have to pry me out of his arms when the groom kissed the bride. I was really feeling him, and the way he had treated me this weekend just intensified my feelings. That's why I couldn't wait for him to get back to the room to experience some of my gratitude.

I took a shower and slipped into this cute little red Victoria's Secret number I had bought the other night. I sprayed on my favorite perfume, Tresor, then slipped under the covers, waiting for my prince to awaken his sleeping beauty. About ten minutes later I heard Dante using the electronic key card at the door. As soon as the door swung open, I saw Dante's face, and it looked like he was enveloped in a dark storm cloud. He gave me the most vicious sneer I had ever seen. He came over to the bed, but instead of taking his clothes off like I had hoped, he pulled the covers back, snatched me by the arm, and lifted me up out of the bed.

I screamed. I had never realized how strong Dante was, and I had never seen this side of him. Actually, I was afraid he was going to hit me. His face was directly in front of mine. His eyes were bulging out and his teeth were clenched.

"Are you . . . are you a stripper? Are you a fucking stripper?"

Shorty had gotten to him before I could. I didn't know what to say. "How—Wha—Who told you that?"

"No, answer my question. Straight up, are you a stripper?" For the first time since we'd met, he was reminding me of the way I was treated by the other guys I had dated before him. "Answer me, dammit!"

"I used to be. I'm not doing it anymore. You're hurting me, Dante."

He let go of me and turned his back, walking toward the window.

"I can't believe this. Why the hell didn't you tell me?"

"Dante, please. You know I had to take care of my family."

"Oh my God. Ain't this a blip? My father is running for office, and here I am dating a stripper. Everything I thought I knew about you was a lie."

I couldn't believe what I was hearing. This man had stuck by me even after he found out my mother was a crackhead, helped me get my brother out of foster care, and insisted over and over that he didn't care what his mother or anyone else thought about me. Told me he loved me just the way I was. I thought I had truly met Prince Charming, and he made me feel like a princess. Yet here he was now, talking to me like a piece of dirt, telling me that what I did for a living mattered to him above all else. I was hurt more deeply than I could ever have imagined.

Beyond my pain, though, I was scared. Dante looked so

angry I didn't know what to do. To hide my fear, I got defensive. "What did you think about me? You knew I lived in the projects. You knew I worked in a club."

"I didn't know it was a strip club. I thought you worked as a barmaid. I didn't know you were taking off your clothes!"

"I was a barmaid. I was just topless while I was doing it," I protested, though I knew that wouldn't make any difference to him.

"Why didn't you tell me?" he demanded to know.

"I was scared, Dante. I just needed more time before I felt I could say anything. It's not like I was proud of what I was doing."

"So you thought it would be okay to string the preacher's son along until *you* felt the time was right? You didn't think I deserved to know this and make my own decisions?"

"Would you have accepted it if I had told you, Dante?"

He remained silent, which told me everything I needed to know. Despite all of his sweet talk, he was just as judgmental as his damn mother.

"The point is I'm not doing it now. I'm getting ready to start school. I'm getting my life together. I can't change who I've been, so if you can't accept my past, then I don't know what to tell you."

Dante looked at me in disgust, then spun around and left the room, slamming the door behind him. I fell upon the bed and cried like I had never cried before. I loved Dante and I had hoped he was going to ask me to marry him someday, but now everything had fallen apart. I didn't know who to blame. Was it my mother's fault for leaving me to fend for myself and my brother while she was out getting high? If she had given me a more secure home, maybe I wouldn't have taken the path I did to survive.

Maybe it was Shorty's fault for not minding his own damn business.

No, I couldn't blame Shorty. I was the one who had purposely chosen to keep this secret from Dante. It should have been my responsibility to let him know the truth before someone else did.

Maybe, though, Dante held some of the blame in this whole mess. After all, he had me believing he was Prince Charming. I thought I could feel secure in his love for me, but he had just proven me so very wrong. Maybe we all shared some blame, but none of that really mattered to me as I lay on the bed sobbing. I'd just lost the best man I'd ever had, and the only one I'd ever truly loved.

36

Donna

The sun was blazing in the room when I woke up. I had no concept of what time it was or where I was. I just wanted to find the bathroom so I could pee. That's when I realized Shorty was in the bed with me. At first I was confused, then it hit me. *Fool, you married him.* The events of my wedding day reeled across my mind in a blur.

When I'd put on my gown and veil and seen my reflection in the mirror, it had finally started to feel real to me. I was the bride, and a hundred and fifty guests were waiting to see me walk down the aisle. My father had just come in to tell me how much he loved me. It was too late for me to back out now, so I did my best to forget about the dream I'd just had. This was no fairy tale I was living; Terrance wasn't going to come and stop the wedding. He had proven himself to be a lying, selfish son of a bitch, and I knew I would be better off when I was finally able to acknowledge that fact and move on. Eventually I would learn to accept and maybe even be happy about being married to Shorty.

When my father escorted me down the aisle, all the guests stood to watch and welcome me. I had seen this tradition many times before, but this time I was overwhelmed. Their smiles and good wishes were for me; this was my day. For a brief time, I was able to forget about all the drama and heartache leading up to this day and just bask in the glow of being the bride. Even my mother, when I approached the front pew where she sat, reached out and squeezed my hand. She looked ready to cry, just like my father. Then I saw Shorty.

He was waiting for me at the altar, looking so handsome in his tuxedo. His eyes locked on mine, and I felt his adoration so powerfully that I just froze. As he stood up there waiting eagerly for his bride, a pang of guilt shot through me. I knew I couldn't give him more than the tiniest bit of my heart, which felt locked in a steel cage ever since Terrance had hurt me, but Shorty was giving his love so generously. It wasn't fair to him, and I was the one to blame.

I wanted to turn and run from the church, but my feet wouldn't move. My father put his hand on my shoulder and turned me toward him, bringing me back to reality. I had gone too far to turn back now, and as much as I couldn't give Shorty my whole heart, I knew it might hurt him even more if I left him here at the altar.

"I love you, Donna," my father said as he lifted the veil off my face and kissed me.

I made it through the rest of the ceremony as if I was a puppet. I responded to the reverend's questions and repeated after him in all the appropriate places, but my body was numb and my mind was blank. There was a momentary feeling of panic when he said, "You may now kiss the bride," but I performed my duty then also, and before I knew it, I was Shorty's wife.

The reception was a blur. I stood with Shorty to greet the guests in the receiving line, and though their congratulations were genuine, most of the time I was too numb to even recognize who I was talking to. I wished that could have been the case when I looked down the line and saw Terrance approaching with his new wife. My knees got weak and my stomach felt like a volcano, but Shorty sensed my anxiety and held me closer to keep me from falling on the floor. It took every ounce of strength I had not to spit in Terrance's face when he told us how happy he was for us. Shorty managed to shake his hand instead of punching his face, then we both turned away to greet the next guests in line.

Terrance had enough sense to stay away from me for the rest of the night, but it was still emotionally draining for me to even know that he was in the room. That, along with the fact that I had to pretend to be so happy in front of my family and the guests, left me completely exhausted. By the time Shorty carried me over the threshold of our honeymoon suite, I barely had enough energy to remove my gown before I was asleep.

It was probably better that I had passed out, because I don't think I could have faced Shorty. He was obviously ready to consummate our marriage, and my emotions were too raw to even face that issue. I knew I wasn't ready, but now that the sun was shining into our suite on our first day as a married couple, I couldn't avoid it forever.

I slipped into the bathroom, wishing I could turn back time to before I got pregnant, but my body wouldn't let me even pretend that was possible. My breasts were sore, my stomach cramped, not to mention the fact that I felt like I was going to throw up. This was not a good way to start what I knew was going to be another rough day.

When I came out of the bathroom, I looked around for the first time and savored the beautiful décor of the suite. We had a large bedroom as well as a living room area with a fireplace. I went to the large picture window and looked out at the beautiful New York City skyline. The view was awesome.

"Hey, Sleeping Beauty."

I jumped with a start. Shorty was awake.

"Hey." I waved from the window.

"Come over here and give your new husband some sugar." He held out his arms to me.

I walked to him and gave him a hug, feeling again the guilt I had experienced at the altar. I just did not love him the way a woman should love her husband, and I wasn't sure that kind of passion was something you could learn to feel. Either it was there at the beginning or it wasn't. I was afraid I was destined to a lifetime of feeling unfulfilled, and that I was offering the same kind of life to Shorty.

For the time being, though, he seemed oblivious to the road we had ahead of us. He leaned in to kiss me, but I pulled away.

"Shorty, I haven't even brushed my teeth."

"I don't care about that. You're my wife. You can kiss me with the worst halitosis."

"Well, I do care." I ran my hand through my hair. "God, I must look a mess. I slept in my clothes. Why didn't you wake me up?"

"Baby, you were out for the count. Wasn't any waking you up. Trust me."

My stomach started to growl, more from nerves than anything else, but I used the excuse to buy some more time. "I'm hungry, Shorty. I need to get something to eat."

"Aw'ight. I forgot you're eating for two. Let me order room service. I'd like to feed you breakfast in bed." He was so accommodating, and it only made my guilt more intense. It was obvious that he was happy we were married. I wished that I could be feeling the same way, but happy was so far from my true feelings.

When the room service cart arrived, Shorty propped up the pillows and put the small serving table before me. He cut up my pancakes and my omelet, then fed me lovingly. I managed to relax a little, and we played around and teased each other throughout the whole breakfast. It reminded me of how well we used to get along before I met Terrance and my life became so complicated. I hoped that one day I might be able to put my past behind me and just accept Shorty's love.

After he finished eating his breakfast, he became serious. "Donna, you know we haven't consummated this marriage. You promised when we were married you'd—"

I lifted my hand, cutting him off, then swallowed. "I know what I promised, Shorty. Just let me go take a shower first. Then I'm all yours."

I think he had to work very hard to keep a grin off his face at that point. I got up from the bed and walked to the shower.

The whole time I was in the shower, my stomach was in knots. Though we got along well and I appreciated Shorty's generosity toward me, I just couldn't imagine myself making love to him. Those feelings just were not there, but once I stepped out the bathroom, I was going to have to grin and bear it. Hopefully, he'd be quick so I could be done with it. I stepped out of the shower, dreading what I knew I had to go in the bedroom and do. It turned out, though, that I wouldn't have to do it that day, because when I looked down, the drops of water on my thigh were mixed with a trail of blood. I let out a terrified scream.

37

The First Lady

It had been a while since T.K. and I had made love, so I must admit I was smiling as I made his breakfast. Lord, did I love that man, and last night he showed me just how much he loved me, too. It was so nice to have the kids out of the house so we could spend some intimate time together. I spent more time with T.K. in a week than most women spent with their husbands in a month, but I couldn't remember the last time we were in the house alone without worrying when or if one of the children would be home. Who knows, though? Now that Donna and Shorty were married and Dante was spending so much time with Tanisha, perhaps I'd be able to get to know my husband in a much more intimate way again.

"Hey, Ma." I looked up to see Dante enter the kitchen wearing pajamas. He surprised me. I had no idea he was even in the house. *Lord, I hope he didn't hear me screaming last night.*

"Good morning, Dante. Would you like some eggs?" I tried to keep up my usually calm demeanor.

"No, thanks. I'm just gonna have some coffee." He took a

mug from the cupboard and poured himself some coffee from the pot on the counter before sitting at the table. I didn't mention it, but he looked like something was troubling him. I was praying that it wasn't the fact that he had heard his parents making love last night. "Where's the bishop?" he asked.

"He's upstairs getting dressed for church. When did you get home? I didn't hear you come in."

" 'Bout three."

I glanced at the ceiling and said a quick thanks because by that time T.K. and I had finished making love and were asleep. "I thought you were spending the night at the hotel with the rest of your friends."

"I was, but I decided I wasn't really in the mood to celebrate, so I came home."

"I hope you're not still angry at Shorty, are you? He's a part of the family now, and sooner or later you're going to have to speak to him. Otherwise there are going to be some very quiet Sunday dinners around here."

"No, it's not that, Ma. Believe it or not, Shorty and I made up last night. I don't have no beef with him. I have some other things on my mind." He rubbed his eyes.

"Well, maybe I have some news that'll cheer you up." I sat down in the chair next to him.

"I doubt it," he answered.

"Oh, just listen for a second. You might just get a kick out of what I have to tell you." I put down my coffee mug and smiled.

He sighed as if nothing I could say would cheer him up. "Go ahead, Ma."

"I had a little talk with Anita Emerson last night," I said, waiting for his response.

His eyes became dark and serious. I had his attention now. Anita must have been more of a pain in his ass than I thought. "About what?"

"About you. I don't think she'll be bothering you or Tanisha anymore."

He tilted his head and stared at me silently, probably unsure how to respond.

"Dante? Did you hear me? She not going to bother you anymore."

"What do you mean, bother me?"

I gave him a patronizing smile. "It's okay, son. You don't have to pretend anymore. I know all about you and Anita."

He almost dropped his cup of coffee. "You knew?"

"Don't look so surprised." I grinned. "A mother's supposed to know these things."

"Mom—I . . ." He couldn't even finish his sentence. I don't think that in a million years he would have thought I knew about him and Anita. Like Anita, he must have thought they were so thorough. "How long did you know?"

"Long enough to know you two were pretty serious for a while."

"If you knew, why didn't you say something?"

I hesitated for a second. "What, and drive you into her arms further? No, thank you. You thought you were in love, Dante, but I knew it was only a matter of time before you'd split up, especially with Deacon Emerson around, so I just sat back and waited."

"What do you mean? How'd you know she'd choose Deacon Emerson over me? I thought she loved me."

"I think she did. But you were missing one key element that a woman like Anita needs—security. When faced with love or security, an older woman will take security every time. She wants to feel like she's being taken care of, and you were a young college student. You couldn't give her that, Dante."

"So you're saying that her marrying Deacon Emerson had absolutely nothing to do with love?"

I knew my words were hurting him, but he had to hear the truth.

"Yes, that's what I'm saying. She chose him for security.

Maybe she figured she could learn to love him later. And from what I can see, she has."

"So why is she after me now?"

"Plain and simple—sex. Anita is thirty-five years old. She's in her sexual prime. Ain't no way old-behind Deacon Emerson can compete with a twenty-two-year-old man, even with Viagra. She wants the best of both worlds. But believe me, she's not leaving him."

Dante shook his head. "You know, Ma, maybe you're a better judge of character than I thought, because that is all she seemed to want. Did the bishop know?"

"No, that's one of the few things I've kept from him over the years. Why don't we keep this as our little secret, huh?"

"Sure, Ma . . . I still can't believe you knew. You're a lot cooler than I thought, you know that?" He smiled for the first time.

"I'll take that as a compliment."

"You should," he said. "I'm also glad you let things run their natural course with Anita. If you had interfered, I would have never known that woman has some real issues. I mean, can you imagine if I had ended up marrying her?"

"Let's not even go there, Dante. Just be happy that now she won't be bothering you with those issues. Not after the conversation we had last night. I'm certain she'll leave you alone so that you and Tanisha can be together."

A frown took over Dante's face at the mention of Tanisha's name. Something was obviously wrong between them.

"Me and Tanisha?" He let out a bitter laugh. "Me and Tanisha are as over as me and Anita."

"What are you talking about? I thought you really cared about her." I gave him a curt look. "Besides, I'm just starting to like her, and you know your father does too."

"I did care for her. I do care for her. Ma, I was gonna ask her to marry me," he admitted, which stunned me, "but I just found out she's a . . ." He turned his face away from me as he said, "She was a stripper."

"Is a stripper or was a stripper? I was told she stopped."

He turned his head quickly toward me. "What did you say?"

I'd paid a lot of money to have Tanisha checked out, and all my sources said she had stopped stripping. Of course, Dante didn't need to know I'd "researched" his girlfriend, so I conveniently avoided that information. His expression told me he already understood that I had done it, so I decided there was no reason to discuss it. "I said, is she still stripping?"

"I don't think so."

I let out a sigh. "Then what's the problem?"

"What did you say?" He raised his eyebrows and asked again in utter amazement. "Ma, are you saying you knew about Tanisha's job and you're still telling me to be with her?"

"That's exactly what I'm telling you, Dante. Believe it or not, I've learned a few things lately. Better yet, I've remembered some things I'd forgotten."

"Like what?"

"Well, I've spent a lot of years worrying about keeping up appearances for myself and this family. That's why when Donna got pregnant, it was so hard for me to forgive her. Your father was able to forgive her right away, but I was too busy worrying about what people would think. Then yesterday at the wedding I saw just how much Shorty adores her, flaws and all, and I saw how many other people at that wedding were happy for the two of them. Sure, some people will still gossip when Donna's baby comes sooner than nine months, but in the end, as long as she and Shorty are a loving couple and good parents, people will eventually forget mistakes they made in the past."

"I hope you're right, Momma. But what does that have to

do with Tanisha? Aren't you worried that my dating her
would wreck the bishop's chances in the election?"

"You did say that she *used* to work in that place, right?"

"Yeah. She stopped when she got custody of her brother,
but—"

I cut him off. "Don't worry about the election. We'll find
some way to spin it in our favor if her background comes
out. I can see the headline now: 'Bishop Wilson's Son Dates
Ex-Stripper Who Reformed Her Life.' "

"But what about me? I just don't know if I can forget that
she was working there."

I reached out and placed my hand on his. "Dante, we all
make mistakes. I've made some of the biggest. What she did
in the past isn't all she is. What really matters is what she
plans to do with her life from this day forward. If you really
love Tanisha, then I think you should work this out."

"Momma, I don't even know what to say right now. You
were always telling me to choose my friends more wisely.
You hated Shorty because he didn't come from the same
background as us. Now all of a sudden you're telling me to
forget Tanisha's past and stay with her. It just doesn't make
sense."

"Like I said, Dante, I remembered some things that were
important, and it may seem a little late to you, but I still want
you to learn from my mistakes. Don't do what I've done for
so many years. Don't worry about what other people might
think. Let your heart guide you."

"You know, Momma," he finally said, "I think you might
be right. But I want you to tell me something, and be completely honest."

"What is it?"

"If Tanisha and I can get through this, I want to ask her to
marry me. I know you're saying you've turned over a new
leaf or whatever, but are you sure—I mean really sure—that
you aren't gonna all of a sudden freak out about the bishop's
campaign and change your mind about her?"

I laughed and looked at him affectionately. "You know, Dante, I might actually enjoy planning another wedding. I'm pretty good at it, if I do say so myself."

He hugged me. "You know, Ma, I'm starting to like the kinder and gentler you."

When he released me, I looked at my son as a man for the first time. "Well, I should be getting ready to get to church. Before I go, though, I'd like to give you something."

"What is it?" I asked.

"It's a ring. It belonged to my great-aunt Elizabeth, and I've been keeping it for years, hoping to give it to one of my children someday. Shorty insisted on buying Donna's ring, so I couldn't give it to her. I want you to have it, so that when the time is right, you can give it to Tanisha or some other girl."

"Ma, you really have changed."

"No, son, I've just realized that you and your sister have grown up and there's nothing I can do to stop it. So I might as well accept it. I guess it's time for me to stop thinking about being a mother and start thinking about being a grandmother."

38

Dante

My mother left the room to get the ring. I sat at the table and wondered about what had just happened. It wasn't easy to digest the fact that my mother was so different from what I had thought my whole life. As a matter of fact, as I looked back, she wasn't the only one who had surprised me. Anita had turned out to be borderline psycho, Shorty had amazed me with the depth of his love for Donna, and Tanisha turned out to have a secret I would never have expected. All of these people who I thought I knew had turned out to be much more than what I saw. When it came right down to it, I had learned a very valuable life lesson. I'd heard it a million times before, but now I really understood what it meant when they said don't judge a book by its cover.

As I waited for my mother to return, the phone rang. I paused to see if my mother or the bishop was going to answer it. When it continued to ring, I picked up the phone. "Hello?"

"Dante!" It was Shorty, and he sounded frantic.

"Yo, dude, what's up? What's wrong?"

"It's your sister, man. She started bleeding, Dante. She might lose the baby."

I jumped out of my chair. "Oh my God. What happened? Where is she now?" I questioned rapidly.

"They're taking her to the hospital—"

I cut him off.

"They? Who's taking her to the hospital?"

"The paramedics. I'm right behind them."

"Why aren't you with her?"

"Because Tanisha's with her."

"Tanisha? What the hell is she doing with her?"

"When I found out Donna was bleeding, I went down to your room to get you but you were already gone. Man, I was freaking out, bro, but Tanisha was so cool, calm, and collected, Dante. If it wasn't for her keeping Donna calm until the paramedics got there, I don't know what might have happened. Yo, I think she might have saved your sister's life."

"Did they say anything? Is she all right? Is the baby all right?"

"The paramedics couldn't tell. She was crying, but she said she wasn't in any pain. There was just blood everywhere."

I said a quick, silent prayer. "What hospital did they take her to?"

"Nassau County Medical Center."

"Don't let anything happen to my sister, Shorty. We'll be there as soon as we can."

"I won't, man. I love that girl."

I hung up the phone and ran to tell my parents.

By the time we made it from Queens to the hospital on Long Island, Shorty had already spoken to Donna's doctor, so he explained what he had been told. It was good news. It turned out that Donna was only spotting blood because of all the stress of her wedding day. She had been in the shower when it happened, so the water on her skin had mixed with the blood to make it appear like much more blood than it really was. The doctors examined her internally and did an ultrasound, and the baby was fine. The doctor wanted to put Donna on bed rest until she made it to her last trimester, but we were all relieved that she and the baby were going to be okay.

Shorty filled my parents in on the drama that had unfolded at the hotel once Donna came out of the shower. While they listened, I went into the triage area, where Donna was being held for observation. Hopefully she would be released in a few hours.

"Hey, little sister. You okay? You really had us all scared there for a while." I kissed her forehead.

"You were scared? How do you think I felt?" she answered, her hand cradling her stomach.

"I know, but the doctor says everything looks good, right?"

"Yeah. I'll be on bed rest, I guess. I might be bored out of my mind, but I'll do whatever it takes to keep this baby."

I smiled at her and placed a hand on her stomach. My little niece or nephew was going to be fine.

"Where's Tanisha?" she asked. "And where were you this morning, anyway?"

"Donna, I don't know if you need to hear about all that right now. You don't need anything stressing you out. But trust me, as soon as I know you're feeling better and the baby's safe, I have some stories to tell you about Tanisha that you're not gonna believe."

She glared at me. "You mean about her being a stripper?"

"Yeah. How'd you know?" First Shorty, then my mother, and now Donna; was I the only one who didn't know about Tanisha?

"She told me on the way over here. You should have seen her this morning, Dante. I don't know what I would have done if she wasn't there to keep me calm. Poor Shorty was running around like a chicken with his head cut off, but Tanisha was there for me. You need to stay with that girl, Dante. I need someone like Tanisha to help me out with you two fools."

I laughed at the image of Shorty in a panic, but my smile quickly faded. "I guess she told you about our fight, huh? I don't know what to do about her, Donna. Even if I try, I don't know if she'll wanna talk to me after how I was last night."

"Dante, trust me. That girl loves you. Whatever you did, she'll forgive you. You just have to talk to her."

My parents and Shorty came into the room just as Donna finished speaking.

"Shorty, where's Tanisha?" Donna asked.

"She left. She said she didn't wanna be here when Dante got here, and that she had a lot of things to think about." The way he answered sounded like an apology.

"Dante, you better go find that girl," Donna ordered.

"I will. I know where to find her," I said, knowing exactly where Tanisha would go when she had things on her mind. I kissed Donna once more then turned to leave.

My mother called after me. "Dante, wait."

I stopped and looked at my mother. She came closer and slipped something into my hand. I looked down at the small box then back at my mother, who was smiling. "Just follow your heart, Dante. Whatever you do, we'll all support you." She kissed me on the cheek then nudged me toward the door. "Now go find Tanisha."

I found Tanisha exactly where I had expected—the observation deck of the Empire State Building. She was standing by herself in a corner, gazing out the window, looking every bit as exhausted as I felt. I wondered if she had slept at all last night. I knew I hadn't.

"Pretty view, huh?" I asked quietly as I approached her.

"Dante . . ." Her eyes were wet with tears. She quickly tried to wipe them.

I didn't know where to start, so I just held out my hand to her. She took my hand, and I hugged her. She cried on my shoulder for a long time before either one of us spoke. When she finally stepped back, wiping her eyes, she said, "I'm sorry."

I placed my finger on her lips. "Shhh. *I'm* the one who should be sorry. I shouldn't have treated you like I did last night. I just got jealous and I felt betrayed."

"Dante, I wanted to tell you . . . I was so scared you wouldn't want to be with me if you knew. I just didn't wanna mess things up."

"It's okay, baby. I shouldn't have gone off the way I did. I didn't even give you a chance to explain anything. I love you, Tanisha. I've never loved anyone the way I love you."

"I love you, Dante, and I want this to work."

"Do you love me enough to marry me?" I pulled out the ring my mother had given me. I hadn't planned on giving her the ring then but it just seemed like the right time.

"Are you serious?"

"Yes, I'm serious."

"But what about your mother? Your father's election?"

"My mother's the one who gave me the ring. She wants me to marry you."

She stared at me in disbelief for a few seconds then said, "Then yes. Yes, I'll marry you."

She jumped up in the air and wrapped her arms around my neck. Our kiss left no question about the feelings that we shared for each other. I wrapped her in my arms and held her tightly, thinking I would never let her go. I had faith that we would be able to work through everything. It was only a matter of time before we'd be walking down the aisle.

39

Tanisha

When I was growing up, I was never sure I would get married, but if I did, I wanted it to be on a warm summer day. On this Saturday at the end of August, the sun was shining and the sky was blue, and it was the happiest day of my life—the day I was to become Mrs. Dante Wilson. My wedding was like a fairy tale, kind of like the marriage of Princess Diana to Prince Charles, only ghetto style. First Lady Wilson even rented a gold and white carriage to be driven from the church down Merrick Boulevard to Antun's catering hall.

I was standing in the bridal chamber, admiring myself in the full-length mirror. My dress was simple yet chic, and although not too revealing, it showed my figure well. I was shocked when Dante's mother told me at the dress shop that she approved. Then again, she did pick it out. I hate to say this, but my wedding was bigger than Donna's. Much bigger. She said there were almost six hundred people invited to our wedding. Most of them I didn't know, but I guess that's what happens when you give the first lady time to plan.

Earlier, when I peeked out into the sanctuary, I saw photographers, video cameras, and news reporters everywhere. There was even a man from *Jet* magazine who was going to take our picture for their "Society World" section. Of course, most of this attention was not for me, but for Bishop Wilson, whose campaign for borough president was running stronger than ever as Election Day approached, but I didn't mind accepting some of the reflection off his spotlight.

I saw Aubrey standing in a small white tux next to Donna's husband. My brother waved at me and smiled. I think he was almost as happy as I was on this day. Dante had been so good to him, and I know Aubrey was looking forward to having a strong man in his life. I smiled back and blew Aubrey a kiss. White roses and corsages flashed by my eyes in a blur as I closed the door.

I turned to Natasha, my bridesmaid. She looked gorgeous in her peach-colored satin dress. "I can't believe how wonderful my new mother-in-law has been. She's footed the entire bill and has attended to all the details," I told her.

"And to think we thought she was a—"

I cut her off. "Natasha, we in church."

"Oops. My bad." She covered her mouth. "Here, let me help you with that veil."

She pinned the veil with its long train to my head, then stepped back to admire her work. She nodded. "There you go. You look good. You look like a beautiful baby doll. If only those girls from the club could see you now."

I turned toward the full-length mirror to see for myself. She was right. My hair fell below my shoulders in banana curls, and with the simple white gown and veil, it made me look more innocent than I had ever seen myself. I guess love does that for you.

The door swung open and Donna came waddling in, round belly and all, holding her hand on the small of her back. In spite of her wide girth, she looked beautiful in her gown. She'd just been taken off bed rest, and I was so happy she was able to be at the wedding as my matron of honor. She had been my biggest supporter in the Wilson household from the day I met her.

"Donna, you look glowing," I said as I hugged her.

"Girl, I'm miserable." She wiped beads of sweat from her forehead with the handkerchief she was carrying. "I feel like this baby's gonna drop any minute. I hope it doesn't come during the wedding."

"Hush your mouth. Don't be jinxing my wedding. Your baby isn't due for six more weeks." I pulled out a chair so she could sit.

"I ain't jinxing your wedding, but I will give you a word of advice. Don't ever get pregnant during the summertime."

I laughed. "I don't care when I get pregnant. I wanna have lots and lots of Dante's babies."

As we laughed, there was a knock on the door.

"Who is it?" I called out.

"It's Aubrey," my brother answered from the hallway. "I got a surprise for you."

"Come on in, Aubrey."

When the door opened, my mouth flew open. Standing in the doorway, holding Aubrey's hand, was my mother. Aubrey was smiling so hard he looked like his face would crack. I was in shock. Even with nearly six hundred guests, she was the last person I expected to see. I had spent so many months refusing to visit her in jail, but in my heart I knew I couldn't stay angry with her forever. As my wedding day approached, I had even considered going to see her. No matter how angry or hurt I had been, it just didn't feel right getting married without letting her know. I had never built up the courage to go see her, so I was overjoyed now that she was actually there.

"Momma!" I jumped up and ran to her.

"Tanisha!" She held me tightly as we both cried.

When I finally recovered from the shock of seeing my

mother on my wedding day, I asked, "Momma, how'd you get here? How'd you know about this? How'd—"

My mother laughed. "Slow down, Tanisha. I'm here, and that's all that matters right now." She reached out and placed her hand gently on my cheek. "I can't believe this is you. Baby, you're beautiful."

"I can't believe *you're* looking so good, Momma. Look at you. You done gained all your weight back." I stepped back and admired her transformation. She was looking so healthy I wanted to cry. For one, it wasn't unusual for her to get down to a size 3 when she was using that stuff. Even her hair had grown out and was pulled into a nice upswept style to complement her elegant chiffon dress.

"Um, Tanisha?" Donna's voice surprised me. I was so taken aback by my mother's arrival that I had forgotten there were other people in the room.

"Oh, Donna, I'm sorry. Let me introduce you to my mother, Marlene. Ma, this is Dante's sister, Donna. As you can see, she's going to have a baby"—I patted Donna's stomach—"and I can't wait to be an auntie."

"Pleased to meet you, Donna." My mother reached out to shake Donna's hand, but Donna pulled her in for an embrace.

"Welcome to the family, Marlene."

"You know Natasha," I said to my mother when Donna released her.

"How you doing, Marlene?"

"Fine, Natasha. I'm just glad to be home."

"I know that's right."

Donna and Natasha both managed to quickly find excuses to leave my mother and me alone. "Come on, Aubrey," Donna said. "Let's go find my brother and see how nervous he is."

When we were alone, I led my mother to sit next to me on the small love seat in the corner. I stared at her in amazement for a moment before I finally said, "I missed you, Momma. And I really can't believe you're here."

"I know," she answered. "I wasn't so sure I would make it here myself."

"I thought you weren't getting out for another few weeks."

"I got an early release for good behavior."

"But how did you know about the wedding?" I asked in total confusion.

"Dante. He's been visiting me for quite a while now."

I was amazed. "He's been visiting you?"

"Yeah. He was coming every week to tell me about you and Aubrey. He's a good man, Tanisha. You're lucky to have him."

"I know," I told her.

"Look, I know you might not believe me, but I love you and Aubrey more than anything in this world. Dante's updates were the only thing that kept me going while I was locked up."

I felt terrible. I hadn't been able to set aside my pain and visit my mother, who was also obviously suffering. Her addiction had stolen so much from all of us, but I had reached a point where I started blaming her, rather than her addiction. She needed help, and I had turned my back on her. My guilt, though, was soon overshadowed by an overwhelming love for my mother, and also for Dante, who had stood by her side when I didn't have the strength.

I held her hand and cried as I apologized. "Momma, I said some terrible things to you at the jail, and then I wasn't there to visit you even once."

"It's all right, baby. That's what helped me get my head together. I'm finally seeing life as it really is for the first time in . . ." She stopped. I think she and I were both overwhelmed as we realized just how long our lives had been in chaos because of her addiction. "Anyhow, this is the first time since you were twelve that I've been without drugs for more than a few days."

I hugged her tightly. "I didn't know you were getting out or I would have invited you."

"That doesn't matter. I'm here, and I love you, baby girl."

We obviously had so much to talk about, but she was right. All that mattered now was that she was here with me.

"I love you, too, Ma. You've made my day. Now everything will be perfect."

"Well, I'm going to have my son march me into the church. I'm going to sit in the front row as the mother of the bride."

She gave me one more hug then left the room to find my brother. I watched her leave, still amazed that she was at my wedding and that it was Dante who had gotten her here. Things were definitely looking up, and I couldn't wait to walk down that aisle and become the wife of the most wonderful man in the world.

40

The Wedding

Bishop T.K. Wilson walked proudly down the aisle of his church, nodding and waving to his friends, family, and colleagues as he made his way to the altar. For T.K., today was a good day. Not only was his son Dante getting married to a woman he absolutely adored, but his daughter Donna, who was having his first grandchild, was just taken off bed rest and would be attending the wedding as the matron of honor. And if that news wasn't good enough, his numbers in the polls had jumped up an amazing ten points in the last week, making him a virtual shoo-in for the borough presidency. As a testament to his expected win, members of the news media were present in force at the wedding. T.K. and his family had become big news, and all the attention was a great thing for his church. Yes, today was a good day for Bishop T.K. Wilson.

When he reached the altar, he looked out among the hundreds of guests and beamed. It was fulfilling to see his church so crowded for his son's wedding. There was no doubt this was going to be a wedding to remember. There was clergy from as far away as Africa, and even his friend

David Dinkins, the former mayor of New York, was in attendance. He sat in a pew near former presidential candidate Reverend Al Sharpton.

When Dante and his best man, Shorty, joined the bishop at the altar, the organ music filtered into the church, signaling to the guests that the wedding was about to begin. The procession began with his lovely wife, escorted to her seat in the front by two handsome young ushers. Charlene looked positively regal, and T.K. was glad. She had worked hard and deserved to feel proud of the grand event she had put together. Charlene had done a magnificent job of pulling things together during the past few months and her hard work had paid off. He smiled at his wife then looked to the aisle, where he saw the bride's young brother escorting another woman to the front. Aubrey left the woman and hurried back to escort his sister down the aisle.

As the bishop watched the woman settle into the first pew on the bride's side, he wondered who she was. He had not met any of Tanisha's family yet, but assumed this must be one of them. Whoever she was, T.K. was puzzled, because for some reason she looked very familiar. The woman looked up, and when her eyes met the bishop's, she paused momentarily. Clearly, she was also wondering if they had met before, but neither one could remember when or where. Their eye contact was only fleeting, because soon the bridesmaids and groomsmen were coming down the aisle and taking their places beside the altar. The bishop's very pregnant daughter was the last to take her place before the organist began "The Wedding March." The church was filled with the rustling sound of six hundred guests rising at once to greet the bride.

All eyes were on Tanisha. Her stunning beauty enchanted many guests as she seemed to float down the aisle toward her groom. Before she reached the altar, she kissed her brother, then joined the rest of the wedding party to stand at the altar beside Dante. When everyone was in place, the bishop asked the bride and groom to join hands. He stood in front of them with a heartfelt smile spread across his face.

"We are gathered here today to join Tanisha Jones and Dante Wilson together in holy matrimony. Now, we all know that weddings are special occasions, but for me, this is an extra special occasion. It's not every day a father gets to preside over the marriage of his own son, and it makes it even more special that my son is marrying a woman as extraordinary as Tanisha. Tanisha, I am so pleased you will soon be a member of my family." The bishop smiled at Dante and kissed Tanisha before continuing. The guests in attendance were touched. They could feel that they were indeed at a very special wedding.

When it came time for the bride and groom to say their "I do's," unlike Donna and Shorty's wedding, both Dante and Tanisha responded loudly and without hesitation. Tanisha even added a little emphasis when she said, "I do, I do, I do!" This brought a laugh from the guests.

The bishop smiled and turned them toward their guests. "If there is anyone among you who has reason that these two should not be lawfully wed as man and wife, please speak now or forever hold your peace."

Of course, there was no one who could possibly object to this very special union, so the bishop turned the happy couple back toward the altar and announced the exchanging of the rings. The bishop turned to the best man, but before Shorty could get the ring box out of his pocket, there was a commotion in the front pew. The woman next to Aubrey jumped up and shouted, "Stop the wedding!" Immediately, every eye in the church was on her.

Tanisha turned quickly when she recognized the voice. "Momma? Oh no," she muttered weakly. Her voice was a mixture of confusion and pain.

"Tanisha, you can't marry him!" the woman shouted in a panic.

"Momma, stop this, what are you doing?" Her embarrassment was evident.

The church erupted with the noise of conversations among six hundred guests wanting to know who this woman was who dared to interrupt such a beautiful ceremony. Of course, the reporters in the church were furiously scribbling in their notebooks by now.

The woman stepped away from the pew and rushed toward the altar. Tanisha gathered up her train and approached the woman, followed by Dante and Bishop Wilson. The group met in the aisle between the front pews. First Lady Wilson struggled to maintain her composure as she watched all her hard work crumbling before her eyes.

"Momma," Tanisha said through her tears, "how could you do this? Why are you embarrassing me like this?"

"I'm not embarrassing you, baby. I'm saving your life. You can't marry that boy."

Tanisha was too distraught to speak, and Dante didn't know what to say either. He had spent so much time with Marlene and thought they had developed some sort of a bond during his visits to the jail. Protesting the wedding was the last thing he would have expected her to do.

"Why can't they marry?" the bishop asked, stepping closer to the woman Tanisha had identified as her mother. Everyone in attendance seemed to lean in closer, as if they didn't want to miss a word of the woman's explanation.

Marlene's tone softened ever so slightly as she looked into the bishop's eyes and said, "Because you're her father, Thomas Kelly."

There was an immediate gasp from all in attendance as photographers' bulbs flashed and video cameras whirred. This would be headline news, better than any reporter in the building could possibly have ever dreamed.

T.K.'s eyes widened as recognition settled in. He hadn't been called Thomas Kelly in over twenty years, and now he knew who this woman was. Yes, she had gained some weight since he'd last seen her and the years hadn't been kind to her but he definitely knew her. He also believed her when she said that Tanisha was his daughter. His skeletons had just fallen out of the closet.

"Marlene?" He spoke barely above a whisper.

"Yes, Thomas, it's me, Marlene."

"Oh my God. This can't be happening," First Lady Wilson muttered when the reality of the situation hit her. Shortly after that she fainted.

41

Dante

I felt like I was on an episode of *The Twilight Zone* or, even worse, *Jerry Springer.* Here I was thinking the bishop was a perfect man, then I find out he not only had a child outside his marriage to my mother, he didn't even acknowledge the child existed for more than twenty years. So much for family values. And as if that wasn't bad enough, the child he seemed to have forgotten also happened to be the woman I loved. I had almost married my own sister earlier in the day. Things couldn't possibly be any worse.

Once Marlene made her announcement, chaos took over the church. My poor mother fainted on the spot. I had to fight my way over to her through the crowd that seemed to instantly materialize in front of the altar. Most of them were reporters and cameramen ready to record my family's most horrifying moment for the evening news. I almost slugged one guy.

As soon as I was able to get my mother back on her feet, I led her across the altar toward the back exit, where Shorty had already escorted my sister to safety. My mother went out the back door and headed to Shorty's car while I stopped and took one last look at the scene inside the church. Like a pack of wolves, the news crews had surrounded Marlene and Tanisha. I could only hope that they had enough common sense to keep their mouths shut. Aubrey still sat in the front pew, looking scared and bewildered. My father was somehow managing to pretend he didn't hear the questions from the reporters as he held his head high and tried to regain some semblance of order in his church. I doubted he would be able to do that, and I wondered if that would ever be possible within his own family. It hurt me to think it, but the word *hate* was at the forefront of my mind as I looked at him.

Shorty drove my mother, Donna, and me back to the house in complete silence. I was too numb to even think about stringing together enough words to make a complete thought. Donna sat in the front seat next to Shorty, making no sound, but I watched her shoulders heave and knew she was crying. Every few minutes I looked over at my mother to be sure she was okay. She sat eerily still, staring out the window with absolutely no expression on her face. I was worried she might need medical attention if she didn't snap out of it soon. Again when I thought about the bishop, I thought about hate.

Inside the house, we settled in the den and stared at each other in continued silence. I don't think anyone knew where to even begin discussing what the hell had happened. Donna's eyes were red and puffy, and my mother's eyes still looked like she was a million miles away. I started to think of Tanisha and the fact that she was my sister. It didn't take long before my stomach erupted and I had to run to the bathroom to throw up, something I'd already done several times since I'd been home. As I stood at the sink to rinse my mouth, I stared at my reflection in the mirror and wondered what I was supposed to do now. I was in love with a woman who I could never be with, and as far as I was concerned, it was all the bishop's fault. I slammed my hand on the sink, releasing some of my anger. There was no doubt in my mind. I hated him.

When I returned to the den, I found my mother, Donna, and Shorty huddled around the television. Shorty had probably turned it on to distract them from their troubled thoughts, but it proved to be no help. Every local station had interrupted their regular programming to bring viewers a news flash, a peek into the shattered lives of the Wilson family.

Popular minister and Queens borough presidential candidate Bishop T.K. Wilson was exposed today for having a love child with known crack addict and convicted felon Marlene Jones. Ms. Jones, who was just recently released from Rikers Island after serving a sentence for possession of crack cocaine, announced that her daughter, Tanisha Jones, was the love child of a five-year relationship she had with Bishop Wilson. Ironically, this information was made public at Bishop Wilson's church, where he was presiding over the wedding of his son, Dante Wilson. Dante Wilson was about to be married to Tanisha Jones, until it was revealed that the bride was his half sister. We will bring you more information on this breaking story as it becomes available.

I shut the television off in disgust. This brief news report was obviously only the beginning of a storm of unwanted attention my family would be receiving. In fact, I knew it was only a matter of time before the news vans would be parked outside our house and the phone would be ringing off the hook. Probably the only thing that had delayed the reporters' arrival was the six hundred guests at the wedding. I wondered how many of them were still at the church, waiting in line for their chance to be interviewed and get their fifteen minutes of fame.

Donna was the first one to finally speak. "I can't believe the bishop would do this," she said, rising slowly from her seat. She began to pace back and forth across the room, holding her swollen stomach as if it might fall to the ground.

"Donna, honey, will you please sit down?" Shorty pleaded. He tried to gently lead her back to the sofa. "I know you're stressed, but think about the baby. The doctor said you should stay off your feet."

"No, Shorty, I don't wanna sit down. What I want is for the bishop to come home and explain what the hell is going on." She balled up her fists, placed them against her forehead, and let out a scream.

"Madonna, calm down," my mother said in a commanding voice. I was relieved to see her coming out of her trance. "Shorty's right. You should sit down. Your pregnancy is stressful enough as it is. We don't want you going into premature labor."

Donna's body seemed to crumple under the emotional strain. Shorty grabbed her and guided her back to the sofa as she sobbed, "I want my daddy."

"Son, are you all right?" my mother asked softly as she reached for my hand. I was still speechless as I sat beside her with tears welling in my eyes.

My mother wrapped her arm around my shoulder and I laid my head on her breast like a child. We were supposed to be comforting her, but she was the one showing incredible strength in the face of all of this. I had always known she was a strong woman, but she hadn't shed one tear. This amazed me, because the public drama had to be tearing her up inside.

"I hate him. I swear to God, Ma, I hate him." I couldn't hold back the tears anymore. I'd never felt so much pain in all my life. I wanted to step outside my body at that point and be anybody but me, because as far as I was concerned, my life as Dante Wilson was in ruins.

My mother stroked my head as she soothed me. "Don't

say that, baby. You just don't understand. None of you will ever understand."

Though her voice was calm, her face looked drained, as if the last few hours had taken their toll on her. For the first time, I could see her real self through her always flawless makeup, and I noticed that she was getting old. Her hair was turning gray around the edges, and a few wrinkles creased her usually smooth olive complexion.

"No, Ma, I understand perfectly. He's a lying, cheating, deadbeat bastard. I can't believe he did this to me. For Christ's sake, my relationship with Tanisha was incest, and everyone with a TV or radio knows about it! He's ruined my life."

I felt like I needed to run to the bathroom again. Every time I thought about Tanisha being my sister, my stomach started to do flips. We'd made love so many times I couldn't even count them.

"Dante, please don't judge your father. He loves you. He loves all of you."

I couldn't believe what she had just said. How could she stand by that—that snake?

"I don't want his love. I don't want anything from him. Right now, I hate the fact that he's even my father."

She sat up, releasing me. "Don't you say that. Don't you ever say that again," she said in that same calm voice. "He may have made some mistakes, but he is always going to be your father."

The door opened, and we all turned to see the bishop enter the house. Donna's sobs became louder, and my stomach lurched. Just the sight of him made me wanna throw up again. My mother rose and went to my father. I wanted to jump up and smack him, yet she was approaching him with such tenderness. His face was blanketed with the look of defeat.

"It's over," he told her quietly. "I spoke to the party chairman and withdrew from the race."

"No, T.K.!" My mother wrapped her arms around his

waist, buried her face in his shoulder, and finally released an ocean of tears.

"It's okay, Charlene. It's going to be okay." He stroked her hair gently as she sobbed against his chest.

"Okay?" I shouted in a rage. "What fucking world are you living in? It's not going to be okay! Nothing is going to be okay, and it's all because of you!"

My mother lifted her head. "Dante, stop it."

"No, you stop it. Stop defending him. Can't you see what he's done? He humiliated you. You're the laughingstock of the church, and soon we'll all be the laughingstock of the whole damn city! I can see the headlines now. Bishop T.K. Wilson and his incestuous family."

"I said stop it! You don't understand." My mother's tears had dried up, and the anger that should have been directed at the bishop was being unleashed on me.

"No, Charlene, let him speak. He's entitled. He's had as bad a day as any of us."

I took a step toward him. "You don't know the half of it, you . . . you fucking bastard. And you've got the nerve to call yourself a man of God. You ain't a man of God. You ain't nothing but a heathenous devil worshipper."

"Don't cross the line, son," he warned.

"Why not? Who are you to tell me what's right and wrong at this point? Look what you've done. Tell me something. How many other times did you screw around on my mother? I bet you've been through half the congregation. How many other brothers and sisters do we have out there, huh, Bishop?"

"Dante, stop it," my mother snapped.

"Dante, when the time is right, I will tell you and your sister about my relationship with Marlene, but not until your mother and I have a chance to talk." He was using that same austere voice he usually reserved for dealing with irate church members, and it was pissing me off.

"Tell me now, goddammit!" If he wasn't going to speak, I would get him to open his mouth another way. My fist flew toward his jaw. He moved out of the way pretty quickly, but I still managed to graze him. Shorty jumped on me from behind before I could get in another swing.

"No, bro. You can't do this. He still your father."

As I struggled to free myself from Shorty's grasp, there was a loud banging at the door. Everyone froze. This was it, the first of the reporters who would be coming to invade our privacy and pry into our pain, all hoping for that front-page story. The banging continued, and Donna finally stepped to the window and pulled back the curtain. She turned back to us with a look of wide-eyed confusion.

"It's Deacon Black and Deaconess Wright."

My mother glanced at the bishop then at me. "It's okay, Donna. They're friends. Let them in."

Donna opened the door and the visitors entered.

"Bishop," Deacon Black said in greeting.

"Deacon, Deaconess." The bishop nodded. "How can I help you two?"

"Bishop, I'm going to get right to the point," Deacon Black said. "We just left an emergency meeting of the deacons board, at Reverend Reynolds's request."

"Reverend Reynolds called a meeting? Good." The bishop's face showed approval. He was probably expecting to hear that Reverend Reynolds wanted to discuss how the deacons could help their bishop, so I know he was taken aback when he heard the deacon's next words.

"Well, I don't know about that. He felt it was the obligation of the deacons board and its ministers to discuss today's events, to discuss conduct he viewed as unbecoming of the pastor of our church."

"Reynolds said this?" The bishop seemed wounded, and everyone else was shocked. We all thought Reverend Reynolds was his closest ally in the church. He was like family.

"He said that and a whole lot more," Deaconess Wright added. "He asked the board to fire you."

"What? They can't do that," my mother protested.

"No, they can't, Charlene," the bishop told her. "But only because the church bylaws say that a pastor can't be fired without an open meeting of the board in which I myself and any member of the congregation are given a chance to speak on my behalf."

The first lady sighed with relief. "Thank God."

"But they can suspend you with pay until the next deacons board meeting. And that's exactly what they did, Bishop." Deacon Black frowned.

"That meeting's not until next month. Who's going to run the church until then?" my mother asked.

"That's the main reason why the deaconess and I came over here, First Lady Wilson. To inform you and the bishop that Reverend Reynolds has been appointed acting pastor for now. And when it's all over, I think he and his new wife plan to have both your jobs."

42

The First Lady

"Bishop Wilson, you've heard the opinions of Reverend Reynolds and some of the other members of the board. They seem to think that the recent media attention to your alleged indiscretions is harmful to the church's reputation, and therefore they are calling for your removal as pastor of First Jamaica Ministries. Before we take this to a vote, we'd like to give you an opportunity to say a few words and answer a few questions if you don't mind," Deacon James Black, the chairman of the deacons board, told my husband.

The deacons board meeting was packed with friends and foes. I, for one, was glad that this day had finally come. We had been through a living hell the last month. The media were still dragging T.K. through the mud about fathering Tanisha and his relationship with Marlene, and the church had not made a public statement either supporting or rejecting their bishop. My good friend, Deaconess Wright, assured me T.K. still had a few supporters in the church, but I knew that Reverend Reynolds had started his own little campaign to erode that base of support. It had become very clear that he was looking to get rid of the bishop and settle right into position as the new head of the church. Unfortunately Deacon Emerson and Anita were now two of his biggest supporters. With T.K.'s future so uncertain, he and I were on pins and needles all month as we waited for this day, so I was relieved it had arrived. It would at least answer the question of where my husband stood with his once-loyal deacons board, so that we might be able to move ahead with our lives, with or without T.K.'s position in the church. I must admit I had no idea what we would do if T.K. was dismissed.

Our relationship with Dante, however, would still need much more time to heal. Dante had moved out right after the wedding. When T.K. and I went to him, asking him to listen to our explanation, he refused. He was vowing never to speak to his father again or forgive me for supporting him, and though it was breaking our hearts, we both knew enough to give Dante time. We prayed that someday soon our son would come back to us, ready to begin repairing our damaged family.

Donna had been angry with her father, of course, but her love for him was strong enough to withstand the truths that were revealed. Although she was back on bed rest and due to deliver within the next few weeks, Donna had insisted on coming to the deacons meeting to support her father, and for that I was grateful. I just wanted to see my family whole again.

I watched my husband as he stood and looked around the room, preparing to answer the board's charges. As he made his way to the podium, his expression was very serious yet stately. This was the man I had loved for so many years; even under the greatest pressure, he displayed such confidence, such courage. He made eye contact with each and every one of the deacons and deaconesses on the board. At some time or another he had helped each one of them, and his eyes were reminders of that fact. He stopped to pause even longer when he reached his protégé, Reverend Reynolds, his eyes reflecting the reverend's betrayal. Ever since he'd come to our church, we'd had that man in our house like he was one of our children. T.K. had taken Reverend Reynolds under his wing, and now it was his voice that was loudest in the call to remove my husband from the church.

"I'll make a brief statement, Deacon Black, but I won't be answering any questions," T.K. announced at the podium.

"Why not?" Reverend Reynolds was quick to protest. "I think you owe us all an explanation for your infidelity and the embarrassment you've brought down on the church."

T.K. chuckled. "I may owe my wife an explanation. I may even owe my children an explanation, but other than God, I don't owe an explanation to anyone else." There was some clapping in the background from a few members who had remained loyal to T.K. throughout this ordeal. "Now, may I go on with my statement, Reverend Reynolds?"

Reynolds sat down and Black nodded his approval.

"As you all know, I've been the pastor of First Jamaica Ministries for the last seventeen years. In that time, we've increased our congregation to become the largest church in the borough. We've built schools and day-care centers, and started countless programs to help this community. I've given my life to this church. I will be the first to say that I am sorry my indiscretions have caused the media to look negatively on our church, but I will not deny my daughter or—"

"So you admit she's your daughter?" Reverend Reynolds asked smugly.

"Yes, she's my daughter." The first time I had heard T.K. say those words, I felt my heart sink, but now I was proud of him. This was a true man of God, admitting his mistakes even in the face of all it might cause him to lose.

"So you did cheat on your wife? Which means you committed adultery." Clearly, Reverend Reynolds had decided to take over the meeting. If I wasn't so dignified, I would have smacked the self-satisfied smirk right off his face.

T.K. ignored Reverend Reynolds and continued to speak to the board. "Now, I am going to make this statement once and only once." He held his Bible tightly. "I love my wife. I've loved her since the day we met, and I swear on this Bible in my hand that I have never, ever committed adultery."

There was murmuring among some of the observers in the room, but T.K. continued without pause. "Now, some of you may believe that and some of you may not, but I will leave here with a clear conscience, knowing that I am right with my Lord. So, if you want to fire me, by all means do so."

On that note, T.K. turned and walked straight out the door. The room erupted in whispers from every corner. Some observers and board members had their doubt written clearly on their faces. To them, it hadn't mattered how many Bibles my husband had sworn on at that podium. Deaconess Wright looked my way, her eyes expressing her sympathy. I took strength from her steadfast support and stood to speak.

"Before you vote, Deacons, I'd like to say something." My voice was calm and even. Reverend Reynolds would not intimidate me, for contrary to what he wanted everyone to think, I knew right from wrong, and my husband was right.

I approached the podium, straightening my hat before I spoke. "As you know, I am First Lady Charlene Wilson, and I've been married for over twenty years to that elegant man who just left. Now, it is my understanding that he has been placed on suspension and may possibly be replaced as pastor of this church because he has allegedly commited infidelities. Am I correct?"

"The exact charges are actions unbecoming a pastor," Deacon Black explained, clearly confused by my question. "But yes, that is our concern."

Reverend Reynolds had the nerve to speak to me, and in such a condescending tone that I had the urge to smack him once again. "First Lady Wilson, we all know that you have to defend your husband, but he has embarrassed the church and cheated on you. Please try to understand. We are just trying to right his wrong."

"Don't you dare try to act like you're defending my honor, Reverend Reynolds. You, who ate at the bishop's table every Sunday, and now try to kick him while he's down. You think I don't know what you're up to? You . . . you Judas!"

"Ahem." Deacon Black cleared his throat. "First Lady Wilson, can we get to your comments?"

"Of course, Deacon," I responded. I had to remind myself not to let Reverend Reynolds rattle me. "If you will indulge me, I'd like to tell you all a story."

Reverend Reynolds tried once again to shake me up. "I'm sorry, First Lady, but what does this have to do wi—"

Deaconess Wright came to my defense. "Let the first lady speak, Reverend." Several voices in the room echoed their agreement with my friend.

"Please continue, First Lady Wilson," Deacon Black said. "Reverend Reynolds, I must ask you to hold your comments until the first lady has completed her statements."

Reverend Reynolds leaned back in his chair and folded his arms across his chest, undoubtedly thinking of a speech of his own to deliver after I finished.

"Thank you, Deacon Black," I said. I took a deep breath and held my head high as I prepared to reveal secrets that had stayed buried for over twenty years. It was time to tell the truth. I owed this much to T.K.

"As I was saying, I have a story to tell you about a young man living a tragic life in Virginia. This man was not a member of any church. The only thing he worshipped was crack cocaine. He and his woman were totally addicted.

"One day, the woman had a reaction to some bad crack. She slipped into unconsciousness and the young man didn't know what to do. He ran for help and found himself at a church, where he met a visiting minister who offered his assistance. The minister took the man back to his home and together they got the woman to a hospital, barely in time to save her life.

"The woman remained in a coma for two weeks. During that time, the minister visited the young man at the hospital daily. Together, they prayed for the woman, begging God to spare her life. The minister also prayed over the man as he fought his own battle against the demons that controlled him. By the end of two weeks, the young man had successfully survived his painful withdrawal from crack, and had found a new reason to live. He found the Lord. He vowed to devote his life to God, because he had much to be thankful for. God had delivered him from his addiction, and his woman came out of her coma and would soon be coming home.

"The minister who had helped the young man was only visiting, to relieve a fellow minister during a month-long sabbatical. The time had come for him to return to his own church. Having found a new life in God and being saved, the young man asked the minister if he could go to New York with him. When the minister agreed, the young man went home to his woman and told her the good news. He was eager for her to experience the freedom he felt now that he had rejected drugs and found the Lord.

"The woman, however, was not ready. She'd had people sneaking drugs into the hospital ever since she had woke up from her coma. She told this young man she would not go to New York and that she liked her life just the way it was. He begged and pleaded with her for days, but it was no use. The drugs still controlled her. She was still using, and trying to convince him to join her again.

"Knowing he'd be in danger of losing his battle with drugs if he stayed with her, the young man left Richmond, Virginia, without her."

At this point, I noticed Reverend Reynolds squirming in his seat, probably trying to distract me. Everyone else in the room, though, was silent and still. With a determined glare at Reverend Reynolds, I continued.

"In New York, the young man joined the minister's fledgling church and stayed true to his vows to the Lord. He stayed off drugs, and even started going to seminary. For two years the minister watched him grow into a fine, devoted Christian, and he knew that someday this young man could achieve great things. The young man became part of his family, almost like a son to him."

Now came the part that I hated to reveal. This was a story I had hoped to be able to keep in the past. This was the reason T.K. had refused to answer any questions. He had been protecting me.

"The minister did have a child, but she was not living up to his high hopes. She was wild and promiscuous. It was only a matter of time before her immoral and fast lifestyle caught up to her and of course it did. The minister was devastated when he learned that his daughter was pregnant, and even worse, that she had no idea who had fathered the baby."

I paused and held tightly to the podium to stop my hands from shaking. The time had come to open the door to my own closet full of skeletons.

"As I'm sure many of you have already figured out, that young man was the man you now know as Bishop T.K. Wilson. The visiting minister was my own father, the Reverend Dr. Charles Jackson, and the pregnant daughter was me."

I heard gasps from several people in the room, including my good friend Deaconess Wright. I was afraid to look at Donna, but I held fast to the belief that God would somehow bring my family through this trial. I struggled to continue.

"My father was lost when he learned of my pregnancy, and it was T.K. who came to him with a solution. You see, T.K. had professed his love to me long before this time, but I was too wild and too troubled to even give him the time of day. Knowing that my pregnancy would destroy my father's career and quite possibly the young church he had started, T.K. offered to claim the child as his and marry me. My father accepted this plan, though of course I protested loudly. In the end, T.K. and I were married, and twenty-two years later, I can tell you that it was the best thing that could ever have happened to me.

"This man, who some of you would like to see removed from his position, pulled himself out of the grasp of addiction and then saved me from continuing down the path of moral self-destruction I had been on. For the past two decades, he has thanked the Lord daily for his salvation. He has been devoted to this church, and I know many of you must admit he came to your aid during your own times of trouble."

My eyes traveled around the room as I looked at each person who had come to T.K. at some time with their own stories of personal failings. In every case, he had helped these people with generosity, and always without judgment. This included Reverend Reynolds, but he obviously felt no gratitude to my husband.

"That's a very nice story, First Lady," he began with ice in his tone, "but it still does not forgive the fact that he had a child out of wedlock. A child he abandoned."

"Reverend Reynolds, that is where you are wrong. The bishop only learned of his daughter's existence on the same day that all of you did. The young woman that he left in Virginia was indeed Marlene Jones, but after he came to New York, they never again had contact. He had no idea that she was pregnant when he left. I can tell you that had he known, he would never have abandoned that child. And you can see for yourself that he will not deny her now. With God's help, he is prepared to forge a relationship with his daughter and do what he can to help Marlene stay free from drugs. And I plan to be by his side.

"So, to you and anyone else who would still insist on removing the bishop from his position, I would remind you that none of us is without sin. Bishop Wilson has sinned, as we all have, but he has proven time and time again that he is devoted to the Lord, willing to right his mistakes, and he is more than worthy of the respect of all of us in this room. He does not deserve to be fired."

The members of the board remained speechless as I left the podium and headed for my seat. I stopped in my tracks when I spotted Dante standing off to the side of the room by one of the doors. The tears streaming down his face told me that he had heard the whole story. I hadn't wanted him to hear the truth about his biological father this way. My heart ached for him, but when we made eye contact, he gave me a small smile and I knew we would be okay. They could do what they wanted with the information they had just been given. As long as I still had my husband and the love of my children, I knew we would be all right.

43

Dante

I wiped the tears from my eyes as I watched Donna stand and embrace my mother. Ma was holding back tears, not willing to give Reverend Reynolds and his cronies the satisfaction of seeing her cry. I was tempted to walk down to where they were seated but decided against it. I needed a minute or two to digest the bombshell I had just heard. Once again, things weren't what they seemed in the Wilson family, and now I had to adjust to the realization that the bishop was not my biological father and that Tanisha was not my half-sister. Ma was right, though; he would always be my father and he would always have my respect. I don't think I'd have the heart to do what he'd done and keep it a secret all these years.

"I would like a chance to speak now," Reverend Reynolds demanded.

Donna released my mother and turned to Reverend Reynolds, who was about to get up. I could almost feel her entire body cringe as he spoke. Talk about a Judas. I wanted to walk down to where he was standing and smack the shit out of him.

"Members of the board, First Lady Wilson has delivered a very impassioned speech in support of her husband. But the fact still remains, though, that the bishop's secret past has caused irreparable damage to the reputation of this church. The media have branded us as a church with an adulterous leader, and no matter what story First Lady Wilson has just told us, it is too late to reverse the negative opinions formed in the minds of the public. What are we to say to the media now? Do you really think it will make a difference to the public that our leader supposedly had no knowledge of his illegitimate child? The point is, we simply cannot support a bishop who had a child out of wedlock. That is not something a man of God would do. It's just—"

"Stop, Terrance! Just stop!"

Reverend Reynolds's mouth snapped shut as he turned in the direction of the shout. His eyes were wide as he stared, along with everyone else in the room, at my pregnant sister, who stood with tears streaming down her face.

"I can't let you do this," she cried.

"What are you talking about?" Reverend Reynolds asked nervously. "It's your father who has done something wrong."

"You are so full of it. And I'm not going to let you get away with this any longer." Donna looked at Shorty, who was now standing beside her.

"It's okay, baby," Shorty said as he held her hand. "Go 'head and tell them."

Donna reached for my mother's hand, and as she leaned against her husband for support, she made an announcement that would leave every person in the room thunderstruck, including me.

"You stand here yelling about how my father should be removed because he had a child out of wedlock, but there is one more thing I think they should know before any decisions are made."

Reverend Reynolds opened his mouth as if he had something to say, but no words came out.

"Why don't you tell them who the father of my baby is, Terrance?"

I felt faint as Donna's words registered. Was she saying what I thought she was? I turned my attention to Reverend Reynolds, who was suddenly looking a lot less confident than he had throughout the meeting. His eyes went from Donna to his wife and then back to Donna. As I watched him squirm, I realized that this was the look of a guilty man.

"Ah, Donna, what are you saying? Everyone knows your husband is the father of your baby, right?" He sounded as if he was begging her not to go any further.

"Don't play stupid, Terrance. My husband is man enough to take responsibility for this child, but you *know* he's not the biological father of my baby."

His wife jumped up and demanded to know, "What is she talking about, Terrance?"

"Nothing, she's lying," he insisted with a wild look in his eyes.

Donna, who had started out leaning on Shorty for support, now seemed to regain her strength. She stood tall and proud and announced to the room full of deacons and deaconesses, "Shorty is not the father of my child, though my child will be blessed to be able to call him Daddy. Reverend Reynolds is the father of this baby."

"That's a lie! That's a bald-faced lie!" he shouted, glancing around the room as if he was looking for someone to believe him. "I'm not her child's father."

"Terrance, you can deny it all you want, but when this child is born in two weeks, you can be sure I will seek a DNA test and hold you responsible for child support."

I looked at Shorty, who was gazing lovingly at Donna, with a newfound respect. He had known all along that this child was not his. He had married my sister for the same reasons the bishop had married my mother. I was stunned and humbled by the knowledge that Shorty was actually a man as honorable as the bishop.

Reverend Reynolds was looking ashen, though still proclaiming his innocence. "This . . . this is ridiculous!" he sputtered. "This is obviously a feeble attempt to save her father's position as bishop. Ms. Wilson, you should be ashamed of yourself for lying to these good people."

He turned to Deacon Black. "She is obviously using the birth of her child as a ploy to manipulate the board and delay your decision. Does she really think that another two weeks will change your opinions? Bishop Wilson is bad for this church, and I demand that the board make its decision here and now!"

As Reverend Reynolds was ranting, Donna had left my mother's side and headed to where his wife was seated. I watched as his wife examined what Donna had handed her. It appeared to be a photograph, and whatever was on it caused his wife's face to crease with anger. She jumped from her seat before the deacons could respond to Reverend Reynolds's tirade.

"Terrance!" she shouted. "Why are you kissing her in this picture?"

"Darling, I . . . I—"

"Don't even try to explain, Terrance. The date on this picture is printed right here on the front. You were in some restaurant all hugged up on her a month after I went shopping for my damn wedding gown! How could you?"

Donna headed back in Ma's direction looking tired but vindicated. It wasn't my mother she was heading to, though. Shorty held out his arms and she went to him. Their loving embrace spoke volumes about how much we had all been through, and gave me faith that, in the end, love would prevail. That's when I decided to walk over and join my family. I walked up behind my mother and hugged her tightly.

While his wife stood by her seat and cried, Reverend Reynolds refused to give up. "Deacon Black, I am not the person you came here to discuss today. Bishop Wil—"

"Reverend Reynolds," Deacon Black said to him with obvious disdain, "the board has heard more than enough from you today. Now, perhaps the best thing for you to do is attend to your distraught wife, and I suggest you do it outside of this room."

Reverend Reynolds finally slumped his shoulders in defeat and left his spot near the podium. He went to his wife, but when he reached for her arm to escort her out of the room, she shouted, "Don't touch me! Don't you dare touch me!" and left on her own. Reverend Reynolds looked crushed as he followed her out.

"Well," Deacon Black announced as the door closed behind the reverend and his wife, "this meeting has certainly brought quite a few issues before the board. Obviously the issue of Reverend Reynolds will need to be dealt with, but the fact still remains that we need to make a decision about Bishop Wilson. I, for one, am still very concerned about the negative media attention that he has brought to our doorstep."

"Excuse me, Deacon. I'd like to speak," I announced as I left my mother's side and headed for the podium.

"Well, Dante, I appreciate that, but I think the board has heard all we need to hear today."

"No, I don't think you have, sir. This church is my father's life, and as his son, I don't think any of you here should feel comfortable about deciding his fate until you have heard what I have to say. Besides, if I remember correctly, church bylaws say that you must hear what everyone has to say before you vote."

Deacon Black looked worn, but he agreed to let me speak. "Very well, son. Speak your mind."

I stood at the podium and looked out at the room full of people, many of whom had been in our home over the years and had come to feel like members of our extended family.

"First of all, I would like all of you who are long-standing members to recall just how much you have seen this church grow under my father's leadership. First Jamaica Ministries wouldn't be half of what it is today without his guidance. He has done much good for this church, needy members of this community, and even personally for many of the people in this room today.

"Now, in the last month and again here today, I have heard many people worrying that the media attention will destroy this church that my father helped build. Well, I say damn the media. They weren't able to destroy Jesse Jackson, and his indiscretions were far greater than my father's ever were. His followers didn't desert him; they stood by him. They refused to let the media shape their opinions, and we as members of a strong black church should do the same.

"I don't think there is one person in this room who could honestly say that they didn't admire and respect my father before this all started. Bishop T.K. Wilson is still that same man, and if you can't see that, then I don't hold out much hope for the future of this church, media or no media. I say hold your vote now, and allow my family and this church to get on with our lives." Almost everyone in attendance began to rise to their feet, then it seemed like every voice in the crowd was chanting, "Let the bishop stay . . . Let the bishop stay . . . Let the bishop stay!"

When he recovered from the impact of the crowd, Deacon Black said, "Thank you, Dante. I would like to second your suggestion. If there are no objections, I think that we should go ahead and hold a vote right now."

The board agreed to hold their vote, and I returned to my mother's side. When it was all said and done, only one board member was still set on removing my father from the church. That one vote came from Deacon Emerson, and I was sure that Anita had had something to do with it, but in the end it didn't matter. My father would be reinstated as bishop to continue his good work in the church and in the community.

My mother, Donna, Shorty, and I left to find the bishop so we could celebrate a moral victory and start healing our family. After that I was going to find Tanisha.

Epilogue

"You sure you wanna do this?" Tanisha asked as we stood holding hands outside the main entrance to Howard University's School of Divinity. It was late January and the new semester was about to begin. Tanisha and I had been standing out there in silence for a good four or five minutes before she finally spoke. There was no need for anything to be said until then because we both knew that if we entered the building, there was no turning back. Our lives would be changed forever.

I turned to her and nodded nervously. "Yeah, I'm sure. Besides, my mother would kill me if I backed down now."

I chuckled, trying to hide my nervousness, but Tanisha didn't laugh. I nudged her and smiled, hoping to lighten her mood. She finally cracked a smile before we started up the stairs. I opened the heavy wooden doors and we walked in, to be greeted by a security guard. "Can I help you?"

"My name is Dante Wilson. I think they're expecting me."

The guard looked down at a clipboard and said, "Yes, they're in the chapel. Can I see some ID, please?"

I pulled out my wallet and handed him my brand-new

Howard University ID card. He glanced at it then handed it back, pointing down the corridor. "Third door on your right. You can't miss it."

"Thanks." I took Tanisha's hand and we walked the fifty or so feet to the large wooden door. The sound of voices emanated from within the room behind it.

"We're late," I said as I reached down to open the door. Tanisha grabbed my arm and stopped me.

"Hold on a second, boo." She looked like she was going to cry.

"What's the matter?"

"Nothin'. I just wanted to tell you how much I love you before we go through that door."

"I love you, too." I smiled, leaning over to kiss her. She wrapped her arms around my neck and we kissed like the world was going to end tomorrow. When we finally broke the kiss, I asked, "Are you ready now?"

She nodded and I reached for the doorknob. Waiting for us inside was a small, select group of our loved ones. Inside the chapel, on the front pew, sat the first lady, the bishop, Marlene, a gangly preadolescent Aubrey, and my sister Donna. Donna held my fat five-month-old nephew on her lap. She was glowing and looking radiant, as if motherhood and being a wife definitely agreed with her.

"Where y'all been? Dang, y'all twenty minutes late to your own wedding," Donna yelled out.

Standing before the pulpit was Shorty wearing a purple robe. He gave us a huge smile. "Are you ready?"

I stepped forward. "Yes."

Tanisha stood at my side and said, "Let's do this." She gazed at me with tears in her eyes.

I looked around at my family. Everyone's life had changed over the last six months. None more than Shorty, who walked into the bishop's office the night after his son's birth and told him he'd gotten the calling. Don't ask me what strings the bishop pulled, but Shorty was now attending

Howard University's School of Divinity and, with the bishop's guidance, was about to perform my wedding ceremony. Needless to say, my mother was overjoyed by Shorty's choice.

I, on the other hand, had enrolled in and was about to begin classes at Howard's School of Law, and believe it or not, I had my mother's blessing. You see, now that Shorty had gotten the calling, my mother had lightened up on me about going to divinity school. I guess all she wanted was to have one son carry on the family business, and now she had Shorty.

With both our families going to live in the D.C. area, Donna, Tanisha, Shorty, and I all shared the same house in order to cut expenses. Everyone was able to help Donna with the baby while she finished up her undergraduate degree at Howard. Tanisha was going to be starting cosmetology in February and was working in one of the most exclusive beauty shops in D.C. as a hair washer.

Even Marlene had moved down to the area with Aubrey, whom she had regained custody of, and she was doing a good job with him. She had gotten a job as a clerk in a social service agency and seemed to have found her life's calling, too. She liked encouraging other recovering addicts. "It helps me stay straight," she would say. Marlene now planned to go back to community college to become a social worker.

As for Donna, she looked down at her fat baby boy, Thomas Kelly, named after his grandfather, then smiled up at her husband. She'd told me in private that she had planned on having her marriage annulled before that day we all confronted the deacons board. She said that was the day she realized how lucky she was and truly fell in love with Shorty.

I had laughed when Tanisha told me Donna rushed straight home from the doctor's office the day of her six-week postpartum checkup so she could consummate their marriage. And boy, had it been worth the wait! She was surprised at what a good lover Shorty was. She respected how he had waited until she was truly ready for him, and she was surprised—the sex was even better with a man who truly loved her and who had proved it in every way.

Yes, Shorty had definitely won her over. Most of all, she loved how Shorty loved their baby. She was even more sprung than she had been with Terrance. She was deeply in love with her husband, the man with whom she wanted to spend the rest of her life.

Donna had learned her lesson the hard way. Just because you love someone doesn't mean that person loves you. She finally understood how Reverend Reynolds had been using her. Theirs had been a one-sided love. Although at first Shorty had had a one-sided love for her, she'd also learned that, as a woman, you can learn to love someone back, particularly if that person is good to you.

My mother was so into being a grandmother that it seemed like she was making weekly trips to D.C., although I think she really enjoyed having the bishop all to herself. The only person that hadn't changed was the bishop. He was still the rock of our family and the church, a good man and a better father.

I watched as Donna cuddled her baby close to her. Shorty coughed against his fist then cleared his throat. He balanced his Bible in his right hand. "Dante Wilson, do you take Tanisha Jones to be your wedded wife, to cherish and to care for until death do you part?"

I looked deeply into Tanisha's eyes. Without hesitation, I said loudly for my close friends and family and the whole world to hear, "I do."

THE PREACHER'S SON

CARL WEBER

ABOUT THIS GUIDE

The suggested questions are intended to enhance
your group's reading of Carl Weber's
THE PREACHER'S SON.
We hope you have enjoyed reading this novel.

DISCUSSION QUESTIONS

1. Is Dante the type of man you would want to date or have date your daughter?

2. What did you think of Tanisha and would you let her date your son?

3. This book could just as easily have been called The Preacher's Kids; what were your thoughts on Donna?

4. What would you have done if you were Donna and the first lady asked you to have an abortion for the sake of the family?

5. There are a lot of things positive and negative said about men of the cloth; what is your opinion of Bishop T.K. Wilson? Would you want him as a father?

6. Do you think Donna was fair to Shorty? And would you have married him in her situation?

7. The first lady seemed to warm up to Tanisha. Why do you think that happened?

8. Were you surprised that Bishop Wilson was Tanisha's father? Could you imagine him and Marlene as a couple?

9. After he found out the woman he loved was his sister, Dante went into a depression. What would you have done if you were him?

10. Were you surprised to find out Reverend Reynolds was married and do you remember his wife from Carl Weber's *Lookin' for Luv*?

11. If you were the bishop would you have kept the first lady's secret?

12. Were you happy with the ending?

Take a look at an excerpt from Carl Weber's

The First Lady.

Prologue

"Hey, Charlene, you ready to get started?"

My good friend and confidante, Alison Williams, smiled as she walked into my hospital room. I tried to smile back when she kissed my forehead, but the abdominal pains I was experiencing wouldn't allow it. So, I lay there in my bed, grappling through the pain as I watched her sit in the chair next to my bed and pull out a notebook and pen. I pressed the button that controlled the morphine drip in my arm, and Alison waited patiently for my pain reliever to kick in. Six months ago, I refused to use any type of pain medication, but now I understood why the Lord invented addictive drugs like morphine and Demerol. Without them, I probably would have died from the pain of my cancer weeks ago. As it was now, I was pushing the damn drip button every fifteen minutes and I was on the highest dose there was, which meant I only had a few weeks left to live.

I wasn't afraid of dying, though. I'd lived a good life, married a wonderful man, Bishop T.K. Wilson, raised two fantastic children, and had the honor of being the first lady of absolutely the best church in Queens, New York. If the

Lord was ready to call me home, although I considered my-self still pretty young, I was ready to go. The only thing I was afraid of was what would happen to my family—more importantly, my husband, T.K., after I was gone. So, I was making preparations to make sure my man was taken care of from the grave.

You see, as good and honorable a man of God as T.K. was, he was still just a man with desires and needs; and men, no matter how bright they may appear to be, are very naive when it comes to women, *especially* slick-ass church women. I could see it now. Fifteen minutes after they put my body in the ground, those church heifers would be in my house try-ing to figure out the best way to redecorate my shit out. Say what you might about my choice of words, but I'd seen these so-called church women in action too many times in the past.

Last year when Sister Betty Jean White passed away, within six months her worst enemy, Jeannette Wilcox, had weaseled her way into that woman's house and was sleeping with her husband. A few months after that they were mar-ried, and if you walk into that house today, there's not one memory that Sister Betty even lived there. So, I could envi-sion T.K. in his moment of grief and loneliness letting some-body manipulate him into doing just about anything she wanted, and I was not about to allow that. That's why, with the help of Alison and possibly my daughter Donna, I was making plans to stop her and any other threats to my family.

I hope you don't get me wrong. I wasn't trying to stop my husband from moving on with his life after I was gone. On the contrary, I wanted him to find someone to spend the rest of his days with and be happy. I just wanted to make sure that whoever the woman was, she had his best interests at heart and wasn't just some ambitious, gold-digging floozy disguised in a church hat and a flowered dress.

I felt the pain medication finally kick in, and Alison helped me as I struggled to sit up. She placed a pillow behind my head then sat back in her seat to take notes as I began to dictate the fourth of seven letters to be given out after my death. The first one was to T.K.; the next two were to my son, Dante, and daughter, Donna. The final four letters, which we would write this day, were to the four women I thought were possible candidates to one day replace me as T.K.'s wife and become the first lady of First Jamaica Ministries.

I started my dictation with a letter for T.K.'s first love, Marlene, the mother of his illegitimate daughter, Tanisha. I never really told anyone this, but I liked Marlene. She had spunk, and from what I heard, a loyalty to T.K. that almost rivaled mine. I must admit, though, that I liked her more when she was living in D.C. with her daughter and my son, who, believe it or not, were married. But that was before I was diagnosed with cancer, when I made it a point to keep any women that might interest T.K. as far away as possible. Now I was happy to hear that she had recently moved back to Queens and had even shown up at a few church services. She, unlike any of the other candidates, had a connection to my family, which made her a very favorable competitor in the race for T.K.'s heart. Her only flaw was that she was a recovering drug abuser . . . but then again, so was my husband.

The next letter was to be written to Ms. Monique Johnson, the first lady of plastic surgery and implants. I'm sorry, but there was no way a forty-year-old woman with two kids could have a body like hers without something going south. Not only was her body fake, but so was her personality. I'd never met a phonier woman in my entire life. She was always smiling in my face and grinning at my man. She knew she wanted him. Rumor has it that she'd had relationships with at least two high-profile members of the church, both of them married. In fact, when Monique was around with her flirtatious self, every wife in the congregation had her man on lockdown. Like I explained earlier, there was no doubt in my mind that Monique had her sights set on T.K. Some of my girlfriends from the church confirmed that her overtures toward him had become even bolder since I'd become hospitalized. I was sure T.K. hadn't even given the woman a second thought with me being sick and all, but a question still remained: Would he be strong willed enough to stay away from her after my death?

After we wrote Monique's letter, the pain was starting to come back, but I fought through it as we started on Savannah Dickens's letter. Savannah was the church's new choir soloist. She was a quiet, attractive woman in her midthirties who kept to herself. I didn't know much about her because she was new to the church and the community, but I will admit I wasn't much for quiet folks because they were usually hiding something. She was, however, the niece of Trustee Joe Dickens, one of the more prominent older members of our church. Joe was looking to become the chairman of the Board of Trustees. I was sure that after my death he would be trying his best to push T.K. and Savannah together in an effort to consolidate power. It was a move I wasn't against, because it would probably benefit T.K. in the long run. What I didn't like was the fact that she was only thirty-five years old. I wasn't objecting to her age so much; she was only ten years younger than T.K. What I was worried about was the fact that she was thirty-five and didn't have any children. A woman under forty who hadn't had a child probably wanted kids of her own, and that was out. The last thing T.K. needed after raising Dante and Donna and putting them through college was another baby to support.

Right before we finished the sixth letter, the pain hit me hard and I had to push the drip. I lay back down and Alison insisted that we'd done enough for the day. God willing, we'd finish the seventh and final letter the next day. It was to my good friend, Sister Wilma Mae Jenkins, one of the church's Holy Rollers. Although I'm not going to reveal its content, I can assure you that it would shake up a whole lot of people.

Six months from now, I'd be dead, but I could guarantee my presence would still be felt.

Can you dictate the lives of your family, friends and enemies from the grave? Those were the thoughts I contemplated as I waited for the new dose of pain medication to take effect. I could picture the scenario now: The first lady of First Jamaica Ministries is dead. Who will win the bishop's heart and become the next first lady? Time would only tell.

Six months later

1

Bishop

I leaned forward in my chair and opened my desk drawer, taking out two glasses and a bottle of cognac that I saved for special occasions. I poured myself a drink and one for my best friend and confidant, James Black. There was nothing like drinking some good old-fashioned cognac with James, especially after a day when the fish weren't biting worth a darn. James and I spent a great deal of time together when it came to both business and pleasure. He was a loyal friend, a former deacon, and now the chairman of the board of trustees of our church. He was also my eyes and ears amongst the members of the church since my wife, Charlene, passed away, God bless her soul, six months ago.

Lately, James seemed to be seeing and hearing more things that I was oblivious to in the church. I hated that because I tried to remain close to all of the members of the congregation, but there are some things that church folks just won't tell their pastor. That's where my wife, and now James, had come in handy. They both had a knack for discovering things before they blew up in my face. My wife, because she was very nosy and intimidating, and James because . . . well, let's just say he was a ladies' man, and I had to turn my head every once in a while to his lustful behavior. Nonetheless, they both got the job done in their own way, and I was appreciative.

"T.K.," James said, swirling his cognac before taking a sip. He stared at me long and hard, as if he was trying to find the proper words to express himself. Normally, this was something James never seemed to have a problem with. I also took note of the fact that he'd called me T.K. instead of Bishop. He only did that when he wanted us to step aside from our roles as heads of the church and deal with each other as men of flesh.

"What's on your mind, James? You got something to tell me? You haven't been yourself all day."

James took another sip of his drink. It was obvious to me he was stalling. "Well, yes, I do," he finally said.

"All right then, man, spit it out," I encouraged.

"All right. T.K., I've been talking to some of the sisters of the church, and well . . . they think it's time." He leaned back patiently in his chair, obviously relieved to get this off his chest. I just wished I knew what he was so relieved about. I didn't have a clue what he thought it was time for.

"Time? Time for what?" I stared at him as I lifted my glass and took a swallow.

"Time for you to make a choice. So, I hope you're ready because life around here isn't going to be easy until you've made your choice."

"And what choice do I have to make?" I asked calmly, still not sure where he was going.

"Whether we're going to have Armageddon around here or peace," he replied between sips, staring back at me with so little emotion he could have been a professional poker player.

I sat up straight in my chair, trying my best to read my friend's face because *Armageddon* was not a word to be used lightly. "What are you talking about, James?"

"T.K., there is about to be Armageddon in this church, and you're about to be right in the middle of it."

There was that word again. James' face still showed no emotion, but now his voice had a chill that had me concerned. Had James been given some Divine message from God that I had been left out of? Was there dissention in the congregation? Were they about to try to vote me out as pastor? I wasn't sure what was going on, but before he left my office, my good friend James Black was going to explain himself.

"James, you of all people know I do not like to play games. So, will you please stop beating around the bush and get to the point?" My voice was firm, and I'm sure he knew I was serious.

"Look, I'm sorry about that, T.K.. I just figured you'd want to hear this subtly." He took a breath before he spoke. "The women of the church are about to tear this place apart, and it's all because of you."

I searched my mind for reasons I might have upset the women of my congregation. "What have I supposedly done this time?"

"It's what you haven't done, Bishop. These women are losing their minds. Haven't you noticed what's going on around here? The women are arriving at church a half-hour early just to assure themselves a spot in the front of the church. I'm not just talking about two or three women. There had to be fifty or sixty of them this past Sunday. And I bet you a hundred dollars there'll be even more this week. It's crazy."

I smiled at my friend with pride. "That's not necessarily a bad thing, James. The word must be getting around that I give one heck of a sermon."

He laughed. "Are you really that naïve? These women don't give a hoot about your sermons. They only—"

I shot him a look and he tried to clean up his words.

"What I mean is all they care about is you." He pointed a

finger at me. "They are all bound and determined by any means necessary to become your wife, the next first lady of the church."

For the first time, I understood what he was talking about, and I dismissed it immediately. Yes, I knew that every congregation wanted their pastor to be married. It just made sense, if you really thought about it. But my Charlene had only been gone six months. That was way too soon for me to even be entertaining the thought of dating, let alone remarrying.

I looked at the picture of Charlene I kept on my desk. Oh, how I missed her. My wife was a spitfire who loved me, my family and this church more than life itself, and to be honest, I wasn't ready to let her go yet. And I didn't think the church was, either.

"That's ridiculous, James. Let me assure you, that's got to be the last thing on these women's minds. Trust me. Like I told you, I know these things. I know the hearts of the women of this church. It's just in their nature to be caring. You can't go taking it the wrong way, James. I sure don't."

"Are you kidding?" He chuckled, but there was a twinge of disdain in his voice. "No offense to your sermons, Bishop, but there's not a hat shop in Queens with a single fancy brim left on its shelves. There are women in this borough who have wiped out their entire savings, and others who have taken out loans just to buy enough hats for as many Sundays as it's going to take to catch the bishop's eye. And how better to catch the bishop's eye than to reserve a place right across from the pulpit every Sunday?"

"James, stop exaggerating," I chortled. "These are good church women who just want to hear the word."

"You can play dumb all you want, T.K.," James said as he poured the last of the liquor into our glasses. "But you can't say that I didn't warn you."

"Well, thanks for the warning, but I'm sure you're wrong."

He held up his glass, a sign for me to toast. I hestitantly followed suit and lifted my glass in the air.

"Here's to me being wrong," James said. Before either one of us could put our glasses to our lips, we were startled by a knock on the door. The concern in James' eyes mirrored my own. That last thing we needed as prominent men of the church was to get caught sipping on liquor. Jesus might have turned water to wine, and even took a sip or two himself with every meal, but God forbid I was caught having an innocent drink with a friend. They'd swear I was a drunk. So, without having to say a word, we simultaneously downed the contents of our glasses. I held out my hand for James to give me his empty glass.

"Come in," I said as I quickly placed the empty bottle and two glasses in my bottom desk drawer. I did so just in the nick of time because as soon as I closed the drawer, the office door opened.

"Gentlemen," Deacon Joe Dickens said as he entered the office.

"How you doin', Deacon?" I asked as James replied with a courteous nod.

"Fine, Bishop. I'm doin' just fine. Heard you two went fishin'. Hope they were biting," the deacon smiled, " 'cause, I'd love to have a few porgies."

"Put it this way, Deacon," I told him. "If you or anyone else ever had to depend upon Trustee Black's and my ability to catch fish, we'd all starve. The only thing we got in that cooler over there is ice."

Laughter filled the room momentarily before Deacon Dickens cleared his throat so that he could speak on what he'd really come for. "Speaking of food and eating, Bishop, my daughter, Savannah, is going to be doing a little cooking this weekend. You know that cobbler you were so fond of at the deacons' banquet last month?"

I smiled at the memory of that cobbler. It was quite possibly the best I ever had. "How could I forget? The darn thing was so good I must have gone back for seconds three times." I patted my belly as I grinned.

"Well, that was Savannah's doing. She made that cobbler."

"Sister Savannah is responsible for that cobbler? Well, I may have to stop by your house a little more often, Deacon, 'cause your daughter sure can burn."

"You're always welcome, Bishop. Matter of fact, along with that cobbler, she's cooking smothered pork chops and collard greens for dinner tomorrow. If I remember correctly, you're rather fond of pork chops, aren't you?"

"Could eat them every day," I said with a nod.

"Well, then you're going to have to come over for dinner tomorrow night. I insist."

I let out a disappointed sigh. "I wish I could, Deacon, but I already have dinner plans to meet with the bookstore committee for tomorrow night and dinner with my daughter and son-in-law tomorrow. How about a rain check?"

The deacon frowned. "All right. How's next Sunday sound? I can't promise pork chops, but I'm sure Savannah will make another cobbler."

I glanced down at my weekly planner then looked up at the deacon with a smile. "Deacon, it's a date. And whether it's pork chops or not, I'll be looking forward to it."

"Good, good," he replied. "How's seven o'clock sound to you?"

"Seven o'clock next Sunday is fine." I wrote it in my planner then made a mental note to tell my secretary Alison to put it in hers.

"Well, gentlemen, I guess it's time I got home. I'll see you at service on." The deacon shook our hands then left, closing the door behind him.

It was obvious that James could barely wait until Deacon's footsteps faded down the hall before he exploded with laughter. "Oh my Lord, that guy is hilarious."

"Why so funny?" I asked.

"What's so funny? You're what's so funny? Can't you see a set-up when it's right in front of your face?" James stood up, shaking his head. "Like I told you before the deacon came in, it's starting, my friend. The battle for who's going to be the next first lady has started, and it looks like the first woman in the ring is Savannah Dickens. And her father's the one who's throwing her in."

"James, my man, you're reading far too much into this."

"Am I, T.K.? Since when does a prominent member of the church invite the pastor to dinner and not at least extend an invitation to any other prominent member of the church who's in the room? I might as well have been invisible."

I sat back in my chair and thought about what he was saying. I didn't reply at first because the more I thought about it, the more his words started to make sense. He did have an intriguing point. Why didn't the deacon invite him to dinner? He could have at least invited him when I declined. Was the Deacon trying to orchestrate a relationship between me and his daughter? It was possible. The real question was if I was willing to be a participant in his plan.

Savannah was single, and she was also a very attractive woman. She had some of the prettiest black hair I'd ever seen. For the first time, I began to imagine her as a woman and not just a member of the church. The image brought a slight grin to my face, which quickly morphed into a guilty frown as Savannah's image was replaced by Charlene's.

"You might be right about the deacon, James, but then again, maybe your dinner invitation just slipped the deacon's mind."

James chuckled. "If you believe that, I got a bridge to sell you out back."

I rose from my chair, reached in my pocket then pulled out some money. "How much?"

James' chuckle became a full-fledged laugh. "You crazy . . . you know that, Bishop?"

"That's what they tell me." I laughed back.

"So, T.K., what do you think?" Oh Lord, he was starting with those crazy questions again.

"Think about what, James?" I said flatly.

"Savannah. What do you think about Savannah? Old girl does have some hips on her, doesn't she?" James traced his fingers in the air like he ws outlining a shapely woman's figure.

"I hadn't noticed," I lied.

"Yeah, right. Sure you haven't." James waved his hand at me. "Look, T.K., you may have the title of bishop, but you're still a man. Don't think I forgot about what happened in the Bahamas."

Blood rushed to my face. "You're never gonna let me forget that, are you?"

"Nope. Never."

"Okay, hold it over my head. Just don't forget I've seen you in a few compromising positions too. At least I was with my wife."

He laughed. "Hey, whatever happened to what goes on in Vegas stays in Vegas?"

"Same thing that happened to what goes on in the Bahamas stays in the Bahamas."

"Aw'ight, I get your point. Look, I gotta get outta here. I got a big date tonight with Sister Renée Wilcox."

I shook my head. "I don't know why these sisters let you get away with your foolishness, James."

"Same reason they're filling the front rows of the church these past few Sundays, Bishop."

"And why's that?" I asked.

" 'Cause a good man is hard to find." James smiled as he opened my office door. "Remember, Bishop," he called as he gave me one last warning. "Deacon Dickens and Savannah are just the first."

I smiled, nodded and waved as James exited the room, halfway closing the door behind him. I proceeded to remove the empty liquor bottle from my desk drawer and stuffed it down in my leather briefcase with the intent of disposing of it in the Dumpster in the back parking lot. I carried the two glasses we'd been drinking from down the hall to the church kitchen to rinse them out.

As I turned the corner to return to my office, I spotted an envelope taped to my door. It actually gave me deja vu because for years, Charlene would leave me messages in the same exact fashion. By the time I got to the door, my hands were shaking and my heart felt like it was going to beat out of my chest, I was so nervous and confused. She'd been dead for six months, but the envelope taped to the door was from my wife's personal stationery.

Somehow, I managed to remove the envelope from the door, make my way into my office and into my chair. I stared at the envelope for the better part of five minutes before I opened it and began to read. The note was indeed from Charlene. Although it wasn't in her handwriting, the words were definitely hers. James was right about one thing: Armageddon was about to start in our church, but what he probably never suspected was that its creator was going to be my deceased wife, Charlene Wilson.